PRAISE FOR *THE BURNED BRIDGES OF WARD, NEBRASKA*

"*The Burned Bridges of Ward, Nebraska* is a brilliant, hilarious, and politically astute take on modern parenting. Eileen Curtright is an amazingly talented and scathingly witty observer of contemporary culture, and she's produced a book full of characters who are believable and sympathetic while simultaneously being laugh-out-loud hilarious."
—David Liss, author of *The Day of Atonement*

D0469454

The
BURNED
BRIDGES
OF WARD, NEBRASKA

The
BURNED
BRIDGES
OF WARD, NEBRASKA

EILEEN CURTRIGHT

Little
a

Published by Little A, New York

www.apub.com

Amazon, the Amazon logo, and Little A are trademarks of Amazon.com, Inc., or its affiliates.

ISBN-13: 9781503950580 (hardcover)
ISBN-10: 1503950581 (hardcover)
ISBN-13: 9781503947610 (paperback)
ISBN-10: 1503947610 (paperback)

Cover design by The Graphics Office

Printed in the United States of America

For Lance

ONE

I had a wild feeling. People looked up from rows of breakfast cereal and sandwich spread and stared at me. I was no longer one of them, and they sensed it. Their lives were bound by the usual rules and routines, but for me the air of the Handy Farmer shimmered with possibility. The smooth shopping jazz piped throughout the store couldn't dull my euphoria. I barreled down the aisles toward my destination, aisle eight, Wines and Spirits. Sparks flew from the wheels of my cart as I rounded each corner. I was capable of anything. I had proven it.

"Mom!" Mitchell said. He was jogging to keep up. "What about these?" My son held up a lurid box of cookies for my inspection. "CHOCO-BOMBS!" the package screamed. "Now with whole grains." The whole grains were a nutritional fig leaf over the ingredients list, which seethed with the letters x, q, and z in strange combinations.

"Sure, whatever," I said. "Throw them in." I kissed the top of his head, and Mitchell did not complain, though one of his fifth-grade classmates might easily be lurking behind the endcap of pork 'n' beans, witnessing this embarrassing display of maternal affection. He had his reputation to think of. Mitchell smoothed his hair where my lips had ruffled it.

"Nice job," Pastor Dan Eubanks yelled from the front of the store, giving me a dual thumbs-up as he exited the building. I waved and put another bottle of wine in my cart. I hadn't been congratulated so widely since my son's birth, but those well-wishes had been tinged with disapproval. People had come to my door with casseroles, to inspect the infant and fish for details. We would have, as they put it then, *a tough row to hoe*. They'd left me noodles baked in soup and a sense of inevitable doom. But they had all been wrong. That was obvious now. And so, instead of modestly downplaying my achievement (*Oh, it's no big deal*, eye drop, shy smile—a response I'd practiced futilely in the bathroom mirror), I was basking in the admiration. I couldn't help myself. I was behaving as if success were my birthright, behaving, in other words, like a man. It came off as conceited. But my joy was uncontainable. As usual, my kid read my mood perfectly. "Can we get root beer, too?" He was already lowering a three-liter bottle into the cart.

"Certainly," I said. We rolled into the express lane, unloading eight bottles of wine, the root beer, and one box of cookies. Shane Glass, the store's aging bad boy, was our cashier. I was still smiling as the chardonnay and assorted reds bumped down the conveyer belt. Shane looked at the wine and then at me. He seemed intrigued by the idea that beneath my lavender scrubs there might beat a heart that had feelings, or at least liked to party.

"What's the occasion?" he said.

"Party at my sister's. I'm a partner in the clinic now."

"Awesome," Shane said. He had a barbed-wire tattoo around his bicep to let the world know he didn't give a fuck. I envied him that, but I'd chosen a different path. I had a child who looked to me to set the example.

"I just hope I don't mess it up," I said, crossing my fingers and wincing in an approximation of proper feminine self-deprecation. A *poor* approximation, judging by Shane's puzzled expression. Because in my heart, I was spiking the football.

Shane was only thinking of the party. He scanned the wine bottles one by one. Yesterday, buying eight bottles of wine would have smacked of despair, but today it felt festive and magnanimous. This was the sort of impulsive thing I planned to do often, now that I had the money and an ownership stake in Nebraska's premier fertility clinic.

"Your sister's place. Up on Pine?" Shane said.

"Yeah. But it's just family. It's very impromptu."

"Gotcha," Shane said. He loaded the bottles into discreet paper bags. I handed one to Mitchell.

"Why do we have to go to Aunt Madge's?" Mitchell said, as we carried the bags toward the car. "Let's do something else."

It was evening and the horizon was lit up by the setting sun. The world beyond the Handy Farmer's lot seethed with opportunities and I was in the mood to embrace them all. It was only coming up with something specific that was the problem. "Like what?" I said.

An old woman in a motorized chair was creeping over a speed bump. Viola Holts was on the loose again, heading into the store for another slo-mo spree. Someone ought to alert management before she stuffed the pockets of her housedress with glazed donuts, but I was too elated to stand in the way of her happiness. I smiled at her as she crested the bump.

"Something awesome," Mitchell said. "Something—" The chair's motor whined. Viola Holts lurched toward us, rolling her wheels over Mitchell's foot. He screamed. Viola shot past us into the Handy Farmer, without a backward glance.

"It's not broken," I said, peeling back Mitchell's sock as I felt the bones in his foot. Blood was welling up from the tread marks beneath his toes.

"She did that on purpose." His eyes were dry. He was old enough to be ashamed of public crying, but I heard the repressed tears in his voice.

"Maybe she doesn't see too well," I said. But we both knew Viola's eyes were still sharp enough for shoplifting.

Someone was sprinting through the lot toward the store; Viola's latest minder, I assumed. I didn't entirely blame him for the "accident." The job was too much for one person. It was time Viola's children faced facts and sent her to a home for the aged and criminally insane. When Mitchell and I hit his peripheral, the runner stopped. He turned to stare at us with his lips parted, aghast, like a citizen who has walked in on a crime in progress. It was Kevin Holts, Viola's son. We hadn't seen each other in more than ten years.

"Kevin!" It wasn't a greeting so much as a kind of involuntary shout, as if I'd found a scorpion nesting in my shoe. Mitchell edged closer to me, uncertain whether this fortyish man in an unseasonable corporate windbreaker was a person we ought to be afraid of.

"Hello," Kevin said. "Rebecca," he added, as if it had taken a moment for my name to surface in his memory. He was leaner than I remembered, with the half-starved look of an endurance athlete.

"This is Mitchell," I said, as he continued to stare. Kevin Holts is notoriously inscrutable, with a Vulcan-like control of emotion that has served him well in high-stakes negotiating. *Who is Kevin Holts?* was the question posed by a recent, not-entirely-flattering profile. A reporter had shadowed him for a week and yet failed to record any spontaneous human reaction, even when a nervous intern spilled her coffee on his pants. But now Kevin's pale face was twitching as if he were stifling a sneeze.

"Kevin Holts," Kevin said. The bottles in Mitchell's shopping bag clinked as the two of them shook hands.

"How long are you in town?" I said.

"Indefinitely," Kevin said. He continued to stare at us. His expression had settled into a grimace that did not invite further questions. But there was no need to ask what had lured him away from the West Coast, where he'd built Crucible, one of those paradigm-shifting tech

4

companies. The reason for his return was already hot-rodding through the aisles of the store with zero regard for public safety. Something had to be done about Viola Holts.

"Your mother," I said, pointing to Mitchell's bloody sock.

"Oh, God." Kevin said. And then he ran through the doors of the Handy Farmer without another word.

❖ ❖ ❖

Mitchell sat at my sister's table, drinking a large glass of root beer and icing his foot while I told everyone the story of the Handy Farmer drive-by. His Aunt Madge and Uncle Ben hovered around him, expressing concern. Nobody, not even Viola Holts, could do a thing like that on purpose—Ben was sure of it. Madge opined that it sounded just like the kind of stunt the old lady would pull. I said nothing about Kevin, and Mitchell, who was methodically chewing cookies, did not pipe in to mention him. He appeared not to be listening at all, but I wondered if he'd intuited my preference for glossing over the encounter. It had the makings of an amusing anecdote—the visionary leader standing speechless in a parking lot, bested by one frail senior citizen. But that wasn't a story I cared to share. The mention of his name would send us cycling through the usual awe-envy-pride-resentment merry-go-round that accompanied any conversation about Kevin Holts in this town. Just the thought of it gave me twinges of a pre-headache. I reached for the wine.

"Who all did you invite?" my brother-in-law said, as I unloaded the bottles onto the kitchen counter. He was wearing an apron that read "Dad's Kitchen, Too HOT to Handle." The festive smell of propane wafted from the patio, and someone had twirled streamers around the kitchen light fixture. A platter of raw steaks sat seeping blood under plastic wrap.

"Nobody," I said, making room in the refrigerator for the white. Usually I washed up at my sister's for holidays, an expected guest but somewhat peripheral to her domestic hub. Tonight, though, was all about me.

Madge uncorked the nearest bottle and poured two glasses. She'd come straight from the office and was still wearing one of her signature red pantsuits with a ballpoint pen stuck through her dark bun.

"Congratulations, Becky. This is . . . tremendous," Madge said, and she clinked her glass with mine. "You've worked so hard for it." She can cry on command, usually during closing arguments, but this time her eye moisture seemed genuine.

I swilled a mouthful of the Handy Farmer's finest and considered the arc of my own career. There had been years under the clinic's fluorescent lights, at all hours, with Mitchell in the care of a series of sitters, some cheery and maternal, some vacant-eyed but presumably drug-free. *Treasure these moments!* That had been the unanimous unsolicited advice. As I staggered around town in a sleep-deprived haze, with my thin, serious baby on my hip and later my stern little child in a stroller, people warned me of the passing of time. But whatever the opposite of treasuring each moment was—that was what I'd been doing. I'd been slogging toward the future, disregarding the moments as quickly as they cropped up. And now my son was taller and older than I could account for.

"So what's next?" Ben said.

Unbelievable. I had swallowed exactly *one sip* of celebratory wine.

Madge glanced at Mitchell, who was eating one of his neurotoxic whole-grain cookies. "Are you going to make yourself another designer baby?"

"There's an idea," I said, smiling as if this remark were not out of bounds. My earliest memory is fighting my sister for a cornflower-blue crayon. We both lost hair in that dispute, and I can still recall the way her calf tasted when I sank my baby teeth deep into it. I don't remember who got the crayon, which probably means it wasn't me.

I followed Ben and Madge out to the patio with my wine, nudging Mitchell through the screen door toward his cousins. He prefers air-conditioning and the company of adults. My nephews, Ethan and Aidan, were bent over the pavement, frying ants with a magnifying glass. They greeted Mitchell with a grunt, and he sat down beside them, sipping root beer and resigning himself to another evening of their company.

"Wouldn't you like that, Mitchell?" Madge said, pointing to her sons. They were a perfect pair, only eighteen months between them; solid, dark-haired children, largely nonverbal in the presence of adults. Their penchant for violence ought to have raised red flags in a mother so familiar with the criminal mind, but Madge saw only the brotherly love that Mitchell had so far been denied.

"Like what?" Mitchell said. My son was looking at his cousins the same way they were looking at the sizzling ants. Mitchell was so different from them, from all of us, in every feature, that in family portraits he looked like a photo-bombing stranger. He took after his father (*or so we assume*, as Madge said), an anonymous genius with no history of heart disease who worked in the space program. Mitchell looked like a needle with feet, with hair that split the difference between red and brown and blue veins that were always visible under his pale skin. At ten, he was fully comfortable with his origin story. He'd been created in my lab under sterile conditions with the best sperm money could buy. Our parents, who lived winter-free in a Florida condo, considered this a tragedy. Madge resented it as a form of cheating. Her boys were conceived naturally and don't come close to Mitchell's IQ. But to Mitchell it was simply *less disgusting* than the alternative.

"A little brother or sister," Madge said. Her voice softened as she imagined for Mitchell a high-performing sibling made to spec. "You *can* get more, can't you?" she said, to me.

"Madge, really," Ben said, dropping steaks onto the grill. An open and honest discussion of reproduction in which the male element had been reduced to a vial of mindless sperm made him, as a man and father, uncomfortable. He blushed over the steaks.

"Good question," I mused. I considered saying that my donor was now out of circulation, and so Mitchell was destined to be a one-off, but this would only prolong the conversation. I focused on the wine and waited for the subject to change. Ants were curling up into tiny balls of dead as the nephews harnessed the power of the sun for their own amusement.

"What I really want is the Phantom," Mitchell said, meaning a ludicrously expensive recreational drone for which a ten-year-old boy could have no legitimate use. His longing for this flying piece of amateur-spy garbage was obsessive and almost romantic. He collected images and trivia with the dedication of an especially motivated stalker. But dream crushing is my least favorite part of motherhood, and so I'd demurred on financial grounds. This put me in an awkward position now, because fertility is rightly called the cash cow of medical specialties. Although I knew, having reviewed the finances before signing on the dotted line, that my particular fertility clinic was currently in a mild slump. Chalk it up to my business partner's mercurial nature and the ever-growing popularity of the child-free lifestyle. But the money was beside the point. Mitchell and I had a difficult conversation in our future, one in which I explained that I never intended to buy him a privacy-invading flybot that might accidentally bring down a commercial airplane. For the moment, I just smiled noncommittally.

"You should do something crazy, though," Ben said, flipping the meat. "Live a little." Ben was an artist who worked in the medium of clay. His lumpy, earth-toned mugs spilled hot liquids down the shirts of all who used them. And yet, people kept buying them, in spite of the burns. Ben saw me as an uptight science drone who needed schooling on all the things that can't be learned in books.

"Not *too* much, though. Maybe just take a cruise," Madge suggested. Her teeth were a little wine stained. Mitchell looked my way, and I shook my head, silently reassuring him that we would never commit ourselves to a floating prison to be buffeted by norovirus, pirates, and costume parties. He nodded. We were on the same page.

"Don't be afraid to think big," Ben said, gesturing with a two-pronged fork.

"I recommend you baby-step it," Madge said. "I've seen too many lives wrecked." My sister had sold so many juries on the proposition that a life of criminal mayhem was something that *could just happen* that she'd begun to believe it herself.

"Oh come on, *Marjorie*," Ben said, with the casual hostility of the long married. "If ever there were a time to throw caution to the wind."

I took a large sip of wine to avoid agreeing with Ben out loud. A new era was dawning for me, and I planned to do something at least moderately incautious at the first opportunity. Something *more rash* than washing lights and darks in a single load but *less rash* than high-wire walking—that was the sweet spot. Madge picked up a two-liter bottle of root beer from the table and began to shake it.

"See this? See what I'm doing?" Even Ethan and Aidan looked up from the ants to watch her. "This root beer is Becky." The plastic bottle was full of brown froth. "And what *you're* saying is take the lid off!"

"Don't!" I said, but Madge unscrewed the cap. Root beer geysered onto the patio, spraying sticky drops over us all and washing away the remaining ants.

"So let's keep the lid on," Madge said, breathless from all the shaking. I wiped root beer off my face and nodded. My sister's demo was pitched at the third-grade level, but she had a point. I'd seen enough late-night docudramas to know that those fifty-minute stories of disaster always began with a woman who "had it all." And now, that woman was me.

TWO

"Oh, he *will* get you pregnant. He's the best," I said. I was in the clinic, sitting behind the reception desk, fielding calls, and staring at the small gilt-framed photo of Front Desk, our receptionist, with her sisters. They were three tall, mousy girls from whom the mall photographer had failed to coax even a single smile, and they were all so alike that I was not entirely sure which of them was the one who worked for us. Whoever she was, she was late again—I assumed she was waking up groggy from the bender that by rights should have been mine. This left me answering the phones, against Dr. Thad's wishes. He feels phones are not my forte, but I'd done a credible job so far.

"Personally, I would not attempt reproduction without him. I'll put you down for our first available," I said, and booked the caller for a consult with Dr. Thad. He worked the front of the house—glad-handing patients and explaining medical concepts with colorful 3-D models of fallopian tubes—and I generally worked the back, sorting sperm and freezing embryos in the peace and quiet of the lab. But Dr. Thad was taking a personal day, and I was spread thin.

My mouth was a little dry from last night's wine, but I had arrived early, as usual, in a no-nonsense ponytail and a fresh pair of lavender scrubs, ready to get down to business. Unlike our errant receptionist, I was keeping the lid on. Kevin Holts was here *indefinitely*. The implications of that had hit me as I bandaged up Mitchell's foot for school. My reputation locally was *uptight workaholic* but Kevin held a contrary opinion. He considered me to be a raving lunatic, and not, I conceded, without some justification.

His opinion gave me pause regarding cutting loose in some moderately rash way, as planned. Maybe the risks Madge warned of were not overstated. Being *capable of anything* cut both ways. It was a bit discouraging, the morning after, to find that a depressing ordinariness reigned, but sticking to business as usual was the safest thing. I envied our carefree receptionist, who was out drinking life to the lees, or more likely, Bold County Lager. The restlessness I felt was worse than a hangover, because there was no hope of curing it with time and aspirin.

Maryellen, our nurse, claimed that Front Desk was named something that possibly ended with the letter *n*, and that she hailed from North Nee, but little else was known about her. Anyway, it was likely our receptionist mattered to someone, and was a valued friend or even an object of desire in certain circles, but to me she was a shadowy figure, a mystery too tiresome to delve into, like parliamentary government or professional baseball. I hung up the phone and what's-her-name walked in, looking disheveled, and not in her usual, small-town-girl-with-low-self-esteem way. Her thin hair was matted on one side of her head and fluffed out violently from the other, and I could not swear that the taupe skirt and beige blouse she had on were not the very ones she'd worn yesterday.

"Rough morning?" I said.

"Traffic. I got stuck behind a combine," Front Desk said.

"That'll do it," I said, noting the purple shadows under her eyes, the puffy lids above them. Front Desk hadn't been home last night, I was as sure of that as I was that her name was one syllable and began with either a *C* or a *J*.

"Nice picture of you and your sisters here," I said. Front Desk just stood there, looking limply confused and palely befuddled.

"I only have one sister," she said in her unnecessarily soft voice. I held up the photo as evidence and wondered if she were still drunk.

"One sister, one brother," she said. She looked rather faint, and I cleared out of her desk chair, letting her take the seat she's paid to occupy.

"Well he's very handsome. You all are," I said, smoothing over the gaffe. "But good looks will only get you so far, Front Desk. Here at the clinic we value punctuality and professionalism." I left her to mull over this bit of advice and went to ready the exam room for our morning appointments. She had so little charisma. I was surprised she was capable of the kind of debauchery that led to showing up in yesterday's makeup.

❖ ❖ ❖

The man sitting in the consult chair across from me was a talker. A patient like this could hijack an entire morning. He was young, younger than I am anyway, with a thin hipster beard riding the edge of his jaw. My eyes traveled between his face and my notebook, where I was doodling a ferret in blue ink as he chattered. I was almost certain we had met before, though where and when I couldn't say. I hoped the wife would jog my memory. I kept my office door open for her as he detailed a lifetime of accidents and injuries. He'd learned to ride a bicycle in a high-pressure situation, falling again and again onto the bar of his blue dirt bike. His father had forced him to remount and pedal on, ignoring his tears. As a teen, he'd sustained an unfortunate whack between the legs with a lacrosse stick, and was carried from the field on a stretcher, pale and vomiting, amid scattered applause. He remembered that both teams stood silently in two lines, with their sticks crossed in tribute, as he was loaded into an ambulance. In college, he'd been kneed in the groin during a kickboxing tournament that got out of hand. At a certain period in his midtwenties, which couldn't, by the look of him, have been more than a few years ago, he'd spent a lot of time in saunas. Perhaps the heat had done permanent damage?

"These are all great questions," I said, stifling a yawn. The "problem of my bedside manner" was something that Dr. Thad and I had discussed many times. Put yourself in the patient's shoes, he recommended. I tried to imagine myself kneed in the groin, but to really get it right, I first had to imagine myself male, and then as the type of man who might kickbox, but ineptly. This was simply too much to take on mentally while also feigning interest. I gave up.

The second consult chair was still empty. Maybe she'd gotten cold feet about making other humans with this man, and kudos to her if that were the case.

"Where is . . . ?" I said, pointing to the empty chair beside him.

"Where is what?"

"Your wife."

"My *wife*?" He laughed.

"Your partner," I amended.

"I'm actually not seeing anybody right now," he said. His gaze lingered on the bare V of flesh above my scrubs in a way that might have been insinuating.

"So you're *not* trying to conceive, Mister . . ." I scanned the file for his name, but it seemed Front Desk hadn't bothered to write it down.

"Not actively," he said, in a tone I found overly cheerful. "And you can call me Calvin." He smiled as if he were unwrapping a special treat for me.

Calvin. It rang no bells. And yet that slight drawl in his voice, the prim dancerly posture. I knew him from somewhere.

"I guess I'm a little confused," I said.

"God, me too," he said, pushing his hair back from his forehead. "I have plunged myself into a swirling vortex of dysfunction. But that's what I get. Never get involved with the parents. That's rule number one."

"The *parents*?" I said. I put my pen down and studied him, trying to make heads or tails of this conversation. He was nodding vigorously.

"Stupid, stupid mistake. But in my field, I'm surrounded by moms. There's a line of them outside my office every day. Every time my phone rings, it's a mom. I don't even know what to say to a woman who doesn't have a child between the ages of five and eleven."

The realization that had been batting around my consciousness like a fly at a window finally broke through. This was Mr. Chester, assistant principal at Mitchell's elementary school, the man who directed school traffic in a three-piece suit, barking orders through a megaphone. It seemed like an inopportune moment to point out our connection. "Calvin, I'm worried we're getting far afield of my expertise here."

"No, believe me, this is the crux of the matter. So this woman and I . . . ," he trailed off.

"The mom?" I prompted.

"Yes. And this is all covered by HIPAA, right?"

"Um, sure," I said. "I mean, probably so."

"I just assumed that at her age, with two kids already, everything was taken care of. You know what I mean. But one night, she confesses that she's been trying to have a baby—with *me*—the entire time. Can you believe that?"

"Not really," I said.

"I mean, kids are my *life*. But I'm not ready to give up my evenings and weekends just yet. So anyway, bullet dodged. But then it got me wondering—maybe there's something wrong with me. Maybe I'm not firing on all cylinders."

He leaned forward in his chair. I had the feeling he was waiting for me to guffaw and dismiss the idea that his fertility was anything but above average.

"Leave a sample, and we'll run some tests," I said.

"A sample?" His face wrinkled with distaste. "No, I don't think so. I was hoping you could just work with the medical history I gave you."

"I'd just be guessing,"

"That's OK. Your best guess, then."

I looked him over, tapping my pen against my lip as I pretended to assess his ability to father children with nothing but my eyes. "My hunch is you're fine. But if something like this happens again—"

Calvin put his hand over his heart. "Never again. You can count on that. I mean, apart from everything else, I could lose my job. From now on, I'm going to be firmly in the public eye. There is no room for missteps. Believe me, I am *through* with the moms."

I stood to signal the end of the appointment. Even if I billed this as a level-five consult, we were way over time. Money was swirling down the drain as he lingered.

We'd moved toward the door. Calvin was standing about a half step too close to me and we seemed to have lurched into the ambiguous territory of *flirtation*. He was handsome in a low-key way I found mildly provoking. Perhaps my random nods of sympathy had sent the wrong signals. "You must know my son Mitchell. He's in fifth grade at Davis."

Calvin's face ran through a series of expressions, like a character actor testing his range. "Of course. Well that explains our . . . rapport." He backed up a half step and assumed a more administrative tone. "These are exciting times at Davis Elementary. Principal Krupka has just stepped down for personal reasons." He mimed drinking to excess from a large bottle. "So I'll be taking on that role." This I hadn't heard.

"That's a shame. But congratulations," I said. "Mitchell will be . . ." *Excited*, I was going to say, but I broke off. Fire drills excited schoolchildren. And food fights. A nosebleed could always draw a crowd. But a change in administration didn't move the needle. Calvin knew that better than I.

"Mitchell Meer. Of course. But I thought *Vicky* was his mother," Mr. Chester said. Vicky was our latest babysitter, a community collegian who frequently picked Mitchell up from school. She was nineteen but built solid and she dressed in roomy pants, like a much older person.

"She most certainly is *not*," I said, raising my voice. The mistake bothered me more than I cared to admit. It was not the first time someone had been confused about Mitchell's parentage.

"Well anyway, thank you for a lovely consult," he said, making his way down the brown hallway toward reception, where I hoped Front Desk would remember to collect his co-pay. I could imagine my sister shaking her head—shaking it in her Davis Boosters T-shirt as Ben delivered five dozen homemade cupcakes for the latest bake sale. Madge was PTO president, and Ben was a classroom dad whereas I . . . well, school administration believed Mitchell was the child of a chain-vaping teenage theater major with a Jesus fish tattooed above the elastic waistband of her track pants. This was no reason to beat myself up. Many loving parents lacked the time to get involved at school. The problem was Vicky. She was overstepping her bounds. Every afternoon she modeled slovenliness, theatricality, and a raging addiction to piña colada–flavored nicotine. Evidently, it was rubbing off on Mitchell. Today would be her last day.

❖ ❖ ❖

I heard the noise of high-velocity advertising as soon as I cracked my front door.

"And that's not *all!*" the rapid-fire TV spokesman was saying. A terrarium with two frogs sat on the coffee table next to a tornado of school papers and a couple of banana peels. This should have made it easier to give Vicky the ax, except that I was late again. I'd paced around my office, imagining various ways the firing might play out. Would I cry? Would she? My motives were not entirely pure and she might call me on them, point out that she'd cared for Mitchell like her own child—wasn't that what really bothered me? *You're jealous of my relationship with your son!* she'd say, puffing pineapple vapor into my face.

Jealous—of my own babysitter? Don't be ridiculous! I imagined myself retorting, with a haughty laugh. I imagined it so long that I was half an hour late leaving the clinic. Now I lacked the moral authority to discontinue her services and would have to put it off until another day, when I was more firmly in the right.

"Hey guys," I said. Mitchell and Vicky were eating frozen personal pizzas on the couch, a practice I have explicitly banned. Neither of them looked up. They were transfixed by the ad for a revolutionary new kitchen tool that lets you prepare restaurant-style bloomin' onions at home with ease. Vicky was sprawled out in her roomy pants, dripping marinara on a Ward College Plainsmen hoodie. Mitchell sat absolutely still, with his usual rigid posture, too engrossed even to blink. I'd once imagined raising a polyglot, beret-wearing child who fed only on organic grapes, but I'd let go of that fantasy. Mitchell had turned out default American: he loved capitalism and footage of people gored by animals, and he preferred food that needed to be heated rather than cooked. I muted the volume on the TV, and the two of them jumped.

"Hi, Ms. Meer," Vicky said. Her calculus book was open in her lap, but its pages were covered by something called *The Sassy Girl's Guide to Guys.*

"Why are there frogs in here?"

"They're toads," Vicky said. "It's a responsibility exercise. There's a note about it somewhere with feeding instructions and whatnot."

"There were three, but one got loose," Mitchell said.

"Loose where?"

"In the house," Mitchell said through a mouthful of crust.

"There's a toad loose in the house?" I said.

"Slight chance it hopped out the door, but more than likely, it's still on the premises," Vicky said. "He'll turn up."

"Well, thanks so much, Vicky," I said, passing her the cash. This was her signal to go, but she didn't budge. At one point, I'd told her to make herself at home, and she had done so—with a vengeance.

"Look! It's Aunt Madge," Mitchell said. The evening news was rolling, and Madge was escorting her client into the courthouse. The client, an accused murderess, was a glassy-eyed blond with a weak chin and an elaborate neck tattoo. She was dressed primly in a Peter Pan collar blouse, which she had definitely not chosen for herself.

"Looks like she's going with the Amélie," I said. The Amélie defense is a Madge specialty—she'll paint the defendant as just a little impulsive and quirky, the sort of manic pixie who might wave a loaded gun around in a fit of whimsy. Juries bought it more often than I would have guessed.

Vicky shuffled out the door with her money, yelling her good-byes over the back of her hoodie. I sat down next to Mitchell and put my hand on his cheek. He looked wary, the way he always does when he suspects a heart-to-heart.

"Mitchell, you're growing up," I said.

"Mom! Not again!" Mitchell said, clutching his chest and flopping over on the couch cushions, faking a heart attack. He twitched and wheezed in dramatic fashion and then went still.

"A lot of kids in your class take the bus home and spend a couple of hours alone."

"Cooper, Mallory, Owen P., and *both* of the Emmas," Mitchell said, rising from the dead and ticking off a list of his latchkey classmates.

"Oh," I said. "The Emmas? *Wow.*"

"And I'm a *lot* more reliable than any of them," Mitchell said, turning the point in his favor. He was already warming to the idea of spending that hour and a half by himself, doing his homework alone, and microwaving his own burritos like a worldly sophisticate. One of the tabletop toads let out an odd, reverberating croak, keening for his lost comrade.

"Find the toad, and I'll give Vicky notice," I said.

THREE

I think I just knocked the wind out of him," I said, carefully sliding the third toad off the edge of a pancake flipper. He landed in the bottom of the terrarium like a rock. The other toads took no notice of their colleague's return, though he'd been missing all night. I'd been stepping out of the shower when I felt something dry and fat pop between my foot and the tiles.

"Mom," Mitchell said. "I think you killed it." His eyes were shimmering above his cereal bowl. He'd ransacked the house for the toad the night before, but toads are masters of disguise, according to Mitchell, though the handout from Ms. Vasquez said nothing of the kind. The toad had not moved since I'd scraped him off the bathroom floor, but I refused to give up hope.

"He's in a defensive crouch to throw off predators. Just give him a minute," I said.

"He really *looks* dead," Mitchell said, peering down through the terrarium lid.

"Don't give up on him!" I said, with cheerful false hope. I was on the point of saying something about the power of positive thinking, but anyone who's reached the age of thirty ought to know at a glance when something is irredeemably fucked, and be mature enough to admit it. "OK, so he probably isn't going to pull through," I said, nudging him gently with a chopstick. No response. "But the other two are doing great!"

"The sub is not going to like this," Mitchell said.

❖ ❖ ❖

"So what did Ms. Vasquez say about the toad?" We were at the park, looking for a wide-open space to test a flying toy. I'd fired Vicky by text, like a coward, and she responded with a series of emojis that struck me as overwrought. Mitchell and I agreed that the results of the toad responsibility test were inconclusive. I'd signed him up for the after-school care program run by the Ward Tennis Club. We had joined a new income bracket, and needed to conduct ourselves accordingly. Mitchell was in a mild sulk.

"Nothing. We had the sub," Mitchell said. He was carrying the remote-controlled helicopter I'd bought him instead of a drone. He'd thanked me, because a helicopter is better than nothing, but somewhat stiffly, because his heart still belonged to the Phantom.

"Well what did the sub say then?"

"He said not to be mad at you. He said *shit happens.*"

"He said that? He can't say that to you." I was already mentally composing an e-mail of complaint to Calvin Chester.

"It's not true?"

"It's absolutely true," I said. As far as glib aphorisms went, "shit happens" was the one that partook most deeply of universal truth. Even as a bumper sticker, it was uniquely capable of uniting people on both sides of the aisle, from all walks of life. But there is a time and a place for that kind of talk.

"Look! The *Bandercooks*," Mitchell whispered. It was unusual to see so many of them in daylight, unless it was in the potholed parking lot of Dot's Liquor, but there they were, *all* of them, just a few yards away, in the middle of Hiram Ward Park on a Saturday morning. They were Ward's most notorious family, most of them thieves or screw-ups, nearly all of them hard drinking and taciturn. A few had even distinguished themselves in the arena of violent crime. They were generally considered a blight on the community, and now they were throwing themselves into the role of public eyesores. Bandercook children were assembled around the edge of the pond, stirring its garbagey waters with long sticks. Bandercook women were smoking cigarettes and comparing piercings at the picnic table. Their teen daughters were slicing onions and putting out jars of pickles and mayonnaise while the mothers talked.

And in the clearing, in a scrum of tattoos and muscle and torn shirts and bare chests, Bandercook men from sixteen to fifty were tossing a football over the dying grass of Hiram Ward Park. Some of them were brothers, some were cousins, some uncles and nephews or fathers and sons—only native Wardians could keep the cursed Bandercook line straight. Bill Bandercook, ever the patriarch, was grilling hot dogs and canned biscuits over a charcoal fire, a can of gasoline at his feet. As a young man, he'd bitten off a rival's ear, or so they said. His brother Abel, father or grandfather to about half of those present, was doing life in a supermax.

Anyone else would play touch football in a park setting like this, but the Bandercooks were slamming each other into the dirt, undeterred by the lack of helmets or pads or a regulation-size field.

"Mitchell, stay here!" I said. But he was already running up to the edge of the game, close enough that a stray arm or leg might knock him over. I followed him to the edge of the grass.

Hayes Bandercook raised his arm to lob an easy pass to Brock, and our eyes met. He stood there, football cocked over his shoulder, staring at me with a mute longing that was, frankly, more articulate than I'd ever known a Bandercook to be. This was not the first time I'd noticed his Bandercook eyes on me. We bought coffee at the same gas station every morning, and often stood side by side, stirring sugar and powdered creamer into our enormous scalding cups without speaking. I looked forward to our weird, silent interaction almost as much as the coffee. But now, with the scent of mud and decomposing leaves in the air and the gasoline fire wafting from the grill, the sensation of Hayes's presence was more acute. I stared back at him. His unruly hair, broad shoulders, and above all that *look*, suggested things to me that were not appropriate to entertain in a family-friendly context. Hayes took a step toward me, and Clive Bandercook tackled him, grinding him into the dirt. The football slipped from Hayes's fingers, and Chad Bandercook scooped it up before it touched the ground, running across the make-shift end zone and setting off a wave of profanity-laced celebration. Hayes began to get up, slowly. Brock stood over him, breathing heavily, not extending a hand. When Hayes was fully upright, Brock pushed him hard in the chest. "Keep your mind on the game, asshole."

Hayes charged at him, knocking him down into the dirt. In a matter of moments, Brock and Hayes Bandercook, both well into their thirties, were trying to beat each other to death in the yellow autumn grass, rolling around over sticks and thorny weeds, kicking and punching with leaves stuck to their bare backs.

Their father looked up from his grill. "Quit it, you pussies!" the old man yelled, but Brock and Hayes, red-faced and swinging, didn't seem to hear. The littlest Bandercooks had been throwing stones into the duck pond, but they began to wander over, some of them barefoot, in sagging diapers, to watch the fight.

"Rus, handle this," Bill said.

Rusty Bandercook laid the book he'd been reading across the arm of his lawn chair and lolled his way over to his brothers, who were struggling in the grass, screaming obscenities. With a practiced air, he poured a can of beer over them, which broke the spell. They separated and sat panting in the dirt, wiping Bold County from their eyes and telling Rusty to mind his own goddamned business and not to be always doing Dad's bidding like a little bitch. Bill brandished his grilling implement and said he'd put a fork in each of their asses and then we'd see who was or wasn't a little bitch. Then he called the children over for biscuits and dogs, while Brock and Hayes spat dirt and blood and brushed the grass and leaves off their chests. Rusty tipped his cap to us, and I pulled Mitchell down the path after me.

Bandercook is as Bandercook does, I thought—a frequent saying in town—shaking my head as we walked away from the scene of public intergenerational dysfunction. I couldn't believe that I had looked at him that way, that I had entertained the thought of Hayes Bandercook even for a moment. Only then did I notice Mitchell, craning his neck and smiling with delight at all this antisocial maleness in the crisp autumn air.

"I wish I was a Bandercook," he said, heaving a sigh. I ignored it. Only a few years ago, he wanted to be a tyrannosaurus.

❖ ❖ ❖

The helicopter was impossible to maneuver. Within fifteen minutes it had crashed into a tree branch and broken into a pile of plastic shards.

"Well," I said, as we surveyed the wreckage.

"Shit happens," Mitchell said.

FOUR

D r. Thad caught me in the break room with a coffee from the Fuel & Flee.

"Oh, Becky," he said, his Louisiana drawl thickening with pity, "why would anyone buy coffee from a place that sells *condoms* and *lotto tickets*?"

There was no answer I cared to give him. I took a long, defiant sip—a critical mistake.

"Pearls before swine," he said, patting the orange Italian monster on the counter, an espresso machine that cost more than Front Desk's annual salary. Then he sipped the crema from a tiny cup and judged me and my thirty-two ounces. "I could certainly understand if you were homeless or a long-haul trucker. Or, say . . . a member of a construction crew."

Again, I said nothing. I could drink what coffee I wanted. He was fishing. But we were not going to discuss this coffee *or any other related subject*. Dr. Thad and I were close, yes, but I drew the line.

"But under the circumstances, it is a most *peculiar* preference." He finished his tiny coffee and let the cup clatter in its little saucer. We had a procedure in five minutes, and I had at least twenty-five ounces to go.

Instead of defending my taste for scalding brown sludge that sat on a hot plate for hours, gaining flavor, I hurled my cup into the garbage can and stormed out of the room. He *knew* and he did not approve. Every time I'd raised my giant cup to my lips, I'd flashed the phone number scrawled on the bottom. Hayes had been unusually slow getting his coffee. He hadn't stepped aside to make room for me, as usual, but when he was finished pouring for himself, he turned and handed me a cup. In my car, I lifted it toward the sun visor and found a phone number written on the bottom.

With his superior intelligence and keen insight, Dr. Thad has a knack for reading between the lines. One day—not today, though—we'd laugh about this. I'd probably thank him. I imagined telling my sister that I'd been conducting a silent gas station flirtation with a *Bandercook*. I might have been able to confess such a thing when we were teenagers, sharing our feelings long into the night beneath the glow-in-the-dark star stickers on our bedroom ceiling. From the top bunk, Madge would have pelted me with judgment and stuffed animals, and that would have been the end of it. Whereas now . . . it was too humiliating. Hayes Bandercook was the opposite of keeping the lid on. He was probably worse than anything Madge had envisioned when she sprayed that root beer in our faces.

A few minutes later, I was back in the break room, rooting through the garbage for my cup. It was gone. My dignity would not allow me to ask for it. For the rest of the morning, I was under caffeinated, and my interaction with Dr. Thad was stiff. We met in the exam room for an intrauterine insemination, and though we put on smiles, we were still very much at odds.

"We feel good about this one, don't we, Becky?" Dr. Thad said, as he stroked Ms. Flyte's sinewy arm. I looked up at him from between her knees. His smile was tight. I hadn't been keeping up my end of the procedural banter.

I slid a catheter past the patient's cervix, up to her chemically primed uterus, and tried not to think of Hayes. I redirected my attention to the uterus in question, which was attached to a woman who had feelings of her own and who needed my reassurance. Her child would not be conceived with a backdrop of calypso music and ocean breezes, or even via a perfunctory exchange during the perfunctory monologue of a late-night show droning away on the bedroom TV. This child was being created among latex-gloved strangers—if not *out of* strangers. Donor gametes was a conversation waiting down the road like a rangy hitchhiker.

"We have a very good feeling, don't we?" Dr. Thad said. The two of us are as practiced as vaudeville performers. My line was something soothing, something positive that made no specific promises. But Hayes Bandercook was pouring hot coffee all over my higher brain functions, and I broke script.

"Morphology isn't great."

"Reyne!" Ms. Flyte wailed, raising her head from the exam table, distressed to hear that the semen we were dispatching to her uterus was populated by lazy dilettantes who lacked the city-sacking drive of more successful sperm. "You *promised* to stay out of the Jacuzzi."

Flyte was a Pilates instructor, lithe and unwrinkled, but pushing forty, and she'd wasted three years on kombucha tea and alternative therapies. I had my suspicions that despite what she'd promised Dr. Thad, she was still subjecting herself to flower extracts and contortions. Reyne Reynolds was present for sentimental reasons, but there was nothing for him to do. He sat in the chair next to his wife's feet, thumbing through an old *Woman's Day*.

"Nina, I swear—" Reyne said, pressing the magazine to his chest to show his sincerity. His voice was familiar from the evening news, where he read the top stories and the farm report with equal conviction, but it didn't work on a person-to-person scale. It was stagy and somehow callous. Everyone was now sure that he'd been sneaking out to the deck and lowering his middle-aged self into the swirling, steamy water, cracking open a beer and giving not a thought to the biological imperative. This kind of thing happens all the time. Dr. Thad calls it "varying commitment levels." Flyte was consumed with a primal desperation for a baby. In another time and place, dressed in animal skins, she'd be messing around with runes and making a barbaric sacrifice to a plus-size fertility idol. She might even be doing that *now*. I had a feeling she would gut me like a pig if she believed it could help. Whereas Reyne was basically OK with becoming a genetic dead end, like the Neanderthals. He probably reasoned that the two of them could travel and eat in quality restaurants.

"Deep breaths, Nina," Dr. Thad said, kneading her shoulders. He set his jaw and looked right into Nina's eyes like a plainspoken man of conviction. "Can I share something with you? When Becky came out of the lab this afternoon, do you know what she said to me?"

What I said was about Mitchell, but we never mention children in front of the patients. Dr. Thad was just improvising now. "She said, 'Dr. Thad, I've run this sample through all the hoops, but I don't care what the numbers say. I *believe* in them. They're fighters, and they'll get the job done.'"

I smiled as if to indicate that I had actually complimented the bellicose spirit of Mr. Reynolds's sperm. This procedure was already costing them, and they were looking at triple that if we had to go in vitro next. "And we're done here," I said, removing the tubes without meeting anyone's eyes.

"You're going to be a beautiful mother, Nina," Dr. Thad said, leaning down to look into her eyes . The tasseled fringe of his Nordic scarf brushed against her forehead. "Just a beautiful, gorgeous mother. Right, Becky?"

"Yep," I said.

❖ ❖ ❖

"What the fuck was that?" Dr. Thad said the moment we were in the hallway. Flyte was still in the exam room, slipping out of the lavender patient gown and into her own clothes. Reyne had already left, explaining he had to "skedaddle" back to Channel 8 News, a lie so desperate and transparent the three of us greeted it with absolute silence.

"I'm having an off day," I said.

"This," Dr. Thad said, drawing an imaginary circle around the two of us with his finger, "only works because you *don't have* off days."

Since the moment my association with Dr. Thad began, more than a decade ago, in the elevator of New Orleans Mercy, our mutual respect has been unspoken, yes, but also unquestioned. It had always gone without saying that *this* was *working*.

"Do you know the amount of hand-holding—figurative and *literal*—it's going to take to undo this?"

"I'm sorry," I said.

"If this blows up . . ." He meant, of course, the Flyte-Reynolds marriage.

"It won't," I said. "You'll fix it." Dr. Thad has saved more relationships than many a couples' counselor; unlike those "he said–she said" hacks, his payday depends on people working it out before the urge to reproduce has entirely dissipated.

"What *possessed you* to mention morphology?"

Nina Flyte chose that moment to emerge from the exam room. She held her chin at a defiant angle, television's favorite pose for strong women in adversity. Dr. Thad went to her. He clasped Nina's hands. He spoke soothingly to her all the way out the door and stood in the building's entryway for a moment, making confident hand gestures as Nina nodded along. He waved as she exited the building.

"Jesus Christ," Dr. Thad said, closing the clinic door behind him. "Why did it have to be her, Becky? The woman is a human marshmallow. When that test comes back negative, so help me, I'm going to have to shoot her with a sedative dart."

"Maybe she'll pull a positive," I said.

"With that kind of morphology? Oh, *come on*. That was just a face-saver for Reyne. His sperm couldn't penetrate a net."

"But—they're fighters," I said.

Dr. Thad rolled his eyes. "His sperm couldn't swim *downhill*."

The phone in my pocket began to buzz. The voice that poured into my ear was devoid of the flat vowels and nasal *a*'s found locally. It was Calvin Chester at Davis Elementary. He was calling in a professional capacity—his, not mine—and he needed to speak to me at my earliest convenience.

❖ ❖ ❖

"Well, Mitchell is certainly pushing the envelope this year," Bev, the school secretary, said when I walked into the main office.

"What do you mean?" It was not my first go-round with the parent-principal conference, but Mitchell had never been in serious trouble. Certainly nobody had mentioned pushing envelopes.

"I'll let the boss tell you," Bev said and took a bite of her Danish, the pineapple kind they sell at the gas station on Twelfth Street. I stepped through the door to Calvin's office. To my horror, in the chair across from Calvin's desk, I saw a pair of freckled knees. I stopped dead in the doorway, staring at those knees, my mind reeling.

"Ms. Meer, I assume you already know Kevin Holts. We're so lucky to have him aboard," Calvin Chester said. Kevin, the owner of the knees, was dressed in cycling gear, which was not unusual. There was nobody in Ward who didn't know Kevin Holts. Framed clippings of his success hung in all the places he'd frequented as a boy. You couldn't get a sandwich or a haircut in Ward without confronting a picture of Kevin leaning against a desk with casual aggression, dressed in khakis and a corporate polo. Unfortunately, I knew him better than most.

"Kevin, this is Mitchell's mother, Rebecca Meer," Calvin said.

"Oh, we go way back," Kevin said. "Nice to see you again, Rebecca." He'd regrouped after our run-in at the Handy Farmer. Now his perfectly bland greeting only reminded me how uncharacteristic his parking-lot reaction had been. He took a long squeeze of water, without a hint of self-consciousness, like it was OK for a grown man to dress in blue spandex and drink from a bottle as long as there were sporty emblems involved. "So here's my perspective on the frog thing—" Kevin said.

"What frog thing are you talking about?" I said. It had been nearly a week since I'd stepped on the frog. I'd assumed the incident was firmly behind us.

"Cal, you told her, right?" Kevin said.

"They were toads, actually. You know, I didn't. I thought it would be better to do it in person," Calvin said.

"That's very sensitive of you, Calvin. But you think these mini-van types respect sensitivity? Like hell they do. All you've done here is project weakness and delayed an unpleasant conversation. Next time, you call her up and you say what you have to say. Boom," Kevin said, slapping one of his blue thighs for emphasis.

"Excuse me," I said. "Why is *he* here?" I said, pointing at Kevin. I was at the point of grabbing Principal Calvin by the lapels.

"Let's all be calm," Calvin said, pushing a box of tissues toward me. I waved them off, and he raised both his eyebrows at Kevin, as if he'd warned him that this was exactly how I'd behave. *Moms.* His impatience with maternal emotions was as clear as if he'd spoken aloud.

"Cal brought me in on this one," Kevin said, popping all the vertebrae in his neck. This was a tic of his, and like most everything else about him, it sickened me. "I'm Mitchell's teacher, so I bring that perspective to the table."

"You're *not* Mitchell's teacher," I said. The two of them exchanged another look.

"Actually, Ms. Meer, he is. Kevin made it official with the fifth grade yesterday," Calvin said. "He's been subbing for a full week. Mitchell didn't let you know?"

"The sub," I whispered. Mitchell had, in fact, mentioned something about it. I should have asked more questions. "But where is the real teacher? Kevin is some kind of an internet salesman," I said.

"Internet *entrepreneur*. My background is in business, yes. I don't apologize for that. And I object to that characterization of my predecessor as a, quote, *real teacher*. Open your eyes! America's workforce is falling behind because we entrust our children's education to aging sorority girls with BAs in child development—which is total junk science, by the way," Kevin said.

"I doubt that you're even certified to teach elementary school," I said.

"*Certified in elementary education?* Do you *want* your son to be taught by someone whose college career was spent making decorations for the All Greek Gala?"

"Yes," I said.

"The average elementary schoolteacher is barely literate," Kevin said.

"Fact," Calvin said, nodding like a disciple gunning for a seat at the messiah's right hand.

"You agree with this?" I said, leaning over Calvin's desk and practically spitting in his eye. There was no point now in keeping a level tone.

"Kevin's style is provocative, but I think he makes some good points. It's the feminization of American culture," Calvin said.

"You're goddamn right it is," Kevin said. "And you know this better than anyone, Meer. You're profiting from it."

"I'm *what?*"

"Tell me this," Kevin said. "How much has the average sperm count of males in the industrialized West declined over the past two decades?"

"By two percent," I said, automatically.

"That's two percent every year, isn't it, Meer?"

"Right. Two percent per year."

"Meaning your average American man is producing 40 percent less sperm today than he was during the Reagan administration. Meaning he's more likely to pay Meer a premium to get the procreating job done. People blame industry, pollution. But I blame the public schools. This place . . . ," Kevin said, looking with disgust at the nondescript gray walls of Calvin's office, "it's a fucking estrogen bath."

"That is the most idiotic thing I've ever heard," I said.

"Look, I'm not here to debate the wider issues. The fact is, Mitch overfed the toads, and they exploded. That's what Cal brought you here to say."

"We gave those toads back days ago. How does their exploding— *exploding*?" I paused wondering if I'd misheard, but they both nodded vigorously. "How does that have anything to do with Mitchell?"

"We discontinued the take-home toad project. There were parent complaints," Calvin said.

"And various other incidents," Kevin said.

"We've made it a community-wide responsibility. It was supposed to be a morale boost. A feel-good project. Toads are endangered," Calvin said.

"Some toads," I said.

"It was room 304's turn to do the feeding, and I sent Mitchell to do the job. I take full responsibility," Kevin said.

"You couldn't have known how things would turn out," Calvin said. "Don't blame yourself."

"Yes, blame the *ten-year-old*," I said, but they ignored me.

"This couldn't have come at a worse time. CLEAVER prep is just gearing up. I'm very concerned about morale," Calvin said.

Was it my imagination, or was there a look of triumph beneath Calvin's serious-principal-conference face? I *had something* on Calvin Chester, that's the way a person without the proper respect for HIPAA privacy regulations might view it. An affair with a parent—that was a story that the other Davis Elementary mothers would have sucked down as eagerly as a post-gym latte. But I considered keeping that secret a sacred trust. Of course I'd judged him. But silently, in the privacy of my own mind.

"Help me understand how the toads exploded," I said.

"Boom," Kevin said.

"I don't think that's possible," I said.

"Some of the gore traveled more than a meter," Kevin said.

"The janitor used the entire stock of vomit absorbing powder to soak it up. God help us if flu season hits early," Calvin said.

"It's pretty fucked up, really," Kevin said. "Best we can figure, Mitch left the entire tub of toad feed in the vivarium. Textbook case of overconsumption."

"I'll be frank, Ms. Meer. Due to the extreme nature of this incident, it's my considered opinion—and our school nurse concurs—that Mitchell is suffering from mild to moderate oppositional defiant reactive attachment hyperactivity disorder," Calvin said.

"Mitchell's problem is that he's immature. And the reason he's immature is that he is only ten years old. This is an *elementary school*. I think you should keep your expectations in line with that fact," I said. As I spoke, Calvin had slipped on a pair of large black reading glasses, which he was too young to need. He wetted his index finger with a sponge pad and began to flip through a file.

"Does this strike you as normal, Ms. Meer?" He read aloud, flipping through various disciplinary reports. "Fighting. Fighting. Arguing. Dress Code. Gunplay—"

"Yes, but that was with a carrot," I said.

Calvin looked up at me over his glasses. "He mowed down an entire table of children with that carrot stick." He continued, turning a page, "Insolence, verbal. Insolence, noncompliance. Insolence, not otherwise specified—"

"I think you've made your point," Kevin said. "The kid's a piece of work."

"You know alternative school shouldn't be looked on as a punishment," Calvin said.

"*Alternative* school?"

"I understand your reluctance. But it's just what the name implies—an alternative form of schooling," Calvin said.

"Shoot straight, Cal. It's a fast track to prison," Kevin said, smiling his let's-all-be-adults-about-this smile, the least sincere expression in his facial arsenal.

"Well in practice, yes. Pretty much," Calvin said, blinking rapidly. "But Kevin feels," Calvin continued, resuming his smooth administrative tone, "and I'm willing to chance it—that he may be able to work with Mitchell. Assuming he's receiving the proper treatment. Which is why I've placed a provisional hold on your son's transfer. Let's all hope that Kevin's influence and prescription amphetamines are going to be the missing pieces in Mitchell's educational journey."

A wave of revulsion began somewhere in the recesses of my plastic lab shoes and rose through me, causing the muscles in my carefully composed face to twitch ever so slightly. Only a sharp-eyed person could have caught it.

"Calvin wanted to bring in the district, but I asked him for the chance to handle it in-house. And to his credit, he gave the go-ahead."

"No, the credit is yours, Kev. Honestly." The two of them beamed at each other.

Kevin stood, capping his water bottle. "No need to thank me; just doing my job. And now, if you'll excuse me, ladies," Kevin said, slapping the door frame twice by way of farewell, "I've got to mold some young minds."

"Isn't he great?" Calvin said, staring after Kevin with naked admiration. He turned to me and dialed his expression down to polite tolerance.

"What happened to Ms. Vasquez?" I said, leaning forward in my chair.

Calvin sighed and rolled a ballpoint pen under his palm—a nervous tic. "Look, we pre-CLEAVER'ed the kids. The results weren't good. They weren't good *at all*, Rebecca."

"And you blame Ms. Vasquez for that? Where does the buck stop, Mr. Chester?" Unless it was a trick of the late-September light—the most fickle and untrustworthy light in the calendar—Calvin blanched slightly at the question.

"It stops with me, of course. And I've got very little time to turn things around. The status of this school as an Acceptable Institution hangs in the balance." Whenever there's a school assembly and an open mic, you can be sure administration will wax eloquent about the "mission" of "educators," but being a principal is just a numbers game: test scores, retention, yearly improvement metrics. Make the numbers work is what it boils down to. The whole thing is a lot like being a bookie.

"And so you just *fired* Ms. Vasquez? She was a dedicated educator, and you threw her under the bus." I hadn't been a huge fan of Monica Vasquez, but in a fight for your life, you use whatever weapon comes to hand.

"Jesus, do you think I wanted to fire Hot Vasquez?"

"Did you just call her—"

"No. I didn't. Absolutely not." He sighed again, and I had the feeling he might be a little in love with Monica Vasquez. He had probably written her some earnest slam poetry or maybe even a slow, folk-rock guitar ballad. "Look, everyone liked her here. If I had only my own feelings to consider, she'd still be in that classroom. But that's not the way it is. I have the *children* to think of," he said, bringing his fist down onto a legal pad on which someone had drawn a squirrel in blue ink. The paper clips in the "World's Best Principal" coffee mug beside the notepad rattled slightly.

"Are you OK?" His eyes were squeezed closed, and I was pretty sure there were tears behind them. It was hard to imagine what kind of credentials Calvin Chester might have for this position. There wasn't any sort of degree hanging behind his desk, just an inspirational poster of some men in a kayak, which, though clearly captioned "Perseverance," raised more questions than answers.

"Fine," he said without opening his eyes. "It's just been a really long day."

"But as for Kevin Holts—"

"You know what happens if the CLEAVER comes back low?"

"You don't get your bonus," I said.

"Mass layoffs. That's step one. Everybody from the principal"—here he pointed at his own chest—"to the lunch lady, out on the street. They bring in new people—all of them hacks, most likely. The scores don't get any better. The next step, they call it a re-org. But that's not what it is. They will close this school. They'll shut it down. Do you understand? They'll bus all these kids to Nee County."

It was a nightmare scenario. Ward isn't exactly Paris, but Nee County's most prominent citizens are the ones who've been given the electric chair. The Nee County kids would eat the Wardians alive, probably literally.

"Kevin Holts isn't going to raise your scores," I said, pinning Calvin's head to the wall with my eyes. "Why is he here?"

"You want answers?"

"I think I'm entitled to the truth," I said.

Calvin sat at his desk, studying his fingernails a moment. "Rebecca, we live in a world of budget cuts," he said, getting up from his chair and pacing the strip of floor behind his desk. "And those cuts have to be made by someone. Who's going to do it? You, Ms. Meer?"

"Why would *I* do it?" I said. I'd voted *for* the school bond at the last election. It had gone down in a defeat, due to a tsunami of antitax sentiment from our town's retirees, who were satisfied that the rising generation already had enough education to empty their bedpans.

"There is a hole in the roof of the gymnasium, dwarfed only by the hole in my budget," Calvin said, getting red in the face—the degree of flushing he's capable of is simply remarkable. "You don't understand why a person of Kevin's stature would volunteer to teach fifth grade. That's right. He's doing this *free of charge*. But what have you done for Davis Elementary? From what I've heard, you haven't contributed so much as a single nut-free cupcake."

"How much did he give you?"

"Just enough for the roof. But I'm confident we can expect more, enough for new floors and electric."

"New *floors*?" Arts had been the first to go, then music. There was still an out-of-tune piano gathering dust in the corner of the auditorium, but I assumed they were just saving it for kindling. The playground equipment wasn't up to code and had been removed, so at recess the children ran around a bare field.

"My focus is facilities. The research shows up-to-date infrastructure correlates strongly with positive learning outcomes."

"Then this is isn't your school anymore. It's Kevin's." That's how Kevin would see it. Crucible—Kevin's amorphous tech company—absorbed other businesses like triple-ply paper towels soak up spills.

"It's still very much my school," Calvin said. "And Kevin Holts is the best thing this town ever produced. He's a local hero."

"Yes," I conceded. "But—"

"In the short time he's been at our school, you are the only parent—the *only* parent—who hasn't been absolutely delighted at the idea of the famous Kevin Holts teaching their kid. Is he an asshole?" Calvin shrugged. "Maybe. That's not for me to say. But he gets respect—more than I do. More than any trained and certified teacher in this school does. Our credentials impress nobody. But his logo shirts and his management book? People eat that shit up."

"You need to understand something. Kevin doesn't help. Ever. He doesn't believe in it. So if he's giving you money, it's because there's something he wants."

"Oh he's got a secret agenda?" Calvin leaned toward me with a patient smile. "Excuse me, but that sounds a little paranoid. He wants the kids to test some educational software Crucible's developing. He flat out asked me, and I said, sure, fine, why not? NBD."

"That's a quid pro quo. That's unethical," I said.

"It's just two friends helping each other out. Nothing wrong with that."

"He's using the kids for product development. You pimped out your students for a roof."

"We're in tornado alley here, and we *need* a gym with a decent roof. That gym is our designated shelter. So yes, I cut a deal to keep your kid safe. You're welcome. My conscience is clear. I'd sell my plasma, if I had enough of it," Calvin said.

A week ago when *he'd* sat on the other side of *my* desk, we were just two strangers talking about scrotal trauma. Now my son was on the brink of expulsion. It felt personal. "Calvin, does all this—is this because of what you told me in your consultation? You know, about the mom? Because I would never share that."

His desk chair squeaked with just the slightest movement. "Why would you even say that? Are you threatening me?"

"Of course not. The opposite."

"I'm pretty sure that, per HIPAA, you're not even allowed to mention that to me here."

"I just wondered if this might be about us." He stood up, and so I had to do the same, though I felt there was more ground to cover.

"Us? Your kid killed the school mascots. *End of story*," Calvin said. I could see him mentally incorporating me into a new anecdote: the archetypal mom who doesn't get it, who can't believe her precious child is capable of doing any wrong. No doubt he had a vast collection of stories like these. Principals probably swapped them wherever they congregated to talk shop. Nothing I could say to him now would alter that perception. He watched as I picked up my enormous purse—in his eyes, my bulging leather bag, spewing change and wet wipes and lip balm, was like everything else about me, a tiresome cliché. I left without saying good-bye.

FIVE

One of Dr. Thad's maxims is that you don't need to solve the big problem if you can solve a small one instead. Get the gametes together in a petri dish, and it doesn't much matter why they can't make the connection out in the wild. *Who cares?* Dr. Thad says, when he's feeling impish, *pregnant is pregnant.* I felt there was a lesson to be drawn from this.

I peeled out of the Davis Elementary parking lot and tried to banish from my brain the image of Kevin Holts's bicycle shorts. He was the big problem, but the small one was Ms. Vasquez, the person who'd been Mitchell's teacher the last time I checked. I presumed she was going through a rough time, but with a combination of a pep talk and the right drugs, she'd be as good as new—*good* being a relative concept— and ready to resume her duties. I simply needed to find whatever ledge she was perched on. *If I were a woman whose world had just been rocked by Calvin Chester, where would I be?* I thought, and the irony was not lost on me.

I drove through the grim streets of Ward in autumn, passing rows of little houses flying seasonal pennants, but their wreathed doors gave no answers. *Everyone's just super in here!* they seemed to boast, though here and there, I saw driveways littered with debris that looked like the shards of smashed-up coffee mugs. Evidently the Plainsmen football team had been on one of their vandalizing streaks, and I was in no mood to judge them. A person can only take so much chipper optimism before being driven to small acts of violence.

But what I needed now—what Ms. Vasquez needed—was a venue in which a person could put aside that cheerful Midwestern facade, as ubiquitous as football jerseys, and just be publicly miserable. There was really only one place in Ward like that: the Old Cheyenne.

Monica Vasquez was sitting on one of the vinyl swivel stools, beneath a flea-bitten feather headdress that hung from the paneling. I guessed she was already three deep, by a certain floppiness in her extremities. There was a shopping bag on the stool next to her.

"May I?" I said.

"Eh," she said, which I decided to take for an affirmative. I moved the bag one stool over, noting that it contained an egg of sandalfoot panty hose (color nude), a store-brand pregnancy test, and a flyswatter, though it was not the season.

"Two more," I said to Elspeth, who was tending this afternoon. Elspeth is beloved for her quickness at the tap and her total lack of curiosity. She put two pints of tomato beer on the bar, and I took a quick swallow. "Calvin told me everything," I said. It wasn't subtle, but nothing about Monica Vasquez suggested a preference for subtlety. She was wearing a sweater with a scarecrow on it and tiny plastic pumpkins dangled from her ears.

"No secrets in Ward," Monica said, which is something Wardians are always saying to each other. And then they chuckle. Instead, a small beery sob escaped from her lipsticked mouth. "He didn't even wait till Friday to let me go."

"That's brutal," I said. An unexpected midweek firing sounded like just the sort of thing Kevin's book, *Man Up! Management*, might recommend, though personally I'd never gotten farther than the jacket copy. "What reason did he give you?"

"He said it just wasn't working for him anymore." Monica dabbed at her eyes with the corner of a cocktail napkin. "He never really got specific. What did he say to you?"

"Let me put it this way: you need to speak to a lawyer. This has wrongful termination written all over it. And I've got just the person." I imagined my sister in her flame-red pantsuit grilling Calvin like a kebab on the witness stand.

"I can't put Cal through a lawsuit," Monica said. "It would kill him."

"I don't think Calvin's feelings are what we need to worry about here."

"You've never seen him cry, have you? His whole body is affected. Chest-heaving sobs. He's a highly sensitive man."

"Monica, he *fired* you."

"Isn't it funny? And yet, by the end, *I* was comforting *him*. I stroked his hair like a little child's. I can't go through that again."

I pressed my temples, hoping to immediately erase that image. "You could appeal to the district. Let the superintendent deal with him."

Monica reached for a handful of chili peanuts with a stuttering mechanical gesture that reminded me of a claw machine digging for plush toys. "Teaching saved my life. If Krupka hadn't hired me three years ago, I would have been dead in an alley by now."

"Dead in an *alley?*" I said. Ward's teacher shortage is well known, but I'd never suspected that Principal Krupka had scraped this near the bottom of the barrel in recruitment.

"I've always felt I could talk to you, Dr. Meer . . ."

"Rebecca," I said. I was wearing my scrubs, as usual, since a morning bar run had not been part of the day's agenda.

"Rebecca," Monica said.

"And I'm not a medical doctor, though I do have a doctorate in microbiology, so 'doctor' is not entirely inappropriate. Go on," I said.

"After—after *it happened*—I went a little crazy. I did some things I'm not proud of."

"Hmm," I said, sipping my murky red beer. "For instance?"

"I burned all my Davis Toad T-shirts. I dropped out of my scrapbooking club . . . and I . . . told Charity—she's our president—that only a color-blind person would use mint-green borders with a harvest-themed page."

"There, there," I said, handing her a tissue.

"But the worst thing is—I took all my Teacher Day presents and I—" Monica's eyes darted over to Elspeth, who was fiddling with one of her large hoop earrings and flipping through a back issue of *Ladyhawk Magazine*.

"Not to worry," I said. Looking at Elspeth, I added, "Unless it's related to B-I-R-D-esses."

Monica dropped her voice to a whisper nonetheless. "I took my Teacher Day presents, and I threw them into the yards of the children who brought them. And I just keep imagining their little faces when they ran outside this morning and saw all those smashed-up coffee cups and ceramic apples—how they thought, *Ms. Vasquez doesn't love us*."

"There's a holiday called Teacher Day?"

Monica sniffed. "There's one like you in every class."

"When did you do this?" I said, keeping to the issue at hand.

"Early this morning," Monica said. "It felt so good, Dr. Meer, but as soon I threw the last 'World's Best Teacher' mug out my car window, I broke down. Now I'm drinking to forget."

People don't drink to forget memories that are only a couple of hours old; Monica was clearly a regret amateur. But the vandalism was impressive and signaled she might have a real talent for ripping up the social contract and living on the edge, or even beyond it, as I presumed there was some sort of seedy ex-teacher subculture she could connect with. It was time to reel her back in to the world of mainstream good citizenship and sanity before she was too far gone.

"Of course you lashed out. You'd been badly hurt. Unjustly hurt. That's why we have to fight this."

Monica shook her head. "Cal said something that stuck with me. He said, 'Monica, I'm giving you a gift, though you may not see it that way now. You might have spent years in that classroom, moving between your desk and the chalkboard like a zombie. You would have grown old teaching kids the trade routes of Champlain and La Salle, thinking, *This is all there is. This is life.*'" A slight shiver traveled up the back of Monica's cardigan. "I hate to say it, but he's right." She grabbed her glass and drained half of it. I did the same. It was a grim picture Calvin painted, and if we were friends, I might have patted her hand and wished her well in her new endeavors.

"But Monica, it's going to be pretty hard to find work now. There's speculation all over town—wild speculation. People will look askance." I didn't know this to be true, but it was a safe assumption. Roseanne Vonik got fired from the Donut Barn for coming to work braless some eight years ago, and the story is still told against her, although, as she argued to management, her uniform shirt was opaque and her cup size small.

"Let them talk," Monica said. "I'm leaving Ward. Who needs this place?"

"The Cheyenne needed it," I said, jabbing a finger toward the dusty feathers hanging above us. A hundred-something years after the last battles and broken treaties—though the eagles still flew and the rivers still ran, more or less—this was all just flyover territory. It seemed a shame. "Stay and fight, for the sake of the children!"

"The children were always the worst part about teaching, for me personally." She was finishing her beer, and I took a very large swallow to catch up.

"Monica, do you know who your replacement is?"

She shrugged, as if this were a matter of indifference to her. "I hate to be the one to tell you, but it's *Kevin Holts*."

"Kevin's not a teacher," Monica said.

"Exactly!" I said, slamming my fist against the bar. Elspeth looked up from her magazine and frowned.

I lowered my voice. "He's not even a real teacher. You have to see that this changes the situation."

"Oh, Calvin," Monica said, drawing a heart in the condensation on her beer glass. "You're too good for this place."

"What?"

"You people—you *parents*—you can't even begin to imagine what his job is like. The long hours, the loneliness, the *impossible odds*, Dr. Meer. You sit here criticizing him, but you have no idea the pressure he's under."

"I'm just trying to help you, Monica," I said.

"Help me? Where were *you* when I needed washable markers and five-pocket folders?"

"This isn't really about me," I said.

"Listen, I'm headed south. My bags are already in the car. I just picked up the last few things for my trip." Monica slid the drugstore bag over her wrist and stood.

"South," I said. That explained the sandalfoot panty hose and the flyswatter, anyway. *"Please* don't leave," I said, following her out the door to the parking lot. "We can fix this. We'll get your job back. I'll call Madge right now."

"Look at that. You can, like, see your breath out here?" She puffed a beery exhale my direction.

"Totally," I agreed, before I could stop myself. Alcohol is a kind of time machine, and Monica and I had ridden those beers back to our teenage years. We'd never be free of the verbal tics we'd cultivated in high school; for me they were always just a chardonnay away. Now question marks adhered to our declarative statements like lint to a sweater.

"I can't spend another winter in Ward," Monica said. She was visibly swaying now, and she put a hand on the hatchback of her ancient Volkswagen Rabbit to steady herself as she looked at me. "But about Calvin. You need to be careful there?"

"Careful how?"

"He says he knows it's irrational, but you've become, like, emblematic in his mind of all that's wrong with American parenting in our times. Everything dedicated administrators are up against: disrespect, entitlement. And you know what? He's got a point, Dr. Meer. He definitely has a point."

I made a dismissive gesture. I was not going to fall into the trap of worrying about Calvin's feelings. "You're in no condition to drive," I said, taking her arm. "Let's go back inside."

"I'm going to sleep it off in the backseat. I'll start my drive south when I wake up."

"Well, that is the responsible decision," I said. I left Monica curled up in the back of her Rabbit, snoring softly. For a moment, I sympathized with Calvin in spite of myself. His days were filled with thorny personnel issues and irate parents. The woman passed out in her car was probably not ideal at the front of the classroom. She wasn't delivering the kind of numbers he needed. And then Kevin had shown up, successful, admired, and seemingly not insane. It seemed like a good trade to everyone but me.

❖ ❖ ❖

Needless to say, my mood upon returning to the clinic was low. I hoped to hole up in my office and bury myself in paperwork, but as I slid through the back door, I walked smack into Dr. Thad.

"You're back," he said, running a skeptical eye over me. A decade in Ward has done little to weaken Dr. Thad's Louisiana accent, which people here find charming. He has a Teutonic, vaguely Alpine quality, and his pale hair and piercing blue eyes now made him seem especially judgmental. "I was beginning to worry," he said. A bit of beer had sloshed over the side of my mug and left a telltale red streak on the front of my scrubs.

"I had some things to do," I said, running a hand through my hair and extracting a leaf from it. This I tucked discreetly into my pants pocket.

Dr. Thad pursed his lips, as if weighing his words. "*Becky* . . . have you been drinking?"

"Just a little?" I said.

SIX

So, I hear you have a new teacher," I said to Mitchell that evening.
I'd waited in the car line with my heart pounding, sure that as soon
as he settled into his seat, he'd pour out the story of the overfed toads
and whatever other goings-on had transpired since morning bell at the
circus that was Davis Elementary under the Chester regime. But now it
was dinnertime, and he still hadn't said a word about any of it.

"The sub is staying. Mr. Holts," Mitchell said, without turning
around. On Thursdays, we eat grilled cheese sandwiches and watch a
nature show called *Serial Predators*. Mitchell was sitting on the floor
with a plate in his lap, watching the South African landscape roll by
in shaky footage shot from the roof of a jeep. A leopard looked right
into the camera, its mouth stuffed with boar. Mitchell finished the last
of his milk, sucking air through the straw. "He says I shouldn't worry
about the toads."

Sometimes when my car crests the little hill in the parking lot,
before he sees me, I see Mitchell standing at the curb with his shoulders
slouching under the weight of his backpack. His neutral expression, the
face he wears when there are no other faces, is a look I recognize from
the hard cases, the patients whose coverage has run out, whose last

round has come up empty. It's an expression of very adult resignation, and the shock of seeing it on childish features has made me brake hard at the empty air, as if I were averting an accident. This evening, with the swollen autumn sun sinking into the ditch behind the school buildings, I'd seen him looking like that.

"About those toads," I said, swirling my spoon around in a mound of applesauce. "What happened to them?"

"Principal Chester spilled the food into the vivarium, and they overate," Mitchell said.

I didn't reply, waiting to see if my silence would make him uneasy. But he sat placidly watching a juvenile boar flee to safety in the bush. The blue light of the television gave his profile an angelic clarity.

"*Principal Chester* overfed the toads?"

"I don't think he understands amphibians," Mitchell said.

"Are you telling me the truth, Mitchell?"

"I think so," he said.

"You *think* so?"

"Well, I wasn't there. But that's what Mr. Holts said."

Lying has not been one of Mitchell's problems. Rather, I think of it as a skill he lacks. If only he *would* say he was sorry for tattooing his classmates with permanent marker in exchange for their lunch money, or that he *did* want to go to the pep rally and wear blue and gold for spirit day, because he *does* take pride in his school, so many of his problems could be avoided.

"Principal Chester says *you* fed the toads."

"That's true," Mitchell said, turning away from the boar massacre to look at me. "But I only fed them the recommended amount. It's right on the back of the container. I noticed most of the food was gone, but I didn't know why. I wouldn't have given them more food if I'd known they were already stuffed."

His lower lip began to tremble. "I thought I was helping them, Mom."

"I know, sweetheart," I said. It said a lot about Calvin Chester and Kevin Holts's combined manipulative powers that I had believed even for a moment that Mitchell was capable of deliberate toad murder.

"I thought I was helping them, but now they're dead."

"Don't be sad. Those toads were pretty stupid. You have to know when to say when."

"Mr. Holts said they lacked personal responsibility."

"I guess that's true," I said.

"And he says man shouldn't weep for the lower animals, so I'm not going to cry about it anymore, OK?"

I rubbed his back in the way that used to put him to sleep when he was an infant. "OK," I said.

"Everyone blames me for the toads, and it's not fair, but Mr. Holts says I don't need the love of my fellow students. I need to focus on becoming an individual. And it's Principal Chester's fault, but we can't blame Principal Chester, because he probably doesn't remember what happened. It was late, and he'd had a lot to drink."

"What?"

"He was intoxicated," Mitchell said. He has a pretty good vocabulary.

"Are you saying that Principal Chester was drinking *during the school day*?"

"No, Mom! *After* school. He stayed late in his office. He drinks because he's lonely. Are you lonely, Mom?" Mitchell asked, looking at my glass of wine.

"Mr. Holts told you all this?" Kevin's total lack of discretion was an unwelcome revelation. I leaned back against the couch cushions and closed my eyes.

"Mom, are you paying attention? Mr. Holts had to drive Principal Chester home, and the whole time Principal Chester was complaining that nobody thinks of him as a man once he puts on his principal hat— but Mom, that's a lie, because he doesn't wear a hat! And he said he'll never get married or even find a girlfriend again ever in his life. Then he got sick in Mr. Holts's car. Mr. Holts drives a Porsche."

Mitchell took a bite of his sandwich.

"Toads can't vomit. That's why they exploded. So Mr. Holts wasn't that mad, because if Principal Chester had exploded, that would have been even worse. He's got calfskin seats."

"I don't think it's appropriate for Mr. Holts to discuss these things with you," I said. "These are grown-up matters."

"Mr. Holts said children should be treated more like adults. If we don't learn to respect ourselves, we'll grow up to be parasites."

"Parasites?" I said.

"The many who feed off the few. Those are the parasites," Mitchell said, wiping up the last of his ketchup with a bit of crust. "Most of the kids in my class are going to be parasites. Can I have dessert?"

"Grab a pudding cup," I said, forcing myself to smile like a TV mom.

SEVEN

There was a knock on the exterior door, which functions as my private access to the clinic. On school holidays, I shuffled Mitchell in and out of this door, because our patients must never, under any circumstances, be confronted with a child on the clinic premises, particularly not one belonging to Dr. Thad or me. It's far better they see us only as allies in their war against infertility, not smug breeders with no skin in the Assisted Reproductive Technology game. Our nurse Maryellen brings her own son, Cooper Zane, in through the front, arguing he's a minor in years only, being fifteen but "as big as a full-grown man." It's probably true that C. Z. is not what women are dreaming of when they get "the baby bug," Maryellen's term for the biologically rooted drive to reproduce one's genes that shapes human culture and existence as we know it.

"Are you going to get that?" Maryellen said, because the knocking had continued as I sat there, musing, and while she swilled soda, on the clock, without a care in the world.

"Why don't you get it?" I said.

"Me? Don't think signing those papers means that you're my boss, Rebecca, because it doesn't." Maryellen is approximately forty-something-years old, but she is not above flipping her hair when exasperated, and she did it now, a swinging punctuation mark of disdain.

"That's exactly what it means," I said. "Now would you please answer the door?"

"*Here we go.* The ink is hardly dry, and it's already gone to your head," Maryellen said, sighing, but moving toward the door. As I'd known she would, because she's both nosy and insubordinate, but the nosy is even more so.

The relentless knocker was Rusty Bandercook, head custodian at Davis Elementary, the very same Bandercook who had poured a beer over his brawling younger brothers a few days before. The general public believes that sperm donors are usually video-game addicts in dirty sweatpants. Our patients like to believe they are all cash-strapped geniuses (as if sperm donation were the male equivalent of stripping your way through college). We cater to a variety of tastes, and so we have both kinds on ice, but neither bio defines the "typical donor." The quintessential donor quality is difficult to articulate, but I've developed an eye for it. Rusty had it in spades.

"What's the holdup?" Rusty said, stepping through the door. "I've got seven minutes, and you're eating into my time." Every step he took, the keys at his hip jingled.

"No, sir," Maryellen said. "You spend your seven minutes elsewhere, and that comes straight from Dr. Thad." The animus between the Bandercooks and Maryellen's people is generational and deep, and when she caught Rusty slipping out the back way with some of our more esoteric reading material stuffed under his uniform shirt—*that's a Bandercook for you!*—she'd gone running to Dr. Thad.

"Where else does he think I should go?" Rusty said. Rusty was strictly an off-the-books donor now, because when Dr. Thad got wind of it, he rightly questioned what possible use we could have for his contributions. I liked Rusty's chances of procreating in the real world—he was reasonably handsome and fairly affable, for a Bandercook. But in the gamete marketplace, he was a dud: short, Caucasian, and without any impressive credentials. "Joe Average," as Dr. Thad said. A total nonstarter. I'd thought there might be a robust market for mediocrity in ART, just as there is in life, but as it turned out, I'd been wrong. We hadn't moved any of Rusty's stock, exactly as Dr. Thad predicted.

"Just a moment, Rusty," I said. "Maryellen, would you go check up on this morning's in-vitro patient? Give her a call, please." Maryellen huffed out of the room, leaving me alone with Rusty.

"Sit down," I said. "We should talk." He took his baseball cap off and put it in his lap. It left indentations in his shaggy blond hair. I hate being wrong, but now it was time to face facts and cut Rusty loose—gently.

"Dr. Meer, can we talk some other time? Because I'm down to six minutes now, and unless you've got some new reading material—"

"About that," I began. The charade that women were lining up to get sperm from Rusty hurt no one, so far as I could see, but it did involve me accepting, paying for, and then personally disposing of a sample for which we had absolutely no use. "I can't take anything from you for a while."

"Demand has dried up?" Rusty said. He looked stricken, and I noticed a certain liquiding of the eyes. He wore the watch his grandfather had bequeathed him on his right wrist. He was the best of the Bandercook brothers, and the family had had some hopes for him, sadly unrealized. Or so I assumed—even Bandercook ambition must consist of more than the family's golden child wearing a shirt with "Rusty B." embroidered above its pocket.

"Not exactly," I pursed my lips. That quality I had first seen in Rusty was playing all over his face. It was a sort of low-grade sadness, something to do with squandered opportunities. It probably hit him hardest when he rolled a yellow mop bucket down the empty halls after hours, or removed a nest of spitballs from the ceiling of the boy's bathroom. *Wistfulness*, that would be the word. It was Rusty's wistfulness that had made me confident, the day I tapped him on the shoulder as he pruned box hedges outside the school building. He might have rejected my proposal, but he would never suspect he wasn't marketable. He *needed* to believe that. Although, truth be told, never in my career has a man questioned the proposition that the world is full of women who want to bear his children and will even pay for the privilege.

"So did you enjoy that family picnic? Any arrests?"

Rusty stood up and reapplied his hat. "I am not here to make small talk. If I can't donate, I'll be on my way." For whatever reason, Rusty is not fond of me.

"One moment. You hail from a farming family, correct?"

"My folks farmed. What of it?" He removed the cap and ruffled his hat hair, trying to smooth it into a more presentable shape.

"You might remember that from time to time, a man from the farming bureau would pull up to the place in a Cadillac, tramp through your cornfields, get dust all over his shiny black shoes, then track that dust all over your kitchen floor when he came in to give your daddy a check—a check *not* to grow."

"Mom and Dad grew soy. Corn's a losing game," Rusty said.

"Whatever," I said. "So that's what I'm doing now." I opened my purse and took twenty bucks from my wallet. "Rusty, this is for *not* leaving a sample."

"My rate is sixty." Rusty slid the bill back across the desk toward me and sat down.

"That's your donation rate. Your fallow rate is twenty."

"Doesn't seem right," Rusty said, but he pocketed the money. "So why are you cutting me off, Dr. Meer? Have I fathered too many? Because I estimate I must have fathered twenty-five to thirty by now. That's hard for a man to achieve outside a polygamous situation."

"You know I can't say." It was tempting to tell Rusty that somewhere in Middle America, his twenty-seventh child had drawn its first breath and that per "industry regulations" he was being retired as a donor, but I did not want to encourage his curiosity about these supposed children. There was a certain sentimentality in Rusty on this topic, and that is always bad news. We call it *ghost daddy syndrome*, and managing it is part of my job.

"Can you at least tell me what the limit is?"

I smiled down at my hands, coyly. *There is no limit.* But Rusty wasn't going to hear it from me. "Absolutely not," I said.

There was a burst of static from the phone on my desk, and our receptionist said, in a tone of deep depression, "Hayes Bandercook is on the line for you. He says it's an emergency."

Rusty pounced on the phone before I could decide on a reaction, picking up the receiver and speaking frantically into it. "Brother, it's me. What's happening? Talk to me, Hayes." It was a touching display of brotherly love, and it lasted about eighteen seconds. "Of course it's me. Why I'm here? That's my business. I said, that's *my* goddamned business. What's the emergency? Oh, is that right? Well, fuck you, Hayes."

The keys at Rusty's hip jingled as he slammed down the phone. "Why is Hayes calling here?"

I folded my hands in a businesslike manner and stared at him. "That's difficult for me to say, since I wasn't able to take the call."

"Well, it wasn't any emergency. I can tell you that much. It sounded to me like he was at Club Schmitz." Club Schmitz is a rough bar near the interstate where Hayes spends his days off playing pool. "You don't want *his* sperm, do you?"

This was a loaded question, and I chose not to answer it.

"Believe me, you *do not* want it," Rusty said, growing agitated. "I'm the better choice by any possible metric. Your customers are not going to be satisfied with Hayes."

"And why is that?" I said, hoping to be talked out of it. Since Dr. Thad tricked me out of my coffee cup, I'd avoided the Fuel & Flee and resigned myself to drinking tiny amounts of expensive coffee in the office. But I still craved my giant cups of gas station swill, and the idea of Hayes Bandercook had only begun to disturb and intrigue me more acutely. It was time to acknowledge the danger of keeping the lid on too tightly. Hayes was becoming a problem. It was better to vent that situation before it exploded. "He's . . . dangerous?"

Rusty snorted, as if the idea were more ludicrous than I could possibly understand.

"Well, what then?"

Bandercooks never speak ill of their own, but I could see that Rusty was struggling not to pour out a stream of abuse on his younger brother. "Only thing I'll say about Hayes—*Hayes* is kind of a joke." Rusty leaned back in his chair and grinned, as if that settled it.

"OK," I said. "Got it. I *doubt* we'll be pursuing this, but just for our records—what's his number?" Rusty gave up the number, reluctantly, and I wrote it down and slammed my notebook shut. Rusty frowned— clearly, he believed that something didn't quite add up.

"I think I'll be on my way," he said. He crossed the room and stopped at the door. "When did you say I can donate again?" He was aiming for casual, but he didn't quite hit it.

I tapped my pencil on the desk and frowned at a picture of dewy tulips hanging on the opposite wall. "Tough to say. There are . . . variables. I'll let you know."

Rusty paused with his back against the half-open door. It was unlike Rusty to linger; perhaps he suspected this was his last visit. I wondered if I should offer him his pick of the magazines as a parting gift. "I heard something about you, Dr. Meer. I wonder if you might be interested to know it."

"Yes?" I said. Immediately I thought of Hayes, of what he might have confided to his brother. But it was not easy for me to put into words what had been happening between us at the Fuel & Flee, and my vocabulary is probably a lot more expansive.

"That new principal? He says you are one crazy bitch." I gasped, and Rusty looked very pleased with himself. "Thought you'd want to know."

"He said that—*one crazy bitch*?"

"Well, no. That was the sentiment. I'm putting it in my own words. Good day." He held the brim of his cap against a sudden gust of wind, which rushed through the door as if someone had thrown it open and blew the papers off my desk.

EIGHT

M itchell, sometimes we have to do things we know we're not going to enjoy, just because it's the right thing to do," I said, shifting uncomfortably in the driver's seat. I was wearing exactly the wrong kind of underwear for a speech like this—the tiny kind that never stay in place because they're meant to be removed, not worn—and it affected my delivery. The speech rang hollow. As I pulled into an open parking space, Mitchell looked at me in a way that suggested that if he were allowed to use the word *bullshit*, he would not hesitate to do so now.

Mitchell carried the birthday present toward the building with a slow, plodding step, like a high-drama inmate being led to the firing squad.

"Keep moving," I said in my prison-guard voice. We passed through the doors of Leap of Faith, an inflatable indoor hell, into Truett Boss's eleventh-birthday party. A towering slide, a bouncy castle menaced by a green blow-up dragon, an obstacle course, and a soft-sided boxing ring filled the room, along with the sound of the continually running air pumps, loud as jet engines. Mitchell and Truett had a long history of animosity. Mitchell hadn't been invited to a Boss party since kindergarten, but now that he spent his afternoons chasing tennis balls with Truett at the club, I supposed things had changed between them.

Truett Boss was standing in the entryway with a "Birthday Boy!" pin stuck to his shirt, studying the facility's fire evacuation route so intently that a puddle of drool glazed his chin.

"Happy birthday . . . Truett?" I said. He looked at us blankly then turned back to the route's hypnotic red arrows and doorways. "What's his problem?" I whispered to Mitchell as we walked past him toward the overflowing gift table, but Mitchell kicked off his shoes and darted toward the slide, dropping his reluctant-martyr act. From a fifth-grade point of view, the party was raging hard. Kids were bouncing and boxing and screaming on every surface, and CHRISTeens with uniform T-shirts and whistles roamed the facility trying to prevent head injuries, while earning unpaid service hours and keeping overhead low. A few parents, mostly mothers, were sitting at a folding table staring at their phones. I put Truett's present on the table and headed for the door.

"Becky!" Madge said, positioning her body between me and the exit. "I've been waiting for you. Come here. We need you." I hesitated, car keys in hand. "Unless you've got plans?" Madge said.

"I've got some errands to take care of," I said. Madge looked me up and down, noting that I was wearing a dress instead of my usual scrubs. My sister has these dark, thin eyebrows and a way of arching them that implies she *already knows* everything you're hiding and that your refusal to come clean is just an embarrassment to both of you.

"Errands? You're dressed like a teen with low self-esteem. What are you up to?"

What I was *up to* was so unmentionable in this context that I followed her across the room and sank into a folding chair without answering. She and Laurel Glass leaned across the table, their heads so close to mine I could smell their shampoo. Now I was trapped.

"You're a doctor—" Laurel said.

"Actually, no. She's not a *doctor* doctor. But she works in the medical field," Madge said.

"How should I put this? Do you notice anything *unusual* about Truett?" Laurel whisper-yelled, over the noise of the air pumps, bringing her earnest, makeup-free face close to mine. She was wearing a pink flannel shirt, and her short hair spiked up in the back as if she'd just rolled out of bed. This was more or less the way everyone looked, and I hated to think how odd, how *disreputable*, I looked by comparison, wearing lipstick at nine in the damn morning. I crossed my arms over my chest, wanting to neutralize any cleavage that might be happening there.

"He seems a little . . ." I hesitated to complete the sentence, unwilling to bad-mouth an eleven-year-old child on his birthday until I knew we were all on the same page.

"Blitzed?" Madge suggested.

"Zombielike?" Laurel said.

"He's certainly taken a keen interest in the fire evacuation plan," I said. The two of them were closer to Amanda, so manners dictated that I let them take the lead in criticizing her child.

"He's hyperfocused is what he is," Madge said. "Can you tell what he's on?"

"On?" I said. "I don't really know. Maybe Benadryl?"

"Be serious, Rebecca. We mean his cocktail. I think Amanda has been tweaking it." I shrugged to convey that I had no idea what they were talking about.

"Doing a custom blend," Laurel said. "Getting prescriptions from more than one doctor. For his A-D-H-D," she said, stringing out the letters when she realized I wasn't following.

"She wouldn't do that, would she? That would be—"

"Unfair! Exactly," Madge said. "Look at our sons." Mitchell and Ethan were swinging at each other with the huge inflatable boxing gloves, while Laurel's son, Braxton, was running headfirst into the wall of the ring, falling down, and repeating the process. "And then look at Truett." Truett was sitting quietly on the carpet, which was deep black and decorated with images of our solar system, studying the tail of a comet with rapt attention. A string of shimmering drool hung from his lower lip.

"He's the perfect child," Laurel sighed. "Anyway, we need you to find out what she's giving him, so we can replicate it."

"You'd want to do *that* to your sons?"

"Absolutely," Madge said. "We need to do it, before they fall further behind Truett."

"Oh Madge, don't." My nephews spent most of their time punching each other and throwing themselves down from high places, yet even so, the thought of them drugged up like that was terrible to contemplate.

"Not *everyone* circumvented the reproductive marketplace, Rebecca. Our genes are only so good."

"Braxton can't sit still for hours at a time, filling in all those test bubbles," Laurel said. "And if he doesn't get promoted to middle school, I will never hear the end of it from Amanda."

"Mitchell can't sit still for five minutes," I said, squirming discreetly in my seat. My tiny underpants had worked themselves into an uncomfortable position and were sure to be making an unsightly lace-print rash on my skin.

"That's why we need you to talk to Amanda. She won't tell us, but she'll tell you. Out of compassion. Say you're finally looking to do something about Mitchell, and you need her help. Go do it right now, Rebecca."

"She's a Christian," Laurel said. "Be sure to mention that."

"Mitchell's not ADHD," I said. Mitchell had abandoned the boxing gloves and was throwing himself through the obstacle course, screaming his head off.

"Mitchell," Madge said bitterly, "is *gifted.*"

"But let me ask you this: what are his grades like?" Laurel said.

"They're OK," I lied. It was only a half lie: *some of them* were OK.

"Do you think those grades reflect his full, innate potential?" Laurel said.

"No."

"That's all we want for our kids—that they do the very best they can. But they can't do their best without—"

"Pharmaceutical stimulants?"

"Exactly," Laurel said. "So you'll do it?"

"I'll try," I said. I was ready to agree to anything that would get me up from that table. I crossed the room toward Amanda, subtly adjusting the position of my underpants, and sending a text: wait

"I'm so glad you're finally ready to do something," Amanda said, when I'd told her, as coached, that I needed a solid Christian favor from her. "It couldn't be easier. Matt and I have seen a world of difference, haven't we, Matt?"

"What?" Matt Boss said. He was bent over his phone, and he didn't look up. He wore a crew cut and a Ward Plainsmen sweatshirt. He'd been the Plainsmen's star quarterback once, and his romance with the former Amanda Walpace was Ward's great romantic saga of the late 1990s. They had been, and in some views remained, a truly dazzling couple. Amanda shrugged as her husband grunted over his phone, swiping furiously.

"Look, I'll show you. Truett!" Amanda called. He was sitting at the bottom of the slide, observing the chaos in the room around him. "Truett!"

"Maybe he can't hear—" I began, though my own eardrums were throbbing from the decibels of her maternal call.

"What?" Truett said. He turned his head slowly, as if her voice had just registered. Amanda wiped his drooly chin with a birthday napkin.

"Nothing, baby. You see how focused he is? He's just taking it all in."

"Is that because of the medication?" I pointed at the drool-wet napkin in her hand.

"Oh, the excessive salivation? That's nothing. That's normal," Amanda said, crumpling up the napkin.

"*That's* normal?"

"It's a normal side effect. Now this is just between us, OK?" She lifted the back of Truett's shirt, revealing a large oval patch between his flesh folds. "See? That's all it is. This is next generation, and it's a game changer. He's an absolute joy to be with now."

"He wears that *all* the time?"

"There's an option to take it off after school or on weekends—but we prefer that he not remove it," Amanda said. "Maybe you should go see what you can do about getting Mitchell on the Phocus patch," Amanda said. "The sooner the better."

"I'll go right now," I said and ran out the door.

❖ ❖ ❖

The Fox Motel is a source for all kinds of custom-blend pharmaceuticals, and as I walked through its dank halls, lined with peeling, flocked wallpaper, I entertained the fantasy of passing on that pro tip to Laurel and Madge. *Ask for Big Country,* I imagined saying, meaning a notorious red-bearded dealer in overalls who sometimes worked out of this location. *He'll take care of you.*

The place was appalling, sordid in the saddest and most pungent way. It smelled like cigarettes and murder—much worse than I'd expected. Even Hayes had balked at meeting here, but I'd rejected each of his counteroffers—Barrelhouse Burger, the shooting range, Hiram Ward Park—insisting on the sleaziest and most secret locale in town. I carefully wrapped the knob in a tissue before opening the door to room 118.

Hayes Bandercook was sitting on a chair in the corner, avoiding the bed—a wise move, because invisible armies of pathogens were probably marching down its paisley coverlet. He muttered hello, looking embarrassed, and I put my purse down without answering or apologizing for my lateness. He'd waited, and now I was here. I'd thought of him every day since the day in the park, and two or three nights I'd even dreamed about him—weird convoluted dreams that woke me up in the very early morning, feeling nauseated and thirsty.

"Why—" Hayes said in his low, sleepy voice.

"Not now." The less we said, the better. Hayes likes to talk, but it's not one of his top skills. He was wearing his muddy brown work boots, but not his lineman's suit. He had on a shirt with buttons and there were ironed-in crease marks in his pants. Even his messy hair had been combed back—he looked like a reluctant child dressed up for church, and I wondered if somehow he'd thought of this as a date. The short brown curtains behind his head let in very little light, so I turned on the room's one lamp. Hayes seemed surprised, but I wanted to see what I was doing, clearly, so that it would keep me from doing it ever again.

I went to join him in the chair. I parted my legs across his lap, sliding down to sit on top him. My dress rode up my thighs. For a moment neither of us moved. His lower lip twitched as if he wanted to speak, but he said nothing. Hayes took the hem of my dress and pulled it up over my head. I heard him make a noise when he saw what I was wearing—a bra I bought without admitting to myself why, the kind that pushes up every ounce of breast meat, so that I looked like a dam about to overflow, and the tiny underwear that migrated upward with every step I took. I couldn't see his face, because my dress was stuck over my head; he'd forgotten to unbutton it. I yanked at the fabric, and Hayes fumbled for the button.

I had known Hayes—known *of* him, anyway—for years. He was most visible after storms, scaling poles and repairing downed lines. I drove past him without looking up and walked by him without saying hello. I had ignored him all over town, through all four seasons, only dimly aware of his interest. But now I had such a weird, relentless craving for this man.

My hands were shaking—I couldn't get to him fast enough. He shifted in the chair to let me unbutton and unzip him, but did nothing else to help me with his clothes. I pulled and slid them off him, and when I had finished, I knew the lamp had been a mistake.

Hayes has the kind of muscles that never went to college. He does not mix protein shakes in a blender or grunt through a thousand reps at the gym. There's a sinewy, solid quality to him that makes you want to run your hands over him, though I had never heard any other woman admit to such an inclination. I bit my lip. The combined experience of seeing and touching him made me feel lightheaded and desperate, like a person who might chew glass or knock on Big Country's door in the middle of the night, begging for a fix. Hayes had just barely begun to touch me—he hooked a thumb under the waistband of my underwear and slid them incrementally downward, as if there were no reason to hurry. I pulled them off with both hands, removing myself from the chair just long enough to do so. I expected to see something amused or smug in his expression, but there was only wariness, as if he could not believe that he was really here with me in the Fox Motel, and that I was back in the chair, licking his neck like an ill-behaved dog.

The wariness did not extend to Hayes's hands, which were moving over me with lightly callused competence.

"Bandercook," I whispered, gripping the back of the chair as I moved against him. Only the thin piece of latex between us, which might slip or tear at any moment, could keep more Bandercooks from coming into this world. "Bandercook," I said, more loudly.

"Please," he said, holding my hips so tightly I'd see the marks of his fingers for days afterward. "Call . . . me . . . Hayes!"

❖ ❖ ❖

I took a shower with my feet wrapped in washrags, hoping to avoid contracting toe fungus, which seemed hypocritical after everything I'd already exposed myself to. When I came out wearing the thin motel towel, Hayes was tying his shoes on the edge of the bed.

"Well," he said, looking at me, but he didn't finish the thought, if he'd had one. There was nothing to say. It seemed insane that the survival of our species was tied up in this odd system of drives and urges. The most irrational and impulsive part of ourselves was calling the shots, reproductionwise, but at least we now had the technology to thwart it. Millions of years of evolutionary history had put me in a crime motel with *Hayes Bandercook*, and now both of us seemed at a loss to understand why. On the whole, I thought, these things were better handled in the lab.

"That was—we can't do this again," I said.

"Understood," Hayes said, watching a drop of water run down my leg to the carpet. I shivered. The room was cold after my shower. I stepped aside to clear his path to the door. The thing that had begun in the park had reached its—natural? inevitable?—its *ridiculous* conclusion, and now it was time to go on with our lives and forget it. Hayes seemed to agree. I tried not to be offended as he walked toward the door, pulling a thick utility glove from his pocket, which he pulled on before he touched the doorknob.

"Good-bye," I said. Hayes turned and scooped me up, throwing me over his shoulder like a stupid caveman. He carried me across the small room and dropped me on the filthy coverlet, where hordes of invisible microbes were also mindlessly coupling, and unwrapped my towel. He pulled off the glove and smiled at me. I opened my mouth to tell him to forget it.

"One more?" he said, tracing a line up my thigh with his thumb. He leaned over to kiss me, and I threaded my hands around his neck and pulled him down.

"Hayes," I said.

❖ ❖ ❖

My hair was still damp at the ends when I picked up Mitchell, fifteen minutes late. He was standing in the parking lot with Madge and his cousins, waiting.

"Sorry," I said.

"No problem!" Madge said, but this was just for the benefit of the children. "What is going on with you?" she whispered in my ear. "Are you keeping the lid on?"

"*Yes.* I just lost track of time," I said.

"You look like you might be about to sail right over the edge. I know the signs," Madge said. For a moment I considered confessing where I had been and with whom. Madge would be scathing—which I deserved—but compassionate. She'd take me home, and while the boys kicked soccer balls over the fence, I would have to sit in her kitchen and confess every detail of the relationship. I imagined the air quotes she'd use around that word, *relationship*, and precringed. I'd be defiant at first, but as she detailed the absolute unsuitability of Hayes or any other Bandercook, I'd come around. I'd agree to meet the boring middle-management divorcé she'd been telling me about for months, Brad or Bryan or something. Maybe there would be a connection. Maybe, over months or even years, Brad or Bryan and I would begin to lay the foundations of a solid, mature relationship. Eventually we might marry, in a small civil ceremony to which Mitchell would wear a rented tux. We'd spend Saturday mornings reading gardening magazines and drinking French press coffee. The idea sickened me. I looked Madge in the eye and summoned up the righteous anger of a practiced, habitual liar.

"Marjorie, I am absolutely in control. I just lost track of time."

"Fine. Geez," Madge said.

NINE

Madge had promised me that running a PTO meeting was foolproof, but the mood in the library conference room was one of skepticism. This was my first time doing anything at all at Davis Elementary, and there were many who felt I did not deserve a leadership role. The resentment from the other parents was palpable. But Madge was embroiled in jury selection up in Nee County and had asked me to take over the food drive, and at the last possible minute, too, "since you've got everything under control."

"Thank you all for coming to this sit-down," I said, removing a film of cellophane from the tray of crudités I'd purchased in the reduced-for-quick-sale cooler at the Handy Farmer.

"A sit-down is what mafia guys have," said a kindergartner's parent. She had a confident ponytail and had pulled a wheelie briefcase in behind her, but now she blushed and looked to the others for confirmation, as if she had spoken out of turn.

"It simply means an informal meeting," I said. For a *formal* meeting you have to go through Bev, and get it on the calendar, but I was steering clear of Principal Chester's office.

"Caitlin's right," Pastor Dan said, clasping a reassuring, pastoral hand over Caitlin's manicure. "A sit-down has criminal connotations. Those things usually end in a hail of bullets." Pastor Dan Eubanks was room dad for grade five, and parent to ten-year-old triplets, his "little miracles." I'm not going to say that I know Pastor Dan from work, but, come on, *triplets*.

"Let's get started," I said, gesturing to the wall, where the thin needle of the second hand was making silent laps around the clock face. We had only fifteen mutually agreed upon minutes in which to work.

"Anyway, the food drive. It's a pretty straightforward project," I began. I was not at all sure that was the case. The food drive was the centerpiece project of the PTO, but Madge had warned me that, from a logistics perspective, it was a "nightmare in a can."

"Wait," whispered Caitlin, pointing to Pastor Dan, who had dropped his head and folded his hands, and appeared to be contemplating one of the barrel-shaped buttons of his fisherman's cardigan. After a moment, he raised his head and removed a blessed cherry tomato from the tray. We had nine minutes left.

"So," I said, clasping my hands together, "the food drive."

"Can I jump in?" Pastor Dan said. "The Eubanks family has always supported the food drive in the past, but this year . . . I don't know. I just feel kind of 'meh' about the whole thing."

This was bad. Pastor Dan is not only the only male, ordained room parent but also, as he says, a real "mover of hearts," to say nothing of wallets. As went Pastor Dan, so would go the sit-down.

"You feel 'meh' about it? What does that mean?" I said. Dan Eubanks typically exuded heartfelt enthusiasm and the scent of Player hair spray—a racy choice, but one that kept his wavy hair camera ready at all times. It was a fine time for him to come down with a case of ennui.

"We do this every year," Amanda Boss chimed in. She was chewing on a browning celery stick. "We bust our asses collecting food for the needy. And when the next school year comes around—guess what? We've got to do it all over again."

"Well, that's true," I said.

"Let me put it to you this way," Pastor Dan said. "What does me lugging in a sack full of canned lima beans really change? Not to mention that poverty here is nothing, I mean nothing, compared to what we witnessed in Guatemala, on our spring mission trip." Pastor Dan pronounced *Guatemala* with an exaggerated guttural quality, like an elderly smoker clearing phlegm.

"So you want to give your cans only to *the* poorest person in the world, is that it?" I said.

"I just think there needs to be some kind of misery bar that's reached before we divert resources one way rather than another. The campesinos in the hills of Guatemala would change places with our poor in a red-hot minute," Pastor Dan said. "There's no question but folks here are riding high by world standards. Riding *high*."

"So either we find a way to ship pork 'n' beans and Vienna sausages to the hills of Guatemala, or we sit back, do nothing, and wait until someone locally is as bad off as a Central American campesino. Then and only then, we act. That's your position?"

"I don't care for the sarcasm, but the point stands, Rebecca. Ultimately, it's a matter of conscience," Eubanks said. "I was speaking with my kids at dinner the other day, and they really turned my head around on this whole topic."

"Your kids?" I said. The Eubanks triplets are photogenic Bible-camp habitués, but they are, after all, only ten years old.

"Now, to give credit where it's due, it was something their teacher said to them. Kevin Holts."

"My ears are burning," Kevin said, leaning in the door. He spent his conference period doing body-weight training in the library. He must have heard us in the midst of all his squats and burpees.

Dan Eubanks stood up to shake his hand. "Mr. Holts, these good people are about to be engaged in a food drive."

"I urge you to reconsider. Think about it: when we tell these kids to bring in cans—to go to their own pantries and load up *their* food for people they don't even know? What are we saying to them? We're saying, you're here to serve others. You have zero rights of your own. Zero." He made a circle with his hand, to better drive home this subtle numerical point.

"But we're not saying that. We're just acknowledging the fact that some people have plenty of food while others are hungry," I said.

Kevin threw up his hands, then let them drop. "And so it begins. The forced redistribution of wealth."

"It's just canned food, Kevin. We are not ending capitalism."

"The issue is not the cans. The issue is altruism itself—whether these kids *do* or *do not* have the right to exist without giving canned food to hungry people. You're telling them they don't. You're demanding that they buy their lives, can by can, from any bum or hourly employee who stumbles along with a growling stomach. And I say *enough!*" Kevin brought his fist down into his open palm.

"Not to mention," Caitlin said. "Is this really the best use of community resources? I mean, the school budget is still pretty tight. Maybe we need to funnel our compassion inward, where it can do the most good for *us?*"

"Exactly!" Kevin said.

"I move that we consider just skipping the food drive entirely," Pastor Dan said.

"We can't not do the food drive," I said.

"Show of hands?"

"Motion carried," Amanda Boss said. Then she pointed a carrot toward the clock. "Time's up. Are we meeting next week?"

"Yes," I said.

"Whatever for?" Pastor Dan said. "We just voted down the food drive. I move that we reconvene next August. Parents?"

I kept both hands at my sides, but even so, the motion carried. Kevin Holts gave everyone high fives as they passed through the door. He stood waiting for me, the last to leave, his palm in the air.

"Forget it," I said.

"Come on, Rebecca. Don't be a poor sport. That was democracy in action."

"That was you in action." There was no situation, however difficult, that wasn't made worse by Kevin's involvement. With a nudge from Kevin, people seemed ready to give in to their own worst instincts. I'd done it once myself. "Can we talk about this?"

"My classroom in fifteen minutes," Kevin said.

❖ ❖ ❖

Kevin was leaning against the door of his classroom, flipping through a fat paperback.

"Meer. You're not wearing a visitor's badge?" I'd slipped up the stairs to room 304 without signing in. Up close, you can see that Kevin has pale-red eyelashes, which I find unnerving, so I stammered a bit.

"I'm kidding. No self-respecting adult should submit to Cal's bullshit rules. I'd have done the same," Kevin said.

"I'm a little concerned about Principal Chester," I said. "Mitchell says he's been drinking."

Kevin shrugged. "He's a pretty good guy, for a statist. But you—are you trying to screw up your kid?"

"Of course not," I said, though the question may have been rhetorical.

"So why did you go and antagonize Calvin? Whatever you did to him, you did not do your son any favors. Mitchell's in his sights now." Kevin adjusted his weight against the classroom door. He very pointedly had not invited me to enter it. "And that's a shame, because Mitch is something else. Just an all-around great kid."

"You think Mitchell is a great kid?" I said.

"Kids like Mitchell are the reason I got into teaching. It kind of validates my whole career."

"You got into teaching *last month*," I said, but without malice, because to my horror, as well as Kevin's, I had burst into tears. Not one of Mitchell's teachers has ever praised him.

"And here come the waterworks. You're a live wire, Meer," Kevin said.

"Sorry," I said, wiping my eyes and struggling to regain my composure. "It's just that Mitchell's teachers usually dislike him."

"Well that's some bullshit, because that kid is special, and I don't mean that in the diminished-capacity sense of the term."

It was too much. I felt a sob rising in my throat, but I bit my lip and forced myself to imagine Kevin sipping a colon-cleanse smoothie in his triathlon unitard, and I got through it. Kevin reopened the book he was reading and began to thumb through the pages, unwilling to engage with more of my emotions.

"Are you out here reading a novel?" I asked, when I could trust my speaking voice.

"*This* is not a novel. This is my teaching manual. Everything I need to know is contained in these pages." He lifted the cover to show me.

"But that's *Atlas Shrugged*," I said.

"You're damn right it is," Kevin said.

"It's a work of fiction."

"I'm pretty sure it's not, Rebecca. The names were changed to protect identities, OK, but all of this shit really happened. It's a kick-ass book."

"You've read the whole thing?" I said.

"I've read enough to get the message. This book changed my life."

"The part of it you read," I said.

Kevin nodded. "Look, I don't want to get into too much of this on school property, but I do want to let you know—I have regrets."

I forced myself to look at him. The pale eyelashes, his Crucible polo, even the way he bent his tall frame to look down at me with his unreadable eyes—these things churned up such a potent mixture of shame, resentment, and confusion that I thought it might be physically impossible for me to just stand there, being civil.

"I regret *all of it*," I said.

"Whoa. You regret *all of it*? Or just the aftermath?" He was blinking rapidly, pointing a finger at me, as if I were a dull-witted student in one of his entrepreneurial boot-camp sessions who had accidentally hit upon a relevant point. It was just as I remembered: no conversation with Kevin can ever be straightforward or easy; he has to pick everything apart. I felt that it would be less unpleasant to smash one of my fingers with a hammer than to continue talking like this, but that option wasn't on the table.

"I hope you can appreciate that this is very difficult for me." I'd made some regrettable phone calls when it all fell apart, our brief and strange "relationship." The things I'd said to his voice mail when it became obvious he wouldn't take the call—I hoped he'd just deleted them without listening. But after some time, he had picked up and told me not to call again, with a cold firmness in his voice that people reserved for telemarketers. It was humiliating to recall it.

"I understand that," Kevin said. "I'll keep this brief. Mitchell," he said. "Now that I've spent some time with him—"

"Some *time*?" I interrupted.

"Not a lot of time, true. But the thing is I MindMapped him."

"What does that mean?"

"It's a program Crucible's developing and, granted it's still in beta, but the idea is that it optimizes educational outcomes by building a computer model of each learner's brain so that media can be targeted to favored modes of cognition."

"That sounds like digital snake oil," I said.

"Look, the thing is, he's a 97 percent match for me. We're essentially the same brain. Now that can happen by chance, maybe, but the most likely explanation is that it's not chance."

"Maybe your program is buggy," I said.

"Right. Could be. I mean, I believe in the team we've got on this thing, but maybe there's some bad code in there. Probably is. That's why we test."

"Good to see you, Kevin," I said.

"Wait, please. It's late in the day to be having this conversation. It reflects poorly," he said. "Of that I am well aware."

He seemed to be hoping I'd chime in, but I said nothing.

"Jesus, this is awkward," Kevin said. "But there's no way—your kid—he's not mine, is he?" He stuttered the question. I'd never heard it before myself, but that stutter figured into his local mythology. It was one of the many obstacles he'd overcome on his road to glory. He'd cured it completely, on his own, simply by willing it gone, so they said.

"Of course not," I said. I stared at him as if he were a potentially dangerous lunatic, and he blushed up to his ears.

"OK, understood." I noticed that he had not shifted his position and that what at first appeared to be a casual lean was actually Kevin pressing his entire weight against the door, keeping it closed. I heard a muffled scream from inside the classroom. "The kids are in there working some things out. I should probably check in."

Kevin opened the door, and a little girl in a bicycle helmet tumbled out into the hallway, belly-flopping on the tiles. "Back inside, Emma T. We don't run from our problems in room 304." A pair of hands appeared, each grabbing one of Emma T.'s ankles, and dragged her back into the classroom. "Nice job," Kevin said, stepping through the doorway. He clapped his hands loudly, and the room fell silent. "OK, people. So where do we stand?"

"Seven in the outer darkness, ten wage slaves, and five industrialists," Mitchell said. "Hi, Mom," he added. He was wearing a helmet and armed with a foam sword.

"That's an excellent morning's work, kids. You can be proud of yourselves. Now drop your weapons and get out your language arts books. I want you to read chapter four in silence, while I check in with the markets. Oh, and for those of you in the outer darkness," Kevin said, raising his voice slightly, "continue with your test prep books. When you're ready to challenge, you may ring the bell."

"What is the outer darkness?" I whispered because silence had fallen in the classroom, interrupted only by the whooshing sound of turning pages and the clack of Kevin's keyboard as he executed a series of rapid stock trades.

"The ones who can't pass the CLEAVER. They're in the cloakroom." A row of children sat in the narrow dimness, working through practice tests, the tops of their small heads brushing the coats that hung above them.

"Kevin, you can't do this," I said.

"I have to do it. Those kids are a drag on the rest of the class."

"It's cruel. Let them come back to their desks!" I said.

"Oh, I will. When they get up to grade level or when they're ready to challenge one of our industrialists to foam-sword combat, they ring the bell. You pass the test or beat an industrialist, and you're back in."

"Does Calvin know you're doing this?"

"This is far more humane than Calvin's plan. He's all about the CLEAVER, whereas my kids now have two ways to succeed: kick ass academically, or kick it literally." He turned back to his screen. "Meer, I'm dealing with some unexpected volatility in the markets. I'm going to have to insist that we table this for now."

"Absolutely not," I said.

He sighed. "Calvin's rounds begin in five minutes. Do with that information what you will."

The trouble with Calvin is that you can't count on him to overlook a small infraction—me in a classroom without a visitor's pass—in favor of tackling the real problems, the ethos of brutal competition that had taken root in room 304 and the fact that the entire curriculum had been replaced with an Ayn Rand novel. "Fine. We'll table it," I said, and after checking that the halls were clear, I slipped through the back door to the parking lot.

TEN

"Never again. I mean it," I said to Hayes, splashing my face with water from the cracked Fox Motel sink and trying to work myself into some kind of shape to appear in the elementary school car line. My ponytail holder was lost forever in the crack between the wall and headboard, and my hair blew out from my head as if from the head of a person who has been rolling around all afternoon on motel mattresses, which, *yes*. But even worse was the sleepy, depraved sensuality I saw in my face. The pert smile of a responsible suburban mother was gone, and instead I had the languid eyes and swollen lips of a woman who has just emerged from an opium den, and unwillingly at that, probably only after some kind of a raid.

"OK," he said, zipping up his lineman's suit, but he grinned in a way that raised doubts. I left first, without a good-bye kiss—because it was *over*, not because I was unable to risk it—and ran into Big Country in the hallway. He hooked his thumbs in his overalls and looked down at me, in a professional, appraising manner, blocking my way.

"Now if I was a betting man, I'd guess you're the type of bitch who likes to paint a stately pleasure dome now and again." His smile was infectious. He meant *bitch* in the best possible way. I could tell. He was big and terrifying, and as white as the creatures that live out their lives in the dark of deep-sea caves, but he had a certain courtliness, and the interpersonal skills of a born salesman. I trusted him immediately. "This is your flavor, isn't it?" He pulled a package with three tabs of Xanadu from the small front pocket of his overalls, letting me take a quick look.

I shook my head. "Chardonnay," I said. "Mostly."

"Huh," Big Country said, smoothing his red chin beard to a thin spike between his hands. "Well, you ever get an idea you want to ride the dragon, you come see Big Country, OK?"

"I'll do that," I promised.

❖ ❖ ❖

"Sure, it *could* happen," I said, and Nina Flyte and Channel 8's Reyne Reynolds leaned forward in their consult chairs, ready to gobble up this paltry offering of hope from my hand, like two goats at a petting zoo licking up feed corn. Reyne Reynolds's fighters *hadn't* gotten the job done, and we were here to talk in vitro.

"So there's still a chance!" Reyne said. This wasn't the reaction I was going for, but I always find it difficult to converse with people who can't fathom statistics.

"It's not, strictly speaking, impossible. But what I'm telling you is that the *overwhelmingly* likely thing is that you will never conceive a child naturally. I really don't feel confident that you're going to achieve a pregnancy unless you go in vitro."

Reyne Reynolds adjusted his tie like a man about to make a counteroffer. "What if we just give it some more time?" he said. I drummed my fingers on the desk, wondering where Dr. Thad was hiding himself this morning. He'd scrawled "in vitro—totally" on a sticky note in their file and left me to handle the rest. But I needed him here, to make these people understand that by just continuing to have sex as usual, they were simply wasting time—theirs and mine. But, I supplied the hard facts, Dr. Thad supplied the optimism and charm. It was a winning formula, and it just didn't work without him.

"Problem is, *time* is exactly what you don't have. As we sit here, dithering, you two are aging—you especially," I said, gesturing to Nina. She whimpered slightly, as if I'd pinch-twisted the flesh on her wiry arms, or attacked her in some needlessly cruel manner—but I was simply stating facts. Reyne could shuffle in here in twenty years, leaning on the arm of an inappropriately young wife, and though we'd have to search even harder for some decent spermatozoa, it wouldn't be much trouble to make him a late-life trophy baby. But Nina was about to be put out to pasture, fertilitywise. *Newsflash: nature unfair to women!* I wanted to scream, but I contained myself.

"That's an interesting point of view," Reyne said. In the Midwest "interesting" is inevitably negative. It functions as a euphemism for *incomprehensible*, *horrendous*, or even *fucking stupid*. "I just don't see how the mere possibility of a child should cost me more than a midsize sedan," Reyne said.

"Reyne!" Nina said.

"Babe, for what she's asking, we could own something late model and four door. Own it free and clear. Drive the damn thing right off the lot."

Nina Flyte began to sob, pulling a large handful of tissues from the box on my desk.

"Becky, what's happening here?" Dr. Thad said, striding through my office door. He looked crisp and relaxed in his lab coat and tie, with some fancy pen his wife had given him gleaming in his pocket. Nina smiled up at him through her tears.

"We were discussing the possibility of treating their infertility with *time*," I said.

"I think that's an excellent idea," Dr. Thad said, putting a hand on Nina's shoulders. He plucked another tissue from the box and dabbed her eyes for her.

I sank back in my desk chair, shocked to my core. The numbers spoke decisively. Reyne and Nina were more likely to discover a deposit of uranium in the little yard outside their condo than they were to produce a child by the standard method. Dr. Thad knew this as well as I did. He often works like a jazz musician, improvising his way through patient conversations with consummate skill, even art. But if this was some sort of strategy, I couldn't follow it. "You *do*?"

"I think the best thing to do is to just"—Dr. Thad began kneading Nina's shoulders—"relax." I couldn't believe what I was hearing. "Just relax," is the top fertility advice given unsolicited by obnoxious relatives. It has no place in medical practice.

"Relax?" I said, sputtering the word. I had risen from my desk chair without meaning to. Reyne and Nina were staring at Dr. Thad and me, who, for the first time ever, appeared not to be a cohesive medical team but two individuals having an argument.

"It's my *medical opinion* that this is a special case. So we give it more time. Keep going with the yoga," he said to Nina, stroking her head. "A lot of times there's a spiritual aspect at play. I think more yoga is going to do you a world of good."

"Well," Reyne said, pushing back from the desk in a way that signaled the conversation was over. "I'm glad you came in when you did, Dr. Thad. Your nurse almost talked us into God knows what."

Dr. Thad didn't correct him. He put a hand on Nina's waist like he was leading her to the dance floor and ushered her out of the room. I bit my lip to keep my thoughts to myself, but Reyne was slow to exit. He lingered a moment, smiling at me in a gloating way.

"Microbiologist!" I said. I couldn't stand it another moment.

"What's that?"

"I'm not a nurse. I'm a microbiologist," I said, breathing deeply to get my feelings under control. Never before had Dr. Thad allowed me to be referred to in such terms. *Nurse*. It was like a slap in the face.

"You're all about the money, aren't you?" Reyne said, leaning in close and dropping his voice. "I knew it the first time I saw you. You look at us, all you see is dollar signs."

"You don't know anything about me," I said.

"And I don't want to, either. I'm just glad Dr. Thad is the one in charge here, because you—well as far as I'm concerned, *you* can screw a Bandercook." That's a common insult in Ward, but it was a shock to hear Reyne's smooth newscaster voice saying something so vulgar. I bent double over my desk, gasping as if someone had punched me directly in the ovary. Reyne took it as an admission of guilt. "Truth hurts," he said, smirking. He went to join Nina.

The *truth* was that engaging in sexual relations with a Bandercook—with *one* of the Bandercooks—was never entirely absent from my thoughts. The idea burned steadily in me like a low-grade fever, and it did hurt, though not in the way Reyne intended. I was beginning to scare myself. I'd assumed the situation would run its course, that I would quickly lose interest once our silent coffee flirtation became something more dangerous and substantial. But just the opposite had happened: I'd begun to fear I was slowly unraveling. I misplaced my keys, forgot to pay the electric bill. I backed over the rosebush next to my driveway. I'd sit at an intersection as the light turned green, staring into space, until Mitchell yelled *Mom!* from the backseat or the cars behind us began to honk. I would read two columns of newsprint only to realize I'd retained nothing at all.

Each night when I looked over Mitchell's homework, I'd feel a headache coming on, and the urge to drop the worksheets on the table and pour myself a glass of wine instead was almost overwhelming. Even in the lab, my mind wandered Hayes's direction. Dr. Thad had certainly noticed something amiss. During a sort, I'd meticulously discarded all the girl sperm from a sample when the patients were aiming for a daughter. I'd caught my mistake in time—barely. Dr. Thad had laughed and said, "*This* is why we have malpractice insurance," but his confidence in me seemed shaken.

❖   ❖   ❖

"Oh, there you are," Dr. Thad said, when I came out of my office. Reyne and Nina had gone, and he was leaning against the reception desk, rifling through the candy dish in search of butterscotch. I stood staring at him, waiting for the apology and explanation, which I assumed would be forthcoming.

Dr. Thad unwrapped a candy. "I'm going to have to ask that you stop giving me that look. You're absolutely bristling with hurt feelings and reproach. It's adorable."

"Is there some reason you don't want Flyte and Reynolds to reproduce?"

"Becky!" Dr. Thad said, pinching my cheek between his fingers. "What a thing to say!"

❖   ❖   ❖

Maryellen dropped by my office, stirring faux-hazelnut artificial creamer into her coffee cup, which said "Mom" in a variety of world languages. "Did you see what I left you?" she said, pointing to my desk. A glossy brochure that I had mistaken for a stray piece of junk mail was nestled on the top of files. I picked it up and studied it. A well-groomed blond woman crouched on the tiles of her spacious modern kitchen, pressing her fists to her temples in obvious distress. "It shouldn't hurt . . . to THINK," the caption said. I raised an eyebrow and read on.

"Are you easily distracted? Do you constantly check your phone or other gadgets? Are you bored by your job? Have you ever taken a rash step that you could not later explain? Do you want to do that again?

Does your mind ever seem to 'wander'? Do you frequently feel compelled by forces beyond your control?"

"Why am I looking at this, Maryellen?" I said, feeling my face get hot. *Yes!* I wanted to scream. *Yes to all of the above!* It was as if somebody had looked into my very soul, seen my pain, and translated it into marketing copy. But I frowned at Maryellen and said, "This sounds nothing like me."

"Not *you*, dummy. *You-know-who*," Maryellen whispered.

"Adult attention deficit hyperactivity disorder?" I said, feeling a stab of joy. There was finally a name for the condition I'd been battling the past few weeks, and a cure that didn't involve peeling the clothes off Hayes Bandercook. That course of treatment had entirely backfired. The more I saw of Hayes, the more I wanted to see him. Meeting a Bandercook in a motel once was a harmless lark, going back for seconds was a troubling trend, but three—or was it four times now? *That* was rock bottom, or maybe even some layer below rock bottom—the red-hot molten core of dysfunction. I was ready to admit I needed help. Just not to Maryellen.

"No, Maryellen, I *don't* know who. I don't know anyone who is suffering from this imaginary condition, and neither do you. This is absolute nonsense," I said, scanning the brochure for the number to a twenty-four-hour help hotline.

"Think," Maryellen said, rapping the side of her skull with her fist. "Use your common sense."

But it hurts to think! I wanted to say, but my dignity would not allow me to make the confession, not to her. I pressed the pads of my fingers to my lips, pretending to use my common sense. Maryellen can get very heated about "common sense," a commodity she believes she possesses and which she feels gives her a more valid worldview than her better-educated employers. "Hmm . . . could it be, uh . . . one of the Bandercooks?" I said throwing out the first name that came to mind.

"The *Bandercooks*?"

"Yes. For instance, Rusty, or possibly . . . Hayes?" Maryellen was staring at me as if I'd just dropped an f-bomb. "You know, Hayes the . . . electrical guy?"

"Oh, I know him very well," Maryellen said, in a way that indicated she didn't think much of him, nor of his parents and grandparents before him. "What in the world are you doing mixed up with those people?"

"I'm not *mixed up* with them," I said, faking a slight chuckle.

"Those two are—" Maryellen retracted her chin into her turtleneck sweater to indicate her dismay at all the unspeakable things they were. "Anyways, the person I mean is *Dr. Thad.*"

"Dr. Thad is fine," I said. He'd rolled in late a few mornings, but I hardly took that for evidence of pathology.

"Is he? And will he be fine next month? Look here," she said, underscoring a line of copy with her fingernail. "This is the kicker."

"Do your symptoms typically worsen between the months of October and February? Ask your doctor if Phocus is right for you." I read aloud. "Maryellen, *everything* worsens between those months. Especially here," I said. Ward in summer was drab enough, but winter Ward was an icy hellscape of drear. People put on weight, drank to excess, got in fistfights, had brainless accidents, and ordered things from late-night infomercials. The whole town came unglued.

"But when does Dr. Thad get all loony? Just *think* about it," Maryellen said, wiggling her eyebrows to urge me on to the right conclusion.

"Hmm . . . ," I said, resting my chin in my hand and again pantomiming deep cogitation.

I briefly indulged the fantasy of telling Maryellen that in spite of her proven track record, I was going to have to let her go and replace her with someone less aggravating. "Stop relating to her as *a person*," Dr. Thad advised me once when I raised the issue of giving Maryellen the boot. "Does this box of tissues annoy you? Are you offended by these forceps? They're simply tools. We don't have to engage with them on a human level."

"Well?" Maryellen said, drumming her fingernails on my desk, like a trio of galloping horses going nowhere. She was close enough to me that I could smell her high-end hair spray. She bought it from a salon in Omaha, making the drive whenever the canister got low, with her two bichons frises yapping in the backseat, and her weird son, Cooper Zane, listening to British folk singers of the seventies through his headphones, because the dogs, to their credit, will not stand for this music to be played over the car's speakers. These details, poured into my ears against my will as we prepped the exam room or locked the place up for the night, now made it hard to think of her as just another office supply. *Tissue box. Forceps.*

"What are you glaring at me for? Do you get it or don't you?"

Maryellen and I were going to grow old together in the middle of the godforsaken prairie without ever understanding or liking each other, and that was that. "I'll have to give it even more thought. You may be on to something. Why don't I go think about this in the lab, and you think about it *while returning patient calls?*"

Maryellen harrumphed out of my office, the rapidity of the friction between her pants legs as she exited presumably indicating her level of irritation.

I called the hotline as soon as she was out the door.

ELEVEN

Mitchell swung his dangling legs back and forth on the edge of the exam table. "Classic, so classic," Dr. Eli Bacon said, scribbling notes on a tablet as I described Mitchell's subpar grades and his various disciplinary incidents. "He's definitely ADHD. We could do the test, but frankly, I don't see the point."

"I think, as a scientist, I'd feel more comfortable if we *did* do it," I said.

Dr. Eli raised her eyebrows above her tortoiseshell frames. Eli was short for Elizabeth, evidently. "There's no way that test will change my recommendation. Not even if it's negative. These days I'm dispensing preventive treatment for ADHD, and he's a juvenile male, so he's high risk." She dropped her voice. "What did you come in for if you don't want the drugs?"

"I do, but—Mitchell, could you wait outside a moment?"

"Yes!" Mitchell said, delighted to be free of the exam room. He closed the door behind him, and from the sound of it, began running laps up and down the hall.

"Look, my son is fine. But I think that *I* have ADHD," I said. "Can you write up something for me?"

"OK," Dr. Bacon said. She put down her tablet and pulled off the tortoiseshell frames, letting the glasses dangle from a pink metal chain around her neck. "Is this a sting? Who are you with? Are you working for the FDA?"

"God, no. It's nothing like that. It's just that—lately—I'm having trouble focusing on my work. My mind keeps drifting to other things."

"What kind of other things?" Dr. Bacon said, without any discernible sympathy.

"Actually other thing. With a person. A particular thing with a certain person."

Dr. Bacon's look was withering. "*That* is not something I can help you with. Do you think this is the most pleasant way I can imagine to spend my morning? Let me tell you, it's not. But I do it anyway. Like an adult. You get some coffee and do your job, no matter how contrary to your preferences that might be. Don't drive up the cost of pharmaceuticals for children in need by using these drugs in such a cavalier manner. Don't even *suggest* it."

"OK," I said, chastened.

"Give that back," she added, and wrenched the scrip she'd written from my hand. "You can get your drugs somewhere else." Dr. Bacon could not resist making an *exit* from the room, storming out dramatically in her kitten heels. I noted that she'd left her prescription pad, handily prestamped with her signature, on the exam table. I deliberated a moment, then ripped some pages from the pad, and plunged them down to the bottom of my purse. A smoldering obsession with a Bandercook was *very far* from normal, and if Dr. Bacon wouldn't treat me, I'd do it myself.

❖ ❖ ❖

"So what did Dr. Bacon say? What's wrong with me, Mom?" Mitchell said as we drove the pancake-flat highway toward home. He looked like he was bracing for very bad news. He looked as if I might be about to tell him we were going to amputate a leg, that if he was unable to sit at his desk, paying attention and applying himself, then he could kiss his days of being a biped good-bye. My child thought I was capable of that, or anyway, of something dire and unpleasant. He even seemed to think he deserved it.

"There's nothing wrong with you, sweetheart," I said. I knew the moment I looked into the small, cold eyes of Dr. Eli Bacon that I was not going to infuse his little blood stream with Phocus. Everyone said it was a pharmaceutical miracle, but I was now sure that for most people, it was one of those fads that would be absolutely inexplicable a few years later, like pants with a multitude of zippered pockets or products made from pomegranates. Nothing would induce me to conduct an indefinite pharmacological experiment on my son's growing brain, however convenient and fashionable it was to do so. As for myself, that was a different matter. Obviously *I* needed it badly, both for my own sake and for Mitchell's. He deserved a mother who was actually as appalled by the idea of meeting a Bandercook for a motel liaison as I would have pretended to be if someone else floated the idea in public.

"But my grades?" Mitchell said.

"Your grades aren't a medical problem. You can get better grades if you work harder." I looked over at Mitchell, a thin, pale boy with eyes so full of life they made me less reluctant to get out of bed in the mornings, and I tried to muster the appropriate level of concern for his future earning potential. I should let him know that the Wharton School of Business would not look kindly on an applicant who had made a D in spelling and that top law firms would take a dim view of a potential hire with a history of food fights, but I just couldn't bring myself to do it. My heart swelled with love for my energetic, poorly focused, underperforming son. The world would be a sadder place I thought, if I made him into a salivating automaton of concentration, a boy content to fill in test bubbles hour after hour until the bell rang at the close of school.

I would be a sadder person if he were anything but exactly the child he was. He was perfect—no, of course, he was not, not in the standard sense of the term—but he was my son, and even his eccentricities and his inconvenient traits were as precious to me as anything in the world. "You know what? Who *cares* about your grades! Just go there and try to learn something. That's all that matters. You're in the fifth *fucking* grade," I said, pounding the steering wheel with my fist.

"Mom!" Mitchell said, wide-eyed and horrified. "You cursed!"

"Sorry," I said. Shorn fields flew by us on either side of the highway, and over our heads, colossal prairie clouds were gathering in the wide sky. "Fifth fricking grade," I said.

❖ ❖ ❖

"Now what would the adult dose be, do you think?" I whispered, as my hand closed over the paper bag Bethany Miles was offering me. The online forums varied widely in their advice on the ideal dose of Phocus oral. I was proceeding on the advice of skiinnycat88, who seemed to be very well informed, but it was tough to determine from her avatar whether she held an actual pharmacist's license. I wanted a second opinion.

"What's that?" Bethany said. She had on a blue vest and a nametag that said "Pharmacist: five years of service." She was standing behind the counter under the neon "Consultations" sign, and I'd assumed her attitude would be *Welcome to the land of pharmaceuticals!* but she was wearing the grim expression of a suspicious border guard.

I raised my voice slightly. "I'm just wondering what dosage would also be appropriate for someone a little bit larger and older than Mitchell." There was a cardboard partition to protect my privacy from the Handy Farmer's other customers, mostly senior citizens waiting for flu shots, but I wasn't confident it would do the job.

"You're not thinking of taking this yourself?" Bethany was keeping a grip on the bag. The moment was becoming strained.

"Of course not," I said. I had filled out the scrip to Mitchell's name to avoid raising red flags, Dr. Bacon being a pediatrician as well as a heartless, judgmental drama queen.

"Because it's written for Mitchell, and I can't by law release it to you for any other application."

"I understand," I said, pulling the bag my direction. Her grip was like iron.

"I certainly hope that you *do*. From what I hear, he desperately needs this treatment." I snatched the bag of pills and put it in my purse.

Shane Glass was dust mopping on the other side of the partition, not even pretending he couldn't hear us. "That's pretty sick about the toads, Dr. Meer. Your kid is like a young Ozzy. So metal."

"It was just an unfortunate accident," I said.

"Yeah, but"—Shane looked over his shoulder to see whether any of the seniors were listening, but they were absorbed with sudoku and their own problems—"I heard he *bit their heads off.*" His voice was filled with awe.

"That's disgusting. What gave you that idea?"

"That's just what I heard," Shane said, shrugging.

"Well as usual, the gossip is all wrong," I said, loud enough so that the entire pharmacy waiting area could hear me. Shane mopped off toward the back of the pharmacy area, whistling.

"Can you ring this up here?" I said, pushing a jumbo pack of quilted toilet paper across the counter. It'd been sitting at my feet, forgotten, as I grappled with her over my ADHD prescription.

"Nope," Bethany said. "Take it to the register up front."

"But there's nobody working that register."

Bethany rolled her eyes and picked up the in-store pager. "Shane to the front. Shane to the front register," she said. "Give him just a minute."

I wandered down aisle seven, "Seasonal Items," carrying my giant pack of toilet paper, waiting for Shane to park his dust mop. When I got to the register, Hayes Bandercook was ahead of me in line. He was dressed in his off-duty clothes, standard issue Bandercook attire, a fading concert T-shirt and pants that didn't even contemplate an idea of coolness. But I knew it was him and not one of his brothers by the angle at which he held his shoulders, the shape of his head, the color and wave of his hair, and the way he tapped one foot, fidgeting with nervous energy. I had inadvertently memorized every detail of him. He went pale when he saw me and ducked his head without saying hello. So it was going to be like *that*. I stared at the calendar behind Shane's head until my eyes burned.

"Try the fruit punch next time. It's way better," Shane said, removing a sports drink from Hayes's basket and ringing it up.

"I like the lime," Hayes said.

"But have you *tried* fruit punch? It's all Hawaiian and shit. Notes of guava."

"I'm happy with the lime," Hayes said.

"OK," Shane said, throwing up his hands dramatically. "Just trying to broaden your horizons. Some people aren't open to change, I guess. Wait a second—what have we got here?" Shane said, his tone changing to surprise as he scanned the next item, something in a cardboard box.

"Shane," Hayes said. Whatever Hayes was trying to convey with his tone, which was pitched somewhere between a plea and a threat, it was completely lost on Shane, who was engrossed in studying a box of condoms.

"Hell yeah!" Shane said, nodding his approval. "The value pack! Congrats, buddy," Shane gripped Hayes's arm. "I am so happy for you. Man, it's been a while, right? Next time get the lambskin though. Trust me. It's a whole other experience."

Hayes slapped some cash on the counter as Shane bagged up his purchases.

"So I gotta ask. Who is it?"

"It's your mom," Hayes said quietly, taking the bag.

Shane laughed, spitting out the fruit punch–flavored sports beverage he'd just sipped. Hayes was already heading through the doors without a backward glance. "Sheila?" Shane yelled after him. "No, man. I do not approve. Don't settle. You're a handsome guy. You can do *way* better than Sheila."

"Find everything you were looking for, Dr. Meer?" Shane said, scanning my toilet paper. I nodded, unable to speak. "Quilted for comfort—that's the good stuff," Shane said. "Excellent choice."

❖ ❖ ❖

In the car, I washed two of Mitchell's pills down with a bottle of flat Diet Coke that had been riding in my cup holder since the day before. For just a moment, I considered resting my head against the steering wheel and sobbing. But Sheila Glass called keno at Club Schmitz five nights a week. It made sense, I told myself, despite the age difference. They were probably soul mates.

"I wish you the best," I said, toasting the two of them with my flat soda as I swallowed a third pill for good measure. I really needed to get my head in the game. *The game of life.*

TWELVE

I woke with a renewed sense of clarity and purpose. It was definitely the drugs. As I moved through my morning routine—shower, breakfast, sack lunch for Mitchell—I was not only more efficient, I was more aware. I was noticing things I'd never taken the time to really study, like the beauty of the sunrise or the thin line of grime coating the bathroom floorboards. My newfound clarity was a mixed bag.

Friday morning is reserved for lab work, and it's the best part of the week, just Dr. Thad and me alone in the cold and quiet, so in sync we're like one person. Lately, I hadn't been pulling my weight around the office, and our thinning bottom line reflected that. But now I was back on my game and ready to demonstrate to Dr. Thad that our partnership was not a mistake.

I found the door to the clinic unlocked, but it was dark inside. "Dr. Thad?" I called.

There was a body lying slumped across the waiting room couch. So it was going to be *that* kind of a day. I hung up my coat and flipped on the overhead. Fluorescence is nobody's friend, but Dr. Thad looked especially corpselike under the tube lights, all puffy eyes and graying stubble.

"Becky?" Dr. Thad said, throwing an arm over his eyes to shield them. "What time is it?"

"Seven thirty," I said. I walked past him to the break room to start some coffee.

"A.M.?" he called after me. I put another scoop of grounds in the basket and shook my head. There are three main scenarios by which Dr. Thad can destroy our practice. Scenario One, the odds-on favorite, is that Dr. Thad will throw his sobriety coin out the sunroof of his car as he speeds down O Street to Dot's Liquor, where he will park across two spaces and stride through the doors like a conquering hero—he is still a beloved former regular at Dot's—to trade his recovery for a bottle of Dublin's Bane.

Scenario Two is divorcing his wife, Angie, and this, too, has a lot going for it, because the Sorenson marriage is notoriously tumultuous. Drop by their cul-de-sac and push through the rustic door of their faux Tuscan unannounced, and the odds are better than good that you will find Dr. Thad careening through the place like a wild-eyed Scarlett O'Hara, while Angie abandons her Midwestern reserve to hurl knick-knacks and accusations. Problem is, Mrs. Dr. Thad put him through medical school and is entitled to a large cut of the business upon their divorce. Ex-Mrs. Dr. Thad would evolve from a mere thorn in the side to a terroristic agent of chaos. It's just too ugly to contemplate. All things considered, Scenario Two is probably my least favored way for everything to go down in flames.

Lastly, Scenario Three. This is the ever-present danger that Dr. Thad is taking his work home with him again, so to speak, although more likely he'd be taking her to the hotel and casino over at Loop City. Volatile, dark-haired patients are a constant threat—adultery with a piquant twist of malpractice.

I heard Dr. Thad getting up, groaning with the stiffness that comes with sleeping on waiting-room furniture past a certain age. "Dr. Thad,"

I called out, as the machine began to spit coffee into the pot. "I don't mean to pry—but are you in some kind of a downward spiral?"

A moment later, he was standing in the doorway glaring at me. "Becky, I *really* don't need your judgment right now," he said.

"I'm not judging you," I said. I would *never* presume to judge Dr. Thad. But by the puffy face and bloodshot eyes, I thought we were looking at Scenario One. "Can we call your sponsor?"

"That's not what this is," Dr. Thad said.

"No?" I said, giving him a quick scan and moving down the diagnostic checklist. "Problems with . . . um . . . Angie?" Everyone calls Angie "Mrs. Dr. Thad" around the clinic, so saying her name always feels unnatural. The only response from Dr. Thad was a groan, as if to confirm my diagnosis: Scenario Two, divorce. He sipped the coffee I'd just handed him.

"Becky, I really don't know how much longer I can stay married." Then he sighed the way middle-aged husbands do when they feel like martyrs because of all the adulterous opportunities they've let slip by them.

"Which one is it?" I said, doing a mental inventory of our needy, brunette patients. Call it a hunch, but I felt we were looking primarily at Scenario Three, adultery and malpractice, with Scenario Two, divorce and financial ruin, just tagging along for the ride.

"It's not that simple," Dr. Thad said, leaning in closer to me, hoping to sway me with one of his tough-yet-vulnerable looks.

"Yes it is," I said.

"Becky, it's not what you think. I've never felt this way before."

"Just tell me who it is, and I'll take care of it. You don't want to do anything stupid." I considered his rumpled, bloodshot appearance. "Anything *else* stupid. You'll thank me later. You always do," I said.

"Not this time," he said. "This is something . . . *profound*."

"I doubt that very much, Dr. Thad," I said. Scenario Three has the potential to ruin Dr. Thad's entire career, and the world is not going to be deprived of his considerable talents. Not on my watch.

"Becky, sometimes I wonder if you have any human feelings at all," Dr. Thad said. My tone had been resolute, *not* cold, but it can be tough to discern the difference. He put down the coffee and left, slamming the break room door behind him. I hoped he was going home to apologize to Mrs. Dr. T., and to put on a fresh lab coat so that we could get on with the work that awaited us, but there was just no telling.

❖ ❖ ❖

"Well, good morning," Maryellen said, hanging up her puffy scarlet-and-cream Ward Plainsmen jacket and unraveling a matching hand-knit scarf. She was wearing an orange sweatshirt with triangles of black duct tape applied to represent the features of a jack-o'-lantern, which was just skating the line of the office dress code. Trailing behind her, with his bad complexion and his eyes fixed on the carpet, was her son, Cooper Zane.

"You'll never guess who I just passed in the hall," Maryellen said.

"Linda?" I said. "Carl from upstairs?" Cooper Zane was shuffling along in canvas shoes, with the confused manner of a missing elderly.

"No, bubble brain! Dr. Thad! I said, 'Dr. Thad, you're headed the wrong way!' But he just barreled past me in a big hurry. What's that all about?"

"He had an errand to run, I think."

"Well I hope the errand was to go change his clothes, because he was wearing the same ones he had on yesterday."

"Huh," I said, shrugging my shoulders. "Good morning, Cooper Zane," I said, and the boy's long lashes fluttered. He mumbled something in the direction of the carpet. "No school today?"

"I opted him out. They're covering *the facts of life* in health, and I don't want him exposed to that kind of thing."

"Then there's no better place for him," I said. "You can set up your school books in the break room."

"We're strict Church of Hiram," Maryellen said, watching her man-size child plod down the hall, his backpack slung over one shoulder. "And with his good looks, the less he knows, the better." She turned to me when Cooper Zane was out of earshot. "So *what* is going on with Dr. Thad?" she said.

Not once in the long years of her employment as our nurse have I ever dished to Maryellen, though she's always trying to insinuate herself into my confidence, with open-ended remarks about how it's "hard out there" for "us single girls."

"Dr. Thad is fine. He's running an errand," I said.

"Well, I guess it's on a need-to-know basis, then," Maryellen said. "I'll just keep my head down and my thoughts to myself."

Fat chance of that, I thought. Maryellen has kept a running commentary of her entire eight-year tenure with us, narrating such dramatic events as the breakage of a pencil or the yearly onset of her seasonal allergies with cable news levels of coverage. I am sometimes nostalgic for Roy, our previous nurse, who was let go after stealing testosterone supplements to improve his performance on the dirt-bike circuit.

"Maryellen, I'm going to need all the star-ampersand-star files from the past three months on my desk as soon as possible." The files of all our needy, brunette patients are flagged with a special marker, its significance known only to me. This simplifies the tedious job of identifying the problem patient whenever a situation of this kind arises. People tend to assume that the human heart is too complex for a rudimentary filing system to reveal its deepest secrets. This is simply not the case. If I were at liberty to share my track record on resolving so-called affairs of the heart with an ordinary spreadsheet and a phone call, many eyes would be opened. But suffice it to say, experience has taught me that once I knew who she was, I could have the whole thing squared away by lunchtime.

❖ ❖ ❖

Maryellen did not reappear with the files. Occasionally she forces me to assert my authority in this way, and so I wandered into the waiting room to find her. "I thought I made it clear, Maryellen, that I needed those—what in God's name are you doing?"

Maryellen was standing on a ladder, stringing spun nylon cobwebs in the corners of the reception area. Our receptionist was pasting a crescent moon above the fire extinguisher, and Cooper Zane had emerged from the break room to position a skeleton cross-legged against the wall. The entire waiting room had been decked out with foam pumpkins, paper bat silhouettes, and a motorized reaper that bobbed its head and cackled in response to noise or movement.

"It's Halloween!" Maryellen said. "You've got to get in the spirit."

There are no holidays within the confines of the clinic. Not a wreath, not a sprig of holly, not a decorative gourd nor a stuffed bunny has ever passed our doorway. Holidays are tied to the seasons, seasons to passage of time, and time is never on our side.

"Why not just get a giant hourglass and put a sign on it that says, 'Your Ovarian Function,'" I suggested.

"Maybe for April Fools'," Maryellen said, positioning a pipe-cleaner spider on some web.

"Halloween is a difficult time for our patients, Maryellen. From sunset on, *children* will be tramping through their neighborhoods. *Children* will be ringing their doorbells. *Children* will be standing under the porch light in their adorable costumes demanding candy. Can you imagine how awful that is for them?"

"I bet seeing all those kids cheers them up," Maryellen said. She had climbed down from her ladder and opened the door to the hallway, and was now festooning our doorplate with a handful of spiderwebs. "Isn't this fun?"

Front Desk nodded, then immediately blushed, shamed at having cut loose like that in front of me. My eyes widened at her impudence—perhaps this girl was capable of more than I gave her credit for.

"It's unprofessional and inappropriate," I said, including Front Desk in my look of censure. Her hair wasn't the deep chestnut that called to Dr. Thad like a follicular siren, but you wouldn't exactly say she was blond, either. I thought she might pass out under my scrutiny, but Maryellen gave her an encouraging slap on the back and she rallied.

"Oh, don't be such a grump, Rebecca! This will take their minds off their troubles. Everyone's a kid on Halloween!"

"Those spiderwebs will remind them of the insides of their empty, aging uteri," I said. "Take all of this down immediately."

Maryellen made a face.

"I hope for your sake that you've cleaned up this mess before Dr. Thad returns."

"And when will *that* be?" Maryellen said.

Rather than answer her, I strode through the waiting room in a brisk, businesslike fashion and nearly stumbled over a small object.

"Whoopsie!" Maryellen called out, running over to grab my elbow and steady me—likely more a stalling tactic than actual concern.

"Will you look at that?" she said. The two of us studied the carpet. The object responsible was a cork, and not a wine cork, but the mushroomy kind from a bottle of champagne. It seemed to have rolled out from under the loveseat on which Dr. Thad had spent the night.

"Oh, frick," Maryellen said. We stared at it, remembering the time two years ago when we found Dr. Thad passed out in front of the waiting room aquarium and had struggled to carry his inert bulk to the car. Dr. Thad's vehicle is far too sleek and sporty to easily accommodate a prostrate body in the backseat, and it had taken quite a bit of effort to stuff him in there. Then we'd had to drive him home to Mrs. Dr.

T. in that condition, and since Angie is something of a baller in what Maryellen calls the Blame Game, the whole experience had been distinctly unpleasant for everyone involved.

Our eyes tracked to the wastepaper basket discreetly positioned behind a silk fern. A long, green-necked bottle protruded from its rim. I held the cork up to the light and wondered if anyone drank champagne alone. I found it hard to believe that Dr. Thad, even given his troubled history with alcohol, would have chosen to end his three-year stretch of sobriety by pouring a bottle of Brut down his throat solo. But I tried to believe it. I tried very hard, as I stood frozen in the waiting room, staring at the cork like an imbecile.

"What the heck is going on around here?" Maryellen said.

"Not to worry; it's mine," I said. Only a very public renunciation of alcohol had saved Dr. Thad's reputation locally the last time we'd been in a Scenario One situation. But you don't get a second chance at a second chance, not in this town, not in this business. We are keepers of secrets, Dr. Thad and I. An airtight sense of discretion—a constant, vigilant self-control—is necessary to retain the trust of our patients.

"You were drinking wine *in the office*?" Maryellen said.

"Champagne," I corrected. "I was celebrating." A dozen better stories suggested themselves the minute it was out of my mouth: patients celebrating a birth, teenage hooligans illegally drinking on the premises, a school art project to turn champagne corks into holiday centerpieces. Maryellen would have accepted any one of those with a knowing nod of her fluffy head. But I had thrown myself on this grenade without thinking.

"Celebrating what? *Halloween?*" Maryellen looked skeptical.

I tried to look cheerful, and not unlike a woman who might drink Louis Roederer in the waiting room with some of her best girlfriends, or possibly alone, straight from the bottle, sometime between COB Thursday and Friday morning. It was critical to conceal from Maryellen that Scenarios One, Two, and Three had united, forming a hybrid superstorm of life- and career-destroying power that none of my care-fully laid plans were adequate to stave off.

"Happy Halloween!" I said.

"Oh dear Lord," Maryellen said.

❖ ❖ ❖

At noon, Dr. Thad had still not returned and, feeling the pressure, I took another dose of Phocus, justified, under the circumstances, and changed into a dress I'd pulled from the back of my closet. "Maryellen, does this dress make me look like a pioneer?" I said.

Maryellen was rearranging the implements drawer. She paused, speculum in one hand.

"Well, a little bit. More like a—"

"A what?"

Maryellen made a motion of zipping her lips. "If you can't say something nice, don't say anything at all. It's how I was brought up."

"Thanks," I said. "It's for Pioneer Day at school." Pioneer Day was the anemic pseudoholiday that had replaced Halloween as a school-sanctioned event.

"Uh-huh," Maryellen said. "You know what? Let me braid your hair. It might make you look less—"

"Less what?" I said, taking a seat on the exam table and pulling out my ponytail.

"Oh, you know. Just less." Maryellen worked my hair into a com-plicated braid. When she finished, she frowned at me, the way she does when we're out of Hazelnut Kiss coffee creamer.

"It's bad, isn't it?" I said. "I don't look anything like a pioneer woman."

"I wouldn't say that. There were *all kinds* of people on the prairie in those days. You know what I mean."

"Not really," I said. I picked up the speculum and considered its possibilities. I'd signed up to bring a period-appropriate activity, something I'd nearly forgotten in my Hayes-induced haze, but now remembered. "Do we have anything lying around here that we can use to build a working butter churn?"

THIRTEEN

The Davis Elementary gym was teeming with children dressed as rustics, in deference to a handful of concerned parents who detected a whiff of Satanism in a pre-Christian Celtic holiday. Calvin himself had no quarrel with Satanism, so far as I knew, but Halloween simply had too much opportunity for self-expression, candy, and actual fun for any school administrator of his stripe to get behind it. So instead of ghouls and licensed cartoon characters, the children were dressed as a group of unarmed nineteenth-century settlers.

I set a plastic mop bucket filled with the contents of eighteen tubs of margarine on the floor of the Davis Elementary gym and stuck a broom handle down into it. "Get to work," I said to a trio of curious third graders and left the scene.

The cafeteria ladies were serving hardtack and corn chowder from the concession stand; a man with muttonchop whiskers sat on a stool and demonstrated how to make a broom out of a willow stick and sorghum. Beneath the basketball hoop, the quilting society ladies had tied on their gingham bonnets and were boring anyone foolish enough to wander within earshot with talk of ticking and stitches.

I stood beside a stack of hay bales, wondering whether I should try chatting with the lunch ladies, the only staff members with whom Mitchell is on consistently good terms, when I heard a child say, "Mr. Holts, are you going *trick or treating*?" She whispered the last phrase, which was not to be uttered on school property.

Kevin was dressed in a corporate polo and pleated khakis, a questionable choice on any other day, but a look that now made him the best-dressed and most credible person in the room.

"No, Emma B. I'll be attending Alterna-Ween. It's an ethical celebration at the county fairgrounds. Are you familiar with the Ward Objectivists?"

Emma B. shook her head.

"Of course you're not. Look at you." She was wearing pink chaps over her jeans, which was not period appropriate. "Well, Alterna-Ween is one of our biggest events. Everyone brings their own bag of candy, purchased from their own resources, to be enjoyed in the company of other rational individuals. Sharing is optional, but discouraged. Handouts? No way."

"Oh," Emma B. said.

"I would suggest that *you* forgo trick or treating as well. Did you know the practice takes its origins from ritual prostitution among the ancient Celts?"

"No."

"Well I don't expect someone your age to understand, but suffice it to say, the word *trick* does not *only* mean a silly prank. Trick or treating is a practice that injures the self-worth of all who engage in it. I believe it has no place in a democratic society."

"But getting candy is fun," Emma B. said.

"Sure it is. But having self-respect is fun, too. Choose whichever is most important to you, Emma B., because you can't have both."

"OK," the child said.

The strains of a fiddle indicated the program was about to start, so I went to the bleachers and sat next to Madge. Principal Chester emerged to scattered applause, wearing a stovepipe hat and a tailcoat, like a short and historically insignificant version of Abraham Lincoln.

"Is that Chester? He looks *bad*," Madge said.

"He's not bad; he's *the worst*," I pointed out. But Calvin did look bad, thin and drawn, like a person who wasn't living well, even, in this lighting, a bit like a real nineteenth-century consumptive. He stepped up to the mic.

"I come to you in the guise of our town's founder, Hiram Ward." Per the history books, Hiram Ward had been a God-fearing bore, not a binge drinker. Yet Calvin looked as if he'd just rolled out of a gutter and put on his tailcoat—which, if you have to wear one, is probably the best way. "This year, our children will be pioneers of a different sort—the first to take on the CLEAVER under the enhanced scoring standard. It will take grit. It will take courage. But at the end of the line, when we've made it—those of us who *have* made it—well, we can take pride in knowing that in four key subjects, according to the benchmarks set forth by the unelected bureaucrats of this noble state, though the road has not been easy, nor the path straight, our progress . . . has been adequate."

"What the ever-loving fuck," Madge said, under her breath, speaking for everyone.

"And now, I ask for your attention, as the townspeople of Ward, circa 1878, present a musical trip through time, back to the days when our fair city was a tiny outpost in the rolling sea of grass."

The Ward Quartet struck up a tune, and when Calvin gave the signal, the children began to sing. What they lacked tonally they made up for in decibels. The song was something about baling hay and shooting buffalo and stealing kisses from a pretty gal. The children stomped their feet and made big stagy hand gestures as they sang. The gym was a sea of rolling video and flashing cameras.

"This isn't all that bad," Madge said.

"It's actually kind of good," I said.

"Don't get carried away. But did you see the puffiness around the eyes? I think Chester had a rough night," Madge said.

"Do you mean to say—he's been *drinking*?" I said, as if this were a new concept.

"Well, wouldn't you?"

"Certainly," I said.

"I would not leave that man alone with sharp objects," Madge said.

Two lines of children appeared in front of the risers to perform a mash-up of the traditional Cheyenne tune "Scalpin' Season" and the pioneer favorite "Red Menace." Half of the kids were decked out in paper headdresses and tempera paint, the other half in farm wear. For the finale, they linked arms and sang about their hearty tolerance for diverse beliefs and cultures and their deep respect for centralized authority. An asterisk in the program noted that the original lyrics had been altered for content, where appropriate.

After a standing ovation, during which Calvin bowed over and over like a tipping bird, although the applause was clearly for *the children*, I found Mitchell in the crowd and congratulated him. He was beaming when he ran to rejoin his classmates, which was not a bit like him.

❖ ❖ ❖

I lingered in the gym, catching up with Madge, whose murder was not going well. Trial began in three days, and she worried that her theory of the case, though a thing of beauty, was simply too complex and subtle for a jury of our peers to comprehend.

"I've got to dumb it down. Like *way the hell down*," Madge said. "We tell ourselves it doesn't matter that our schools are crap, but believe you me, when your life is in the hands of nine subliterates, you'll see that it does matter." She was too preoccupied with her case to ask about the food drive, so I was spared having to tell her that the other parents had voted it down. I hoped that somehow the subject might never come up again. I worried she'd blame me and what she called my "regrettable people skills."

"You seem good, Becky. Like back to normal."

"What does that mean?" I said.

"Normal? Well for you it means intense, driven, and highly repressed. For a while there it seemed like you were . . . Well, anyway. Let's not get into it. Ben and I were worried."

I wished her good luck, and we hugged good-bye, promising to get together as soon as her trial wrapped up. On my way out, I stopped by the vending machine in the hall. I was beginning to feel weird. My pulse was racing, and I had a sudden, terrible craving for Cheez Bears. I inserted my dollar, but the bag stuck in the machine, swinging from its hook. I beat the glass panel with my fists.

"Easy," Calvin Chester said, coming up behind me. "Sometimes a frontal attack is not the best method. Think strategically." He tipped the machine forward and the bears fell into the slot.

"Thank you," I said, retrieving my snack and unbuttoning the top button of my dress to give myself some air. I felt flushed and panicky. I began to worry that the last dose of Phocus had been ill-considered.

"Rebecca?" Calvin said, dropping his voice. "Are you—?"

I intended to leave, but the light in the vending machine behind Calvin began to flicker, blinking on and off like it was transmitting a secret message. In spite of my distress, this caught my attention and held it firmly. It was ever so slightly to the right of Calvin's head, and I stared at it, breathing raggedly.

Calvin took a step closer. "What's happening here?"

I looked at him, though I was still somewhat preoccupied with the problem of the blinking light. "Huh?" I said.

"Exactly. Is there something you want, Rebecca?" He was leaning in very close to me, and he had dropped his voice to a whisper. I felt his breath on my cheek. I opened my mouth to answer him and a small drop of drool fell from my bottom lip, splashing onto his hand, which he had put on my arm at some point while I was studying the pattern of the flashing bulb.

"I see," Calvin said, wiping his hand against his pant leg. He seemed both disgusted and intrigued, and I was in no mood to answer any awkward personal questions about my health care.

"Excuse me!" I said and darted for the door.

❖ ❖ ❖

I returned to the clinic shaky, salivating, and in no condition to deal with Dr. Thad. So of course he was sitting on my desk, flipping idly through the star-ampersand-star files Maryellen had finally delivered, though in exchange for this and the makeshift butter churn, I'd had to promise the two of us would get together for a "girls' night" in the near future.

"What are you doing with those?" I demanded. In his current state, those files were the last thing he needed to be handling. And in my current state, with my blood amphetamine level at roughly Elvis, the Vegas years, the last thing I wanted to be dealing with was him.

"Preparing my talk for Midwest Fertile Con, of course. I assumed you had Maryellen pull these for reference, but I see no common denominator at all. We've got endometriosis, polycystic ovaries, low sperm count, and arcuate uterus all jumbled up. It's sloppy, Becky. And what is that you're wearing?"

"It's a prairie dress," I said.

"Are you sure? The length is more suggestive of a prairie shirt. It's my understanding that a lady of that time never showed more than a sliver of ankle—"

"There were *all kinds* of people on the prairie," I said, feeling defensive. I wiped a small amount of saliva from my lips with the back of my hand.

"True. Well, you look positively dissipated. Like the prairie version of Hester Prynne, I kid you not. Can you change? I find it a little . . . unnerving."

"Certainly," I said, to the man who was still wearing yesterday's tie.

FOURTEEN

I passed a very long night counting the squares on my quilt, mentally listing and relisting the capitals of Latin American countries—first alphabetically, then by date of their founding—and other such pursuits, unable to drift off to sleep. Toward morning I reached for the package insert for the Phocus capsules and belatedly scanned it. It confirmed what I had now suspected for hours, since the moment I drooled on my child's principal: I had massively overmedicated.

I was now coming down hard from a prolonged Phocus trip, and according to karma_chameleon04, the sobriety sherpa at the recovery forum, the next forty-eight hours were critical if I was to avoid either a pharmaceutical or Bandercook relapse. I sat at my desk sorting through the rather substantial pile of star-ampersand-star suspects, but my usual instinct for sniffing out Dr. Thad's passions had left me. My mind kept wandering back to a certain motel room, a certain springy mattress, a certain muscular, criminal/electrical lineman whose name I had both screamed out loud and was embarrassed to mention in public. This was all to be expected, according to the posters who had lived it. I sipped water from my bottle, getting some relief for my dry mouth, at least, and tried to remember a couple of lines from the serenity prayer, but came up empty.

With great effort, I returned my attention to the files. Our dark-haired patients were solid, no-nonsense Midwesterners, young and sporty. But I could see that as the years passed, they'd fill out beneath their game-day sweatshirts, making endless pots of chili to feed the children Dr. Thad and I would give them. They'd grow ever more cheerful, until, in their final senility, they simply smiled vacantly at one and all. That is *not* Dr. Thad's sort of thing, to say the least. And yet it *had* to be one of them. One of these brown-haired star-ampersand-stars was not as she seemed. One of these sensible women was, in fact, a champagne-swilling mass of passion and volatility. But which one was it?

"Each year," Dr. Thad was saying, loudly, just outside my door, "the majority of young people with even slightly above-average promise leave not just Ward, but this entire state. Hence the falling CLEAVER scores, hence the general decline of business and enterprise. If something isn't done, we will be left simply with our crops and our cattle—who already outnumber us—and the exploited temporary labor brought in to process them. We will become *a village of idiots.*"

I closed my eyes and breathed deeply, attempting to concentrate on the delicate work before me. I lay my hands on the stack of files and waited for a burst of insight. *Which one?* I waited. There was nothing. Not the slightest tremor of instinct.

"Which one?" I screamed, aloud, hurling a small potted bamboo shoot that Dr. Thad had given me last Christmas. It shattered into a pile of shards and dirt. Beyond the thin walls of my office, I could hear the stunned silence. I can count the times I've lost my temper on one hand. No one here had ever heard me raise my voice.

Damage control is one of my strengths, and I understood that it was better to address the incident immediately, before everyone began to draw wild conclusions. I stepped outside my door. "You may have heard the noise of smashing ceramics just now," I began, speaking calmly and smiling to reassure my stunned and horrified audience, which included, I was appalled to discover, Dr. Thad himself. He had an arm around a pair of IVF patients, and he was staring at me with the most peculiar expression. Maryellen was clutching her chest, and even Front Desk had widened her pale eyes.

"I'm sorry—" I began again. And then I realized I had nothing more to say. There was no explanation I could give or wanted to give. I ran out the door midsentence, without my coat, brushing past Dr. Thad, and leaving him, Maryellen, Front Desk, and assorted patients in my wake.

❖ ❖ ❖

Hayes might be anywhere along I-80, alone or with a crew, high up in the bucket truck, or scaling a pole, or, if he'd gotten in another dispute with the county, simply standing on the side of the road waving a flag, as punishment, while others did all the drama work. There was no point in looking for him; he worked a radius of at least a hundred miles. "There is no point in looking for him," I repeated out loud, as I drove just past the Ward city limits, all dry mouthed and jumpy, to a formerly run-down outpost of town called the East Bottoms. Most of the Bandercooks who didn't farm lived here, though the area was on the upswing. Young families were fixing up these old houses and parking minivans stuck with honor-student and distance-running decals in the narrow streets, to the consternation of long-timers like the Bandercooks, who were doing all they could to keep gentrification at bay. Hayes's house was in a reasonable state of repair, though he hadn't bothered with even minimal landscaping, unless the rusted-out bathtub on the side of the house was decorative in function.

I rang the doorbell, fidgeting in the cold, with no plan for what I would do if anyone answered. Which someone did, immediately. The chimes had hardly finished sounding and Rusty Bandercook stood in the doorway, still mustarding a sandwich.

"Dr. Meer?" He was wearing his off-duty clothes, standard Bandercook attire, a band T-shirt and a pair of roomy corduroys, to which he'd added a striped fisherman's sweater. He had the piece of sandwich bread in one hand and a mustard-streaked knife in the other.

"I hope I'm not interrupting," I said, pointing at the sandwich.

"Not at all," Rusty said. "Come right in."

"Oh, I probably shouldn't," I said, backing away from the door.

"Hayes won't mind," Rusty said. "He's not even home."

I stood on the doorstep, wanting to run, yet strangely intrigued by the idea of poking around Hayes's house. I knew almost nothing about his life outside the Fox Motel.

"All due respect, Dr. Meer, it is far too cold for this kind of hesitation. You came here for a reason. Nobody just drives through the goddamned EBs . . . unless they're out of sandwich spread. So come on in, and let's get to the bottom of it."

I followed him into the house, noting a sagging gray couch, a wedding-ring quilt folded over the back of a cane rocker, and a framed poster of snowy mountain peaks that had been part of a Bold County Lager promotional effort years back, slightly askew. Rusty took me to the kitchen, and began stacking pink meat circles on his mustard bread.

"Have a seat," he said, and I pulled a carved spindle chair away from the table and sat down. "You don't look well," Rusty said. "I'm going to make you a sandwich."

"OK," I said. My thoughts felt fuzzy and disjointed, and I missed the searing clarity of yesterday. But right now, I was as indifferent as a stoned college nihilist to the judgment of society, and so I took the plate Rusty gave me and also the glass of tap water. It was an excellent sandwich. "Shouldn't you be at work?" I said.

"Personal day," Rusty said, chewing rapidly. "It's a religious thing. Celebrating the solstice."

"That's in December," I pointed out.

"By your calendar. Anyway, I know why you're here."

"Oh?" I said, through a bite of sandwich. It was more than I knew. Now that I was here, I couldn't imagine what I'd hoped to accomplish. The crazy impulse that had driven me from my office had dissipated entirely. Maybe I'd just been hungry. Anyway, Hayes was out running through winter fields hand in hand with Sheila Glass, a scenario in which I had no place. At least, I hoped I had no place. I wasn't sure what my outer limit on debasing myself might be, but I was still cautiously optimistic that a love triangle with a Bandercook and a keno-calling line dancer with a breast tattoo was just beyond it.

"Now the most likely, the most logical explanation is that you've come to apologize and to ask me to resume working as a donor for your clinic. Am I right?"

I shrugged, weighing the relative unpleasantness of confiding in Rusty versus accepting another specimen cup from him.

"Yes, I think we can agree that's the most likely reason for your visit. And of course, you are most entirely welcome here. Can I get you another sandwich?"

I shook my head.

"Well, I won't keep you in suspense. The answer is yes. I will resume my role as donor."

"Great," I said. "Well I should probably be going."

"Wait just a minute," Rusty said, pointing his index finger toward the popcorn ceiling as if on the verge of making a salient point. "That theory doesn't hold, Dr. Meer. You didn't come here for me. You had every reason to believe that I would be at my post at Davis Elementary and no reason to think I would be here in this house, which is not even my place of residence. It isn't logical. And if you can't see that, why then your medical degree isn't worth the paper it's printed on."

"You make a strong case, certainly," I said. I had the urge to take a puff from an art deco cigarette holder while Rusty paced the kitchen tiles like Hercule Poirot addressing all the assembled suspects in the ballroom.

"I think we can agree that running into me was just a happy coincidence. But where, then, does that leave us? Well, let's break it down. Whose house is this?" Rusty pointed at me, expecting an answer.

"It's Hayes's," I said.

"Bingo!" Rusty said. "You're at Hayes's house to see Hayes. Preposterous, you might say. After all, you are a medical doctor. And Hayes—" Rusty laughed, drily. "*Hayes* is kind of a joke." I took a big sip of tap water, too quickly, and some of it trickled down my chin.

"And *yet*," Rusty continued, again index-fingering toward the roof above us. "I submit to you—"

"Is there a bathroom around here?" I said. Rusty wheeled around on his foot and said, in his normal tone of voice, "Of course there's a bathroom around here. What do you think we are? Animals? Down the hall to your left."

It wasn't a long hallway, and yet I took a wrong turn, into Hayes's bedroom, which was neat and impersonally spare, betraying no evidence of his personality, except for a large blond-wood water bed in the center of the room. "What a joke," I said to myself and began rummaging through his drawers. Some last dregs of amphetamine must have been pulsing through my system, because I became immediately absorbed in the task, making a mental catalog of the contents of each drawer—thick work socks and plaid in all of its permutations; the entire family tree of plaid; every genus, phylum, and species of plaid. It was becoming a very extended bathroom trip, but I pressed on, leaving Rusty to assume the worst vis-à-vis the state of my intestines.

I was examining a value-size box of condoms—*unopened*—when the window slid up and Hayes stepped through it, as softly as a cat burglar, for all that he was wearing heavy-soled boots and this was his own home. I assumed he had his reasons. We stared at each other a moment, and I dropped the box of latex onto the water bed like it was a fiery hot iron. It made ripples in the bed's surface.

"I knew I'd see you again," Hayes said, smiling. He is unusually soft-spoken, especially for a Bandercook, and I tried not to think about where he might have acquired all his habits of stealth. There was a light in his eye—he looked *vindicated*, I thought, and then I wondered if that word was part of his vocabulary.

"*Did* you?" I was going for a sneering tone, as I was somewhat put off by his presumptuousness, but given the circumstances, it was a tough tone to pull off. I may have accidentally sounded a vulnerable note. Hayes crossed the room and lifted me off my feet, throwing me on to his embarrassing Burt Reynolds–era bed before I could make any cutting remarks about his recent passion for keno.

"You're like a shy baby deer," Hayes said, scraping my collarbone with his stubble.

"In what way?" I said, but Hayes abandoned metaphorical language for kissing, playing to his strengths. I pushed him away. "Rusty is here!" I whispered.

Hayes froze, suspended above me on his forearms, wide-eyed. "What's he doing here?"

"Making sandwiches!" I whispered.

"Then you have to go. I'm sorry. But this can't happen right now. Hurry, through the window." Hayes directed me toward his open, screenless window, through which little snowflakes were blowing.

"But Hayes, he already—"

"We need to keep this quiet. I feel terrible about this, but it's the best thing, believe me," Hayes said, and he lowered me out into the yard, depositing me in a pile of blackening elm leaves. "I'll be in touch," Hayes whispered and shut the sash. I walked through the backyard to my car. It had been snowing softly for a while now, and a layer of soft white flakes had accumulated in the rusted-out bathtub. I scooped a handful of snow and crushed it in my palm, wondering if it were possible that Hayes was embarrassed of *me*.

FIFTEEN

Thanks a bunch, Rusty," I said raising one latex-gloved hand to wave him out of my office. The other hand, the one holding the sample cup, was hovering above the garbage can, waiting for Rusty to be on his way. He was unusually chatty this morning.

"You're so welcome. I'm supposed to be winterizing the school building right now, but I figured, fuck it."

"I hear you," I said. Outside, flurries were blowing through.

"Expect zero accumulation," Reyne Reynolds said on the morning weather. "This is just a little foretaste of the frozen hell that's coming. Back to you, Deb."

Deb laughed uneasily, and they cut early to a commercial for the law firm of Barton & Theotopolous, "The Dual Fingers of God."

My hand was cramping, and I looked up from my musings to see that Rusty was *still* in my office, doing some musing of his own.

"Once she sets in, winter's not going anywhere. I'll have a good long time to weather-strip those windows and doors."

"That's the spirit," I said.

"Until next time," Rusty said.

One more time, and we're even, I thought. I had planned to take three batches, but I was docking him one because of all the chatting. I dropped the specimen cup in the garbage the minute he was out the door.

"Becky," Dr. Thad said, as the cup thudded into the bottom of the bin. He has a bad habit of coming out of nowhere at inconvenient moments. "Please tell me you aren't throwing semen into the general office garbage. Have some self-respect."

"What does self-respect have to do with it?" I said, *like an idiot,* instead of simply denying it, as any thinking person caught in these circumstances would have done.

"You were so young, Becky. So young when I met you. What passion you had in those days! What fire! And *just look* at you now!"

It's true, lavender is not my color, but Angie chose the office color scheme, and therefore we were all doomed to wear lavender scrubs, which allegedly "pop" against the Navajo Mushroom upholstery, until her whims dictated otherwise. Dr. Thad, I noted, wasn't looking so hot himself. He was pale and tired and he was wearing a Scandinavian boiled-wool sweater coat over his scrubs, though it was only thirty-eight degrees outside.

"We were both very young," I pointed out. I felt I was holding up OK, but under certain lighting, you could see that the years had not been kind to Dr. Thad. He was a delicate flower of the coastal South, destined to wither and die in a climate like this, although a pessimist might say that we're all destined to wither and die, regardless of climate.

"And now, here you stand, throwing a cup of illicit janitorial semen in with the ordinary garbage, when we have a dedicated medical waste receptacle, not to mention a top-of-the-line cryo suite, which we have the moral and financial obligation to fill with primo stuff." Dr. Thad strode from the room, in a significant huff.

❖ ❖ ❖

I gave Dr. Thad a wide berth all morning, and he channeled his disgust with me into another feat of salesmanship, closing on an IVF Deluxe Package with a pair of ag extension agents who'd been flirting with taking their business to our rivals, the Roane Clinic. Congratulations were in order. "Freezing some 'bros?" I said, stepping into the lab.

"You know it," Dr. Thad said, smiling. He was putting four microscopic children on ice. These were reserves, and if things went well for their parents, they'd never be called for. If things went badly—if their slightly more promising siblings failed to take root—and if these 'bros made it through thawing, implantation, gestation, and birth, we'd probably see them around town one day.

Dr. Thad made no mention of our earlier disagreement. I shouldn't have worried. He and I have never felt the need to rehash every little hiccup that occurs in the course of a normal working relationship. Our connection is an intellectual one; the *work* is what matters most to us both. And we simply couldn't spare the time to kiss and make up, figuratively speaking, because we were up to our necks in it today. It was a relief to be in a place where feelings were beside the point, in the clean, orderly confines of a well-run lab.

I turned my attention to the ova of a twenty-eight-year-old Fulbright scholar whose desire to help an infertile couple was exceeded only by her crushing student loan debt. She was a year too old for this, really, but I'd fudged her birthday and accepted her as a donor out of compassion. "Complete confidentiality," I'd said to her, which was true, for now. Sometimes I wondered whether that would hold. A change in the law, and one day a child reared in the greater Ward area might come knocking at her door, calling her Mom.

I never bother raising these occasional doubts to Dr. Thad. *Get over it*, would probably sum up his view. Instead, I said, "I think we've just plugged the Brain Drain." Dr. Thad rewarded me with one of his mellifluous chuckles.

"We've had a lot of expenditures this month," I said in what I hoped was a lightly conversational tone, encouraged by Dr. Thad's genial mood. Acquiring so much high-end sperm and ova had required record levels of spending, and on top of paying for the new cryo suite Dr. Thad had just purchased, we were skating very close to the edge. We only needed a few solid sales to right the ship, but I wasn't a closer, and Dr. Thad's recent absenteeism had hurt us.

"This suite will pay for itself a hundred times over," Dr. Thad said, tucking a stray lock of hair under his paper lab cap.

"This came today," I said, removing the energy bill from my pocket as though it were a minor thing. Dr. Thad's panic attacks are not pretty; avoiding one required tact. "It seems to be past due, which is a problem. And our account balance is on the low side. Even with this morning's sale, we're spread thin. Nothing to worry about, of course. I know these genius 'metes will turn a profit for us soon, but until they do, we still have to pay the bills with something."

"Of course," Dr. Thad said, but I could see I didn't have his attention. He was sorting sperm now, weeding out the girl-making ones on behalf of a thirtysomething couple with a donut franchise near Des Moines who wanted a male heir. "Like there's still primogeniture or some bullshit," Dr. Thad said. "One of you little bastards is going to be master of a donut shop in rural Iowa. Isn't that something?"

"The funny thing is, this energy bill? It actually says final notice. But that's probably a mistake. So as soon as you close on just a couple more of these IVF packages, we'll be fine."

"Becky," Dr. Thad said.

"Yes, Dr. Thad?"

"Where are we?"

"We're in the lab," I said. The cryo lab, I didn't say. The lab that has the sacred duty of preserving the genetic posterity of hundreds of our clients in the form of frozen gametes, stored away for a rainy reproductive day, to say nothing of the embryos.

"And when we're in the lab, Becky, I need to focus. I can't have you distracting me with low-level housekeeping matters. Just take care of this."

My background is in microbiology, not accounting, as Dr. Thad is well aware, but he was under a certain amount of stress. "I've left some messages for . . . um . . . Angie—"

He cut me off. "You can't rely on Angie for everything," Dr. Thad said. "Just pay it."

"The account balance is too low," I said.

"Impossible," Dr. Thad said, and he made a sweeping, dismissive gesture with one of his finely shaped hands. He has his impetuous side, and it is very difficult to argue with him when he's like this, but I persisted.

"If we don't get some fairly large payments soon, there's some question of whether we'll be able to meet payroll."

"What's the number?" Dr. Thad said. I told him.

"Double-check," he said, somewhat sharply, but he's a Harvard-trained scientist, a leader in both the fields of fertility and cryobiology, not a customer service rep, so I've learned not to mind his irritability. I double-checked.

"See for yourself," I said, holding up my phone. The account balance was made even more ominous by the fatal backlighting of the screen. Dr. Thad leaned in next to me and peered at it. The ambient air in the cryo lab is a good five to ten degrees below the comfort level of the average person. Dr. Thad is highly cold sensitive, which is why he wears a very striking Nordic scarf around his neck. To my surprise, he was now using it to wipe beads of sweat from his forehead.

"Are you OK, Dr. Thad?"

Dr. Thad smiled, but it was a sad little smile, implying secret worries. We are nearly the same height, so I can look directly into Dr. Thad's eyes, which are rather steely. At the moment, though, they were drained of the remarkable vitality that has made the clinic the standard of care in the entire Midwest region. From the look of him, it was now confession time.

"Oh, Becky," he said, breathing the words into my hair, because to my utter shock, he had suddenly wrapped me in a close hug. This was an unprecedented event in our twelve-year work history, but I put my gloved hands around him awkwardly, and tried to seem natural.

❖ ❖ ❖

No decent scientist will reject a theory out of hand, without at least consulting the data, and I graduated near the top of my class. Therefore, in light of the circumstances, I was forced to wonder if Maryellen's idea about Dr. Thad's condition—his seasonal looniness—deserved my consideration. "Of course not," I said aloud and turned my attention to the payroll. If Dr. Thad and I both gave up our paychecks, we could just about make it. But the idea—the absurd, Maryellen-generated idea— began to nag at me. We were slogging through a gray November, and even Front Desk, who was highly deficient as an employee and if anything, *hypo*active, seemed to be feeling it. As a student of history, I knew that the theory of gravity had first been proposed to Sir Isaac Newton by his half-witted coachman. "Fine," I said glancing at my screen. "I'll just check it out."

"Who are you talking to in there?" Maryellen yelled from down the hall.

"No one!" I answered, closing my door.

Due to my rigorous record keeping, it was the work of a moment to pull together a cluster map of Thaddean incidents. I took a sip of coffee and stared at my screen. The months of November, December, and January were clotted with dots. The summer months were empty, indicating that all had been peaceful. Not *once* in any calendar year had Dr. Thad romanced a patient, gotten sloppy drunk, or been involved in a brawl earlier than mid-October or later than early March. There was no denying it: Dr. Thad brought out the dysfunction and self-sabotage the way other people brought out garlands and tree skirts—seasonally.

"Is it *possible*?" I whispered.

"What's that?" Maryellen bellowed from just outside my door, where she was probably standing with one of her large ears pressed against the fiberglass.

"Nothing!" I yelled back.

If I could only share this document with Dr. Thad. He could not deny, if shown the dramatic topography of this cluster map, that the data were suggestive, even compelling. And then? What if we could *treat* it? A vision of a life in which Dr. Thad embraced monogamy, sobriety, and nonviolence spread out before me, and it was a beautiful vista. The breakthroughs we'd make! The prestigious prizes they'd throw at us if only Dr. Thad were able to give our work his full attention year-round! The *money*!

But I couldn't show him the map. I could *never* let him know that, due to my close observation of his behavior, not only did he have virtually no secrets from me, but I'd also been systematically cataloging his missteps, with only the purest and best of intentions. No doubt he would find that "super creepy and not unlike the practices of a garden-variety serial killer," which was his reaction when I inadvertently revealed what I knew about his preference for wintergreen toothpaste over spearmint. It was unfair—*anybody* who had routinely been through his medicine cabinet and had an eye for patterns could have deduced as much—but I have not been allowed past the threshold of the Sorenson residence since that fairly insignificant revelation.

I printed out the document, and putting it and the adult ADHD pamphlet in my pocket, headed down the hall to Dr. Thad's office. I had to make him see that his attention deficit hyperactivity disorder was tearing his life, and, just as importantly, our business, apart.

"Dr. Thad?"

"What is it, Becky?" he said, without looking up. He was bent over his phone, shooting down enemy helicopters with a World War II–era tank. I closed the door behind me, and Dr. Thad's head snapped up. "Is this a *closed-door* conversation?"

"If you don't mind—it's rather personal."

"Certainly," Dr. Thad said, but he looked wary.

"I'm just wondering—how shall I put this? Have you ever taken a rash step that you could not later explain?" I was going to lead him through the questionnaire on the back of the pamphlet question by question, then tabulate his score. He'd earn at least a seven, which indicated a high probability of ADHD, and then he'd have to face up to the problem.

Dr. Thad leaned back in his chair and cracked his knuckles. "I assume you're joking." The line of his mouth was just in the neighborhood of a scowl.

"No," I said.

"Of course not. You don't joke. I know this. Just as you know that over the years, I have, at times, behaved impulsively. It might not be going too far to say that rash behavior is a recurrent pattern—a pronounced personal tendency of mine."

I was nodding vigorously.

"In fact, Becky, the day we met, what transpired? Do you recall?"

"You had a fistfight with one doctor over his doctor fiancée."

"And was that, do you think, a prudent thing to do? Is that something I think back on fondly, full of satisfaction with the manner in which I conducted myself?"

"I couldn't say," I said.

"Assaulting my supervisor—that might be called rash behavior, don't you think? And do you know what happened to Dr. Van Heuss? She's active in the antivax movement these days—that's right. She's an absolute slobbering lunatic. And for her, Becky, for *her*, I nearly ruined my marriage and my career. No, I can't explain that, nor would I even presume to try."

This was going better than I'd dared hope.

"Please explain to me why you come in here, interrupt my work, and throw my worst moments, my lowest points up in my face? Answer me this: All these years of patience and nonjudgment, were they all a show? Because I thought you understood me. I thought that you sympathized."

"No, Dr. Thad! You misunderstand me." I'd imagined Dr. Thad denying his problems or coming to a slow, tearful realization. I was not prepared for the rage.

"Then there remains only one possibility. This isn't about me, is it? This is about you. *You're* the one who committed a rash act you could not later explain, and now you've come to me for guidance."

"Yes. I'm concerned that I may have adult ADHD." It was safer to backtrack. Dr. Thad wasn't ready to acknowledge his issues, and it had been a mistake to ambush him like this.

Dr. Thad made a scoffing noise. "These fad diseases have always been with us. In the middle ages, it was Saint Vitus's Dance. Then hysteria. Last year it was irritable bowel."

"Well, yes," I said, pulling the cluster map out of my pocket. "But take a look." Maybe I could get him to acknowledge his problems in principle, without him realizing whose problems they actually were.

"Why, this is nothing but an ordinary cluster map. I don't see how this is at all relevant."

"I've been charting my behavior for years. As you see, the number of inexplicable, rash acts is heavily concentrated in the winter months, which I believe is consistent with a diagnosis of adult ADHD."

"My God. *Each* of these dots represents a distinct rash incident?"

"No, it's on a ten scale, because I had to compress for space. The red dots are for violent or confrontational outbursts, the blue are for episodes of binge drinking, and the green are for . . ."

"Yes?"

"Sexual," I said. An uncomfortable silence ensued.

"Wow," he said, finally.

"I know."

"Becky," Dr. Thad pulled open the drawer to his desk and rummaged through it. "I feel—I can't begin to describe it. I know you like I know myself, and yet, in some ways, you're a perfect stranger. I simply never dreamed you were so volatile."

"Thank you," I said. Dr. Thad struck a match and lit a thin, ladylike cigarette. I sat absolutely still with shock, waiting for him to say *Oh, by the way—I've taken up smoking*, but he did nothing of the kind. He puffed away with perfect unselfconsciousness, like a time traveler from the middle period of the twentieth century.

"You have to treat this," he said, inhaling deeply. He blew the smoke up toward the ceiling with a practiced air. "No, I insist. We can't have you behaving like this. *Not. An. Option.* I'll write you the scrip myself. Phocus, is it? Let's go with the full patch," Dr. Thad said, scrawling something on his dispensing pad. "Now go fill this. Take the rest of the day if you need to—in fact, yes, I feel it would be better if you left *immediately*." Dr. Thad ashed gracefully into his coffee cup and handed me my prescription.

I stood to go. His minty breath, that sandalwood-heavy cologne—were these things simply disguises? I failed to understand how Dr. Thad could keep his smoking secret from me, the one person who knew everything about him. Or perhaps I didn't know. Perhaps I had fundamentally failed to understand Dr. Thad himself. The thought was so terrifying that the familiar things in the room—the office chairs, comfortable but not *too* comfortable; the desk; even the earth-tone walls around me—they all felt swimmy and insubstantial. All my founding assumptions—everything that a moment ago had been solid and reassuring and true—had just been ripped away from me. I felt like a college freshman who had been introduced to solipsism and marijuana in the same evening.

"And Becky," Dr. Thad said, letting the cigarette hang from his lip like an old-time gangster, "your hair."

"What about it?"

"It appears to be growing darker."

"I hadn't noticed," I said, running my fingers through it.

"Well see that it doesn't become a problem," Dr. Thad said, sucking down another hit of nicotine.

SIXTEEN

There is absolutely nothing that Dr. Thad and I can't discuss, but there are certain things we *choose* never to mention. As I paced the room, considering Dr. Thad's naked body, sipping my coffee, and weighing my next move, I had an inkling that *this* would be another of them. I had checked his vital signs immediately upon entering the room, and, finding them all in order, gone off to make myself another beverage. I'm sure he would have approved, if he were not lying face down on an exam table, with his feet in the stirrups, snoring heavily, and unable to offer any input one way or another.

But as for what I was contemplating next—I was *far* from certain he would consent to it, or that he would give his approval after the fact. This gave me pause—the ethics of the situation. For a moment, I thought about asking Maryellen's advice, but Dr. Thad would never forgive me for exposing him like that, morally and physically. I had to decide for myself, and I knew which way I was leaning. I looked into his sleeping face, and tried to imagine how I would answer for it, once he was awake, fully dressed, and bristling with indignation—assuming he found out. He would remind me of his degrees, his stature in the field. He would call this an unforgivable liberty.

But unfortunately, Dr. Thad was not entirely naked. He was wearing one of the pink surgical caps we keep for patients, which he had donned sometime during the previous night's festivities, the particulars of which I preferred not to imagine. The cap was pulled down low over his left eye, causing his unruly hair to puff up in a ridiculous man-bouffant. This hurt his credibility, as did the snoring. I was unable to take his future objections seriously.

I set down my tiny coffee with a sigh, peeled a Phocus patch from its sticky backing, and, gently lifting Dr. Thad's well-developed left buttock, gingerly applied it to the area beneath. I hoped it would go undetected long enough to do him some good. Thanks to my own Phocus patch, I was fully clothed, ready to work, no longer sharing intimate moments with a Bandercook, and producing the ideal amount of saliva. That was all I wanted for Dr. Thad. I sipped my coffee and speculated on how long before he—or more likely *she*—found it.

Dr. Thad was nearly fifty years old and had obviously had quite an evening, so I estimated a full forty-eight hours of recovery were required before he would be back in the proverbial saddle. That was just enough time to take the edge off this downward spiral. But the bigger question was who *she*, the future patch detector, might be. I had narrowed it down to five candidates, plus Angie, who might also still occasionally be benefiting from Dr. Thad's renewed lust for life, or what have you. Now I went through the list, mentally placing each woman in the situation I saw before me, and attempting to determine which of them was most likely to have green-lighted it.

As I considered the various suspects, I glanced at the Phocus patch and noted that it was already beginning to peel itself away from Dr. Thad's skin. The area in question, like all of the Sorenson corpus that I have viewed in the course of various on-the-job incidents, was completely covered in fine brown hair. This hair was now preventing adequate adhesion.

I gently pressed the edges of the patch down with my index finger, but almost immediately they curled up again. Dr. Thad had not moved, so I risked applying more pressure. The top edge of the oval patch was now firmly affixed to Sorenson flesh, but the bottom edge was slightly puckered, and I didn't like the looks of it one bit. There was nothing for it. I hauled off and delivered a slap to Dr. Thad's backside, smoothing the patch and achieving firm adhesion at last, as well as waking Dr. Thad, who yelled "Jesus Christ, Becky!" the moment his eyes flew open. "What are you doing to me?"

"Just trying to wake you," I said.

"That's not the preferred method," Dr. Thad said, snatching the paper hat from his head and holding it in front of his lower half in a belated attempt to preserve some dignity. I could see that he had much more to say, and was far from satisfied with my explanation, but priority one was removing himself from the scene.

He hopped down from the exam table with a level of agility surprising for a deeply hungover middle-aged man, and headed down the hall to his own office. He very sensibly decided the paper hat was best used to shield me and any other possible spectators from full frontal exposure. I was rubbing my hands with sanitizer. When I looked up from the sanitizer nozzle, I saw Maryellen looming in the doorway, and beside her Cooper Zane, who had turned a very becoming shade of scarlet.

I shrugged at them in a what-can-you-do? sort of way. Dinosaurs were on the menu at Ward High today, curriculumwise, and Maryellen is not the sort of mother to let the tender shoot of Cooper Zane's faith be crushed in the terrifying jaws of an omnivore who stalked the earth long before God's self-reported rollout of the domed waters, etc. So she had decided to take her chances and hope that this was one of the days when Dr. Thad wasn't pantsless at the office, and her luck had just run out. You might say it was all part of God's plan, but you certainly couldn't blame me.

Nonetheless, I had a strong feeling that Maryellen was about to give me a piece of her mind, so I held up a freshly sanitized hand and said, *"Nuh-uh,"* signaling my unwillingness to get into it. Nudity is very Biblical, and Dr. Thad's stroll down the hallway recalled the original walk of shame, the expulsion from Eden, with me in the role of the snake, the angel with the fiery sword, or the Lord himself, depending on how you framed it. If anything, this was probably a valuable lesson for Cooper Zane.

"Girls' night. Tonight," Maryellen sputtered. "And that's *all* I'm going to say."

"I can't," I said, automatically, but even as the words were leaving my lips, I realized they weren't exactly true. Mitchell was spending the weekend with the Ward Nature Boys, who were going up to the wildlife preserve in Dawson to shoot at deer and sleep in the snow, according to Mitchell. My brother-in-law Ben was troop leader, and he had assured me that there would be cabins, and though they would *track* deer using an old Pawnee method, no firearms would be involved. I'd had misgivings, but I was very much in favor of Mitchell spending time under the influence of a man who wasn't Kevin Holts. Kevin was too indifferent to nature even to shoot at it, whereas Uncle Ben, I hoped, could fill my son and the other boys with admiration and compassion for our natural world, and for the noble beasts who populated the undeveloped lands around greater Ward.

"You promised," Maryellen said. "It's Friday night, and we're going out."

The prospect of wasting a perfectly good evening at the Old Cheyenne was a grim one. I'd be surrounded by other parents, sipping watery beers, discussing test scores and kitchen remodels. We'd debate the pros and cons of various diets and exercise regimens. A few beers in, someone might tell a slightly off-color joke for which he'd immediately apologize. These were the pallid good times adulthood had to offer, and I had never really developed a taste for them. But a promise is a promise, so I agreed. Maybe under the soothing influence of my Phocus patch, I would be better able to stand the tedium.

"Wear a dress—or maybe not. Maybe just some jeans," Maryellen said.

SEVENTEEN

Maryellen was dancing with a large-animal vet from Nee under the ancient paper spheres that hung from the ceiling, dropping the dust of the long dead upon the inebriated. At the table behind me, someone was telling a joke about the difference between Lutherans and astronauts. I'd heard it before. I twirled my fingers through the bowl of gummy popcorn. It was only nine thirty, and at least three more hours of girls' night stretched ahead of me. The Phocus patch was working, I supposed, because the urge to slip out of the bar in search of Hayes Bandercook was very slight. And yet I took no pleasure in my newfound decency and self-control. Amanda Boss and I had discussed her new kitchen backsplash for *twenty solid minutes*. The enthusiasm I heard in my voice as we debated the merits of one tile versus another made me wonder if I was becoming an even worse kind of monster.

But to my surprise, the scene in the bar was devolving fast. It was two-dollar-pint night, and this seemed to light a fire under the bar stools of the Old Cheyenne. *Let someone else pick up the pieces!* was kind of the unofficial theme of the evening. All around me, people were beginning to make poor choices, and I wanted nothing more than to peel off my Phocus patch and join them. But I was still fighting my way back from the Bandercook brink, and I didn't trust myself.

Calvin Chester was drinking a red beer in a yellow flannel on the bar stool nearest the door to the ladies' room. I needed to go, but there was no way to slip past him without awkward interaction. My ability to read faces diminishes when I'm drinking, and I felt no good would come of speaking to him now. Also it was girls' night, and per Maryellen, girls' night was for sparkly tops and uncomfortable shoes and dancing and a midnight run through the drive-through of Barrelhouse Burger, not for dealing with school administration. I crossed my legs and vowed I would wait him out.

"No, I didn't order that—" I said to Elspeth, who like an evil temptress, was placing another two-dollar pint in front of me. I wanted it, badly, but not as much as I wanted to *not* go to the bathroom until Calvin was sitting elsewhere. There was no way I could drink this beer and achieve that modest goal.

"It's from the principal," Elspeth said. "He said to tell you—damn it, I can't remember. There was a message to go with it." Elspeth shook her head, her braids sliding over her shoulders like thick snakes. "It's gone. It just flew right out of my head."

"What kind of a message?" I asked, but Elspeth just blinked her large lids under the yellow light, unable to characterize it. "Was it something nice?" I prompted.

"Well, yeah," Elspeth said, giving me a look that suggested only a dim-witted or deeply paranoid person would interpret a free beer as a hostile gesture. But Elspeth, who was stone-cold sober, could not retain a message from one end of the OC to the other, which suggested to me that she also could not be trusted to detect any subtle barb that might have accompanied the beverage.

I glanced over at the bar. Calvin was laughing easily and not looking my way. There is only one thing to do with a free drink, and I did it, finishing the whole thing in under ten gulps, staring at the back of

Calvin's head as I did so. He didn't turn around. Nor did he look my way as I brushed past him into the ladies' room.

I chose the stall with the most graffiti. It was a living history of the graffiti-minded in Ward, their lusts and grievances gouged into the door. If you wanted to know who in the area was a cocksucking bitch, for instance, there was no better place to go—other than the men's room, probably. I was pleased to see that my name was nowhere mentioned on the door of stall one, but near the door handle, someone had etched the words "Dr. Thad Sorensen is a SLUTWHORE." I rifled through my purse, found my keys, and began to scratch through the derogatory statement, but the graffiti artist had had remarkable strength, and it was exhausting work. I remained on the toilet, with my underpants spread out between my knees, to obscure my true purpose in the stall. The door gouges were so deep that I settled for just adding a small but emphatic "not" in front of the "a SLUTWHORE," which was far from a compliment, but still represented a marked improvement. Someone with a heavy tread entered the bathroom and took the next stall.

"Rebecca? Is that you?"

"Elspeth?" I said. It was her voice, and her large tan oxfords.

"I just remembered that message. The principal said, 'Go ahead and use the bathroom. I promise I won't talk to you.'"

"Are you kidding?"

"Nope. I told you it was a nice message."

"I guess," I said. I was at the sink now, and I looked over my shoulder as I scrubbed my hands.

"You want me to tell him something back?"

"No thanks," I said. I tossed some paper towels in the garbage can, then walked through the door and right into eye contact with Calvin. I had been prepared to ignore him all night, but now he'd crossed a line. The seat next to him was empty, and I took it.

"Thanks so much for the bathroom pass. But your authority doesn't extend past the confines of Davis Elementary. In the real world, people use the bathroom without getting the go-ahead from you."

"That's what I would have assumed, but I've seen two other Davis mothers use the men's room tonight. And compared to you, they're—well, that's neither here nor there. The fact is, you've all actually got a much better chance of avoiding me in the *women's* restroom, counterintuitive as that may seem."

"I'm not sure what you're talking about," I said.

"When you were sitting over there"—Calvin gestured toward my empty seat across the room—"you kept looking this way, longingly. My first thought was you were giving me that look—"

"Ha," I said. I suppose the kind thing would have been to mask my feelings, but Calvin Chester as an object of anyone's desire—much less my own—was simply inconceivable. Could anyone love a school principal? I doubted it.

"Believe me, there was a time . . . ," Calvin trailed off, looking somehow both smug and wistful. "But things are different now that I'm in administration. All this authority—it pushes people away. It's the reverse of what I expected, to tell you the truth. I don't know what Henry Kissinger was talking about."

"Neither do I," I said, truthfully. For a moment, I entertained a dark hope that Calvin was on the verge of self-destructing. Madge had noticed something amiss, and she has a sixth sense for dysfunction. The drinking, the loneliness: these were positive signs. The two-dollar pints were doing nothing to relax him, and I felt optimistic that if he loaded up the trunk of his Chevelle and headed east on I-80, Kevin Holts's teaching career would come to an abrupt end.

"Anyway, then I remembered I'm sitting by the bathroom door, and it all made sense." Calvin laughed, somewhat bitterly, and stared down at the damp circle left by the pint glass on his empty napkin, reckoning with the fact that he was less desirable than a public toilet. But if Calvin was looking for sympathy, he was in the wrong bar. The Old Cheyenne simply doesn't attract that kind of crowd.

Amanda Boss was stepping carefully in her night-out heels in front of the neon sign for Bold County Lager and teetering into, yes, the men's room. I had not been aware that Calvin Chester was such a pariah, but given that, it was weird that he should insist on positioning himself so squarely in front of the ladies' room, where he clearly wasn't wanted.

"You could sit somewhere else," I suggested, as Elspeth put two pints in front of us.

"First I give up my seat at the bar. Then what?" Calvin said. I shrugged. "I'll tell you where *that* ends. It ends with me drinking alone on the street corner. I'm holding my ground."

I wrapped both hands around my pint glass. *Oh, it's not as bad as all that* is likely what Maryellen—who was now make-out dancing with her large-animal vet—would say. Vague positivity was what the occasion called for, but I couldn't muster it. Wasn't that the old hanging tree groaning in the wind in the parking lot outside? Why yes, it was. The citizens of Ward were not going to literally string up or tar and feather Calvin Chester, as their ancestors would have done, but Amanda Boss had chosen to brave a wall full of urinals rather than brush past him on her way to the restroom. His popularity was low, and I wasn't going to say otherwise.

"Do you know . . . ?" Calvin said, tilting his glass to deflate its layer of foam, but he trailed off, staring at the bubbles.

"What?" I prompted.

He put down the beer and swiveled his bar stool my direction. "I'm just going to come out and say this—a woman has never *drooled* on me before, Rebecca. That was a first."

"Hmm . . . ," I said, sipping the Bold County rapidly.

"It's—honestly, it's kind of hard to interpret, something like that. I looked it up. Drooling is often associated with hunger—it's a very primal response. Kind of animalistic, if you think about it. Some sources even suggest it can be associated with marking one's territory—not to put words in your mouth. I really don't know where that came from. Maybe you don't either. I guess what I'm saying is, I find you very hard to read."

I had continued drinking as he rambled away about my saliva, and now I slammed my empty beer glass down on the bar and stared at him. Then I waved at Elspeth to bring two more, because I was not going to endure this kind of talk with an empty glass.

Calvin cleared his throat, looking a little alarmed by the appearance of the new pints. "So how's business?"

"What have you heard?"

"Just making conversation," Calvin said. He reached for his glass.

"Dr. Thad and I are doing very well. There's a seasonal aspect to fertility work. Most people don't realize that. It ebbs and flows."

"*Dr. Thad?*" Calvin said, raising an eyebrow. I could see that he was surprised, and was now recalibrating some previous impression. "Why do you call him that?"

"It's his name," I said.

"But why the title? How long have you worked together?"

"Twelve years."

"*Oh,*" Calvin said. "I'm sorry—but really—did you say twelve *years?*"

"I did." Calvin looked very much like a person who was trying hard not to laugh.

"And in *twelve years* he's never said, 'Hey, Rebecca, just call me Thad, OK?'"

"He has not," I said quietly. I drew a crosshatched pattern in the frost on my pint glass.

"So are your customers mostly lesbians?" Calvin said, by way of changing the subject.

"They're patients, not customers. Mostly we get infertile hetero couples. But yes, sometimes lesbians, and sometimes single women."

"Single women—that's so sad. It's just unfair to the kid, you know?"

"Oh, I know." He didn't seem to realize how tactless he was being, which made me wonder if he was doing it deliberately.

"I'm going to be a very hands-on dad. Wearing the baby in a sling, bare-chested and all that."

"I wouldn't count on it," I said, through clenched teeth, because a human hand was now resting, as if casually, on the small of my back.

"Why do you say that?"

A slight static charge clung to my sweater, and when Calvin removed his hand—which, so far, he was not doing—the fabric would adhere for a moment to the skin of his palm, lifting the sweater up and away from my back. If so much as a fingertip of his brushed my bare skin I would—I didn't know. I sat there, hating him, offering no feedback on the hand, just going along with it basically, that's how it would seem. Why was I so unable to confront this man? *Get your hand off my back and Kevin Holts out of the classroom* is what I ought to have said, with authority. Instead, I sat there, seething.

"No, really. I want to know. Because before you said"—he dropped his voice to a whisper—"everything was fine. Have you seen something to change your mind?"

"It's not like I can diagnose you sitting at the bar."

"But you *suspect* something," he said. His eye sockets looked almost hollow in the dim light of the OC. "You do, don't you? Tell me what it is."

Without examining my motives, I pushed back in my seat, crushing his hand against the chair back before he had time to remove it. He pulled his hand free as I gave him a serious once-over.

"You have a very scanty beard," I said. "That's not a good sign."

"It's scanty?" he said, reaching involuntarily toward his chin, but stopping himself and folding his hands together on the bar, like he wasn't flustered. "What does that mean?"

This would have been an opportune moment for the polite lie, but sometimes the clinician in me takes over. Plus, he didn't really deserve one. "It doesn't *mean* anything. But it correlates with a low sperm count. Extremely low, usually."

"A *low sperm count*," Calvin repeated, slowly, like it was an unfamiliar foreign phrase.

"Not to mention poor motility. Grade D, maybe grade C at best."

"What are you saying?"

"I'm just saying, don't get your hopes up, you know?"

I ought to have seen it coming. There must have been warnings in the preceding moments—widened eyes or heightened color—the usual signs of impending emotional distress that tell me, in the clinical setting, to end the conversation and bring in the big guns of empathy: Dr. Thad himself. That I suspected nothing, that I was truly blindsided, was testament to the volume of bargain-priced beer swirling through my system, dulling my senses. I had meant to hurt Calvin, to insult and embarrass him, but even through the fog of Bold County, I could see now that I had gone far beyond that.

"So . . . I'm . . . *never* going to be a daddy?"

"That's not what I said."

"It is. It *is* what you said." Dr. Thad would have known just what to do. He has an uncanny knack for rephrasing bad news so that it sounds like neutral news, or even somewhat OK news. That is not my talent. I took a sip of Bold County and studied his face.

"*All I said* is that the odds are very much against it."

"Oh, God!" Calvin said, his voice breaking. He pushed away from the bar, and moved through the crowd toward the exit, rubbing at his eyes. I stared after him in horror.

"Want to close out your tab?" Elspeth asked, watching him go. I passed Elspeth a ten.

"Keep the change," I said. I followed Calvin out into the snowy parking lot.

EIGHTEEN

Calvin Chester was walking into the wind, crossing the icy, empty stretch of O Street with his odd, springy step and heading toward the darkness of the Pine View apartments, a complex popular with single and recently divorced men, a place so unutterably grim that the Ward police did nightly spot checks of its second-floor balconies this time of year. On sad winter nights, ledge-perched depressives in their underpants considered making the parking lot's lone pine their last sight on this earth. Ward PD routinely talked them down before they burst themselves open on the icy asphalt below.

"Calvin, wait!" I yelled, but my voice was lost in the wind. I raced up the wooden stairway after him. "Calvin!" He was opening the door when he heard me, and he turned to look at me. Tears were streaming down his face. He made no attempt to hide them.

"What else can you *possibly* have to say to me, Rebecca?"

"Nothing," I said, kissing him right on the lips without having actually intended to do so. They were cold and utterly unresponsive, but the sight of him, so crushed, by me, was unbearable. I persisted in the kiss, throwing my whole self into it, like I was trying to smother a kitchen fire. He put up his arms and attempted to peel me off him.

I didn't blame him; I was a monster. I wanted to beg his forgiveness, to take back everything I'd said and tell him how sorry I was, that he shouldn't give up on life, love, and fatherhood. I wanted to tell him that he had so much more to live for, that if he split his head open in the parking lot, I would never forgive myself, but it was too late. When I put my hands on him, he jumped as if I'd whipped him with an electrical cord, gasping with shock and dismay. But he was already responding, there was no denying it. Whatever objection he was voicing collapsed into an incoherent groan, and he grabbed me with blind desperation, like a man teetering on the edge of a high place, and pulled me into his warm, unfurnished apartment, down onto the demoralizing beige carpet. Calvin was sucking my lips roughly, like a person who hadn't been touched in a long time, and tearing blindly at my many layers of clothing. By the time we were finally undressed on his surprisingly stiff and prickly carpet, I knew this was not going to go well. His skinny torso was attached to a pair of muscular arms, and his narrow hips were set above full, womanly thighs—his, not mine. He looked like several different men stitched together. *Like Frankenstein's monster.*

Time seemed to stop, and not in a good way. My knees were raw from carpet burns, my lips were chapped, all I wanted to do was sleep off the two-dollar pints, but instead I was straddling my child's principal in his totally empty living room, stifling a yawn, and racking my brains to remember just one of the "guaranteed to blow his mind" tips so often featured in women's magazines, whatever could get us out of this situation in as quick and face-saving a manner as possible.

Calvin and I obviously did not read the same magazines.

Finally, looking equal parts confused, annoyed, and lustful, Calvin flipped me onto my back, proving that sometimes it's better not to overthink these things. I made a reasonable amount of noise, and after a polite interval, he collapsed on top of me. We lay there for a moment, too rug-burned and exhausted to speak. Then he got up, brushing his hair from his eyes and looking at me like I'd hurt him in some especially cruel way.

"Was that—did you just have pity sex with me?"

"No," I said, covering my breasts with my coat. "Not even close." He was propped up on one arm, and his pointy underarm hair was fanning out like a weird sea creature.

"Then stay the night," Calvin challenged me. It felt like a dare we would both regret.

"Where?" He had some books stacked in the corner but no sleepable surfaces.

"In my bed, obviously,"

"You have a *bed*?"

❖ ❖ ❖

Early the next morning, having endured an entire night of spooning under a floral comforter (a relic from a previous relationship, I assumed), but, thankfully, *not* a repeat, I left. Calvin sat up in bed as I passed through the door of his bedroom fully clothed, with my coat already zipped. We looked at each other and didn't say a word. Outside, the cold air of the Pine View parking lot felt like a much-needed slap in the face.

I passed three people I knew between the icy doorstep of Calvin's apartment and the street half a block away, where I'd left my snow-covered car. Ward can be like that sometimes, usually when it's most inconvenient. If I'd been engaged in some act of quiet heroism, I definitely wouldn't have run into anyone, but now, with yesterday's eyeliner raccooning around my eyes, a serious hangover, and the mountain of snow on my car giving public testimony to the fact that I hadn't been home last night, it was just one awkward encounter after another. I ran the gauntlet of hurried pleasantries with Front Desk, who was tearing into a cruller right there on the street, then Shane Glass, who winked at me in his skull hoodie, walking his ambling bad boy's walk away from the smoldering ruins of *his* evening, and then Matt Boss, who looked up from his phone to stare at me, and then bent his crew cut over the screen and texted Amanda. Or so I assumed. All this I endured while still smelling strongly of Calvin Chester's cologne or possibly body spray. I had just finished scraping the last of the ice off my windshield when my brother-in-law appeared. He was pulling a dolly stacked with crates full of potter's clay.

The sun was rising, and its vague pink light reflected off the snow.

"Morning," Ben said, raising a mitten.

"Aren't you supposed to be with the Nature Boys?" I said.

"Well, I sure did want to be, but funny story—"

"Then who's chaperoning?" I said.

"Now that's what I'm about to tell you. Funniest thing. Kevin Holts has been helping me improve site traffic to my online store, being as the bottom's pretty much dropped out of the pottery market locally—"

"Ben, who is with my child?"

"Lo and behold, an order comes in for two hundred mugs, but the catch is they've got to ship by Monday or it's no deal. I went to Kevin and I said, now this order has come in—"

"Ben. Are the Nature Boys wandering around unsupervised?"

"Now of course not, Rebecca. You know me better than that. So I said to Kevin, 'I'm going to have to decline this order, I have a prior commitment.' And Kev says to me, 'Nonsense, Ben, this could be your big break, *I'll* take the Nature Boys—'"

I was already getting into my car. I peeled out onto O Street, leaving Ben to wind up his story to an empty curb.

NINETEEN

As I closed the miles between Ward and the wildlife preserve in Dawson, I began to feel sicker. By the time I opened the gate to the preserve and began driving down the rocky entrance road, which rearranged all my internal organs with each painful bump, I'd come to terms with one fact. The fact was that when I opened a bleary eye and saw Calvin Chester's arm around me, and felt his bare legs tucked up under mine, when I looked over into his sleeping face and the memory of all that had transpired between us hit me like a pool cue between the eyes, and when I then retched for reasons both physical and psychological—*that* was the best I was going to feel all day.

As I proceeded down the bumpy path toward the cabins, I reached for another antacid. I looked up just in time to see my car making contact with a horned animal. The noise of the impact was enormous, as if the deer had detonated a large amount of explosives just at the moment my car ran him down. My head whiplashed back, and the air bag filled the front seat. I sat for a moment, stunned and horrified, then I got out of the crumpled car, pushing the door open with difficulty. Beneath the wheels, the wounded animal was thrashing its head back and forth.

"Rebecca?" Kevin said. He was running toward me, dressed in thermal wear, and I saw my own face in the lenses of his tiny, round, light-reflective sunglasses. A ragtag band of Nature Boys circled around the horrific scene.

"Are you hurt?" Kevin said.

I shook my head.

"Mom! What have you done?" Mitchell said, his voice breaking. The deer was in obvious pain, blood pouring out all over the snow.

"Jesus," Kevin said, looking at the mangled deer, which was making horrible honking groans of agony. "What's our next move here, Rebecca? How do you want to handle this?"

Truett Boss began to wail. I crouched over my knees and gushed hot vomit into the snow.

"OK then," Kevin said. "I guess I'll be taking the lead." He turned to address his troop. "Boys, wait here with Ms. Meer. Do not approach the animal. I will be right back." He ran off in the direction of the cabins. I vomited again, with a semicircle of sobbing Nature Boys in their gold scarves and little blue stocking caps for audience.

"Sorry," I whispered to the deer, causing the boys to sob more emphatically. The deer thrashed its antlers around in the blood-soaked snow.

Kevin returned with a small silver object in hand, which in my distress I did not immediately recognize. "I'm going to need everyone to stand back. Behind that fire pit, everyone," he said to the wailing boys. "Rebecca, can you?" Kevin said, cocking his head in the way he wanted me to lead the boys.

"Come on, kids," I said. "Let's go wait over here."

Kevin slipped on a pair of noise-canceling earmuffs and fired three times into the deer. Its guts burst open, splattering intestine all over the snow.

"Coooooool," one of the boys said. They were still crying, but they were less hysterical now, mesmerized by the site of Kevin Holts firing into the deer like an executioner. He removed the clip and turned to address them.

"Now boys, I want you to know, this firearm is for self-defense, not hunting. It's not the proper gun for hunting. You'd want something else for that—something with less firepower, I'd guess," Kevin said, wiping a bit of deer blood from his forehead. "Something that would preserve the meat and hide for some possible use."

We heard a rumbling coming down the road in front of us, and a green park ranger's truck pulled up. "God*damn* it. This is not your day, Meer," Kevin said under his breath, as a ranger in a big green coat leapt from his vehicle and ran to the scene of the accident. He wore his hair in a feathery mullet beneath the peaked dome of his ranger's hat, and a tiny well-groomed mustache adorned his lip, recalling the casually rugged masculinity of a vintage cigarette commercial. But unlike the men who'd sold extra-tar smokes to earlier generations, he was anything but composed and self-contained.

"Oh no. Oh, Jesus, no. Not Pretty Johnny Flowers. Not the Duke!" The man collapsed on his knees, stroking the buck's head, his eyes welling with tears. "Who did this? Who *did* this?" he screamed. He beat his fists in the bloody snow in anguish. The boys cowered. My nephew Ethan pointed a small finger in my direction and stepped back behind Kevin's legs.

"It was me—it was an accident," I said.

The park ranger stood, squaring his chest like an angry gorilla, getting in my face. "This is a wildlife *preserve*. He was safe here! He was supposed to be safe!"

"I'm so sorry," I said.

"Ma'am, there are consequences when an animal like that is struck down on a wildlife *preserve*. Not just to the ecosystem. I mean legal consequences. First and foremost, there is a five-thousand-dollar fine. You may be sentenced to no more than ninety days in prison."

"Mom!" Mitchell screamed, throwing his arms around me and sobbing once again. I was crying now, too. I'd plowed right into a blood-soaked nightmare, and the green-hatted ranger of fury was going to make me suffer as the Duke had—I could see it in his eyes.

"Easy now. Let's talk this out," Kevin said. "We didn't have time for introductions in the midst of this terrible tragedy. What can I call you, sir?"

"I'm Eric Underneedle. You can call me Ranger Eric."

"Ranger Eric, my name is Kevin Holts," Kevin said, pausing to let this sink in, but Ranger Eric didn't seem to have heard of him. "And I want you to know that the Nature Boys and I are just sick about this accident. Just sick about it. There is no question that we'll pay that fine. I'll cut a check here and now, and do so gladly. It's the least that magnificent animal deserves. But I think we can agree that this was an accident, a terrible, terrible, accident, and therefore, a civil matter. I could get legal on the phone, but I hate to involve lawyers. I'd hate to pollute the memory of Pretty Johnny with any sort of ugly legal squabble. That's not what he would want. In fact, I'd like to make that five thousand dollars just the first, if you'll allow me, in an annual donation. Given in memory of this noble beast, so tragically struck down in his prime."

The ranger wiped his eyes and sniffed.

"You're going to be OK, buddy," Kevin said, pulling him into a hug. "We'll get through this." The two of them patted each other's backs vigorously, then broke the hug.

"Did he suffer?" Ranger Eric said.

"Not for long," Kevin said, shaking his head somberly. "I made sure of that."

"I thank you," the ranger said. "That, at least, is something."

❖ ❖ ❖

It took hours for the towing company to come for my car and for the corpse of Pretty Johnny Flowers, the Duke, to be dragged out of the snow and loaded into a park-service truck. The best solution, Kevin said, studying the bare branches over my head and not making eye contact, was probably for me to ride back in the van with the boys in the morning, unless there was someone I cared to call? There was not, I admitted.

Kevin took the Nature Boys on a short hike to lift their spirits. As we trudged along the preserve's boring flat trails, Kevin amused them by telling stories of famous and influential people he'd met back in California. The mood lightened with the day, which was becoming exceedingly sunny. Rays of winter light were stabbing me right in my whiplashed, hungover skull, as if no detail was too small for the universe to see to, when it came to the matter of maximizing my suffering. But I felt I deserved it. Occasionally Mitchell would reach out to me and squeeze my hand. The other boys stared at me with fascination bordering on awe, and whenever I looked at them, they dropped their eyes and ran ahead down the trail.

". . . and that *barmaid* was none other than three-time Oscar nominee Sandra Bullock." I could hardly hear Kevin's name-dropping anecdotes over my pounding headache. I staggered along behind in my high-heeled boots, just hoping not to vomit again.

Pretty Johnny Flowers was just a smear of viscera in the snow when we returned, and it occurred to me that I owed Kevin something—a thank-you, an apology, five thousand dollars annually. We filed into the Nature Center, and I tried to find the words to convey the feelings that were welling up in me, alongside the nausea. But Kevin wasn't looking at me at all; he had clipped me out of his field of vision entirely. He directed the kids past a cardboard cutout of a smiling Ranger Eric Underneedle—*in happier days*, I thought—into a room full of backlit dioramas of prairie dogs. The Nature Boys trooped through, into a carpeted indoor amphitheater, and another park-service employee,

Ranger Gretchen Floss, began clicking through slides on the completely nondescript flora and mostly humdrum fauna of our native state. Kevin slipped out into the hall, and I followed him.

"Kevin," I said.

He paused with his back to me, and then, moving slowly, like he was mustering the resolve to deal with an especially unpleasant task, he turned around. "Yes?"

The noon sun poured through the floor-to-ceiling windows of the center and gave Kevin, now that he was finally looking at me, a clear view of my face. *"Yeesh,"* he said bending to look at me. "You might want to go freshen up. There's nonpotable water in the facilities. Go now. Seriously."

I went and scrubbed at my face with wet paper towels. The black rings of girls' night eye makeup had long ago migrated down my face in the style of Gene Simmons. I was terrifying.

When I emerged from the bathroom, Kevin was leaning against the wall, waiting for me.

"Rebecca, I don't know where to begin. I'm a future-focused person. I'm a positive person. Maybe if I went up on a hilltop and just meditated, just let the wind wash over me and the sun shine down, maybe then the right words would come."

"You'd freeze to death first," I pointed out, but he ignored my negativity.

"But right now? I don't have that kind of perspective. So all I'm left with is this: what a colossal fuckup."

"Yes," I conceded.

"Let's just skip over the five-point buck, the goddamned pride of the preserve for a minute, because, yes, deer run out in front of cars, sure. It happens. But why are you even here? You show up looking like last night's mistake, smelling strongly of Player Pour Homme, for what reason exactly?"

"I'm not sure," I said, much too nauseated to deal with this line of questioning. All I wanted was a dark room, a bed, and some extra-strength aspirin. "I was worried about Mitchell."

"Mitchell was fine. They were *all* fine. Now? A little bit traumatized. There's no getting around it. Those boys saw something today they will never forget."

The sound of wailing filled the hallway, as the doors of the amphitheater burst open. Nature Boys streamed out, streaming tears.

"I'm so sorry," Ranger Gretchen Floss said, twisting her hands. "There was a slide of the Duke, and they all just lost it."

"No apologies needed. It's not your fault, Ranger Gretchen." Kevin dropped to one knee and spread his arms wide. "Troop hug! Come on, everybody get in here." The boys clung to him, even Mitchell.

"Do you know what the Pawnee believed about deer? They believed that when a deer was slain by a mighty hunter, its soul departed its body and went up into the sky, where the chiefs of old still live. And some nights, if you look up to the stars, you'll see them. Sky Chief. Sun Chief. Chief Ruling His Son. They ride on horseback through the stars, and all the great bucks who ever lived ride with them. Well, boys. The stars got a new buck today. The finest one of all."

❖ ❖ ❖

At dinner—hot dogs for the boys, green sludge for Kevin, pureed in his tiny travel blender, and for me, nothing, it was still too soon—the boys talked only of Pretty Johnny Flowers, the Duke, in the stars. When the winter day faded into night, Kevin took them out in the snow to stare up at the sky.

"He's there! Right there! You guys, I saw him," Truett Boss said, and everyone agreed.

We slept on cots in the cabin. Kevin lent me his sleeping bag, claiming he had more than enough warmth from the roaring fire he'd built, which sent smoke billowing up the stone chimney, and his form-hugging long underwear. As the boys drifted off to sleep, Kevin whispered.

"That is a *tenacious* fragrance, Rebecca. Not many men I know wear it. Fewer women."

My back was to him, and I didn't turn around. "That was really beautiful, what you said about the deer. I never knew that about the Pawnee."

Kevin shifted on his cot. "It was total fucking bullshit. I was just cleaning up your mess."

As the boys fell asleep all around us, I knew Kevin's eyes were boring into my back. I imagined that if I looked over at him, I would see those eyes glowing in the dark with tiny flames of judgment. So I didn't turn around. I put my hand up my girls' night blouse and began peeling my Phocus patch from my lower back, slowly, so as to make no sound. I'd been such an innocent when I slapped it on, so full of hope for the person I could become. Now I understood that it couldn't really help me, that there were some things even lower than Hayes Bandercook.

TWENTY

"A bout the food drive," Calvin said, dropping in next to me as I walked across the parking lot to pick up Mitchell. I'd just parked our new car, a light-green Ford Granada with a rust spot on the door that resembled the state of Florida. I'd picked it up at Second Chances Auto in Nee "for a song," as the salesman put it, due to its fragrant interior.

"The food drive? We're not doing the food drive," I said. It had snowed earlier and would snow again, but the children were outdoors in the cold, running around the soccer field. The hoods of their coats flapped behind them; it wasn't cool to wear your hood that year. Nobody had yet lost an ear to hypothermia, but I expected it would happen before spring. Calvin was looking at the children, not at me, and he was clean-shaven. He seemed younger and even more sincere without the thin line of beard—painfully, boy-band sincere. I avoided looking at his jawline, just to be tactful. We hadn't spoken since I left his apartment, and now we were both stiff and hesitant, as in sync with our awkwardness as we had been out of sync on his horrible carpet.

"We most certainly are. And we're going to need a *W* on this one."

"Excuse me?"

"A win. We need to win it."

"How do you win a food drive?"

Calvin stopped in his tracks, just in front of a speed bump, and looked at me straight on. A fading light threaded itself through the school buildings, and our shadows conferred like two hunched Ichabod Cranes. "You're *joking*, right?"

"Aren't the winners the hungry people who get a bag of groceries?"

"I guess they're winners . . . in a sense. But what I'm saying to you is that our haul needs to be bigger than any other school's in the district. A lot is riding on it."

"What exactly is riding on it?" I had spent several dark hours waiting for the sun to rise over the Pine View apartments, staring into the unblinking face of an obese cat as Calvin slept coiled around me like a spring, and I was not at all sure where that left us.

"More than you know," he said. "It's important for all the children that we dominate this thing, but for the fifth grade more than most. I've given some thought to your qualms about our current faculty situation."

"Not qualms. Violent objections. The situation in fifth grade—it's *untenable*. Do you know that there are children forced to spend the entire day in the cloakroom? They can't come out until they score a pass on the practice CLEAVER or battle their way out with swords. Foam swords."

Calvin hunched into his coat, trying to cover his chin with its collar. "It's possible that my hire was too radical. A tendency for bold, decisive leadership is a weakness of mine."

"Nobody's perfect," I said, flexing my cold fingers under my fuzzy gloves.

"It's not fair to expect everyone else to keep pace with my vision."

"Are you offering me—" *A quid pro quo,* I was about to say. *Win the food drive and Kevin goes back to the internet?*

But he didn't want it like that, out in the open, so he just nodded quickly and said, "I'm offering you a chance to beat the record, which is five thousand cans."

"*Five* thousand cans? There are three hundred children in this school. How do you expect me to do that?"

"You're going to have to be just absolutely ruthless to even come close. But coming close isn't going to be enough. I need you to *win* this, Becky."

"It's Rebecca," I said.

"Really? Because Thad calls you Becky."

Thad! It was like a knife to the heart, as he'd no doubt intended. Why was I the only person not on a first-name basis with Thaddeus Sorenson, MD? Why was I, his right-hand man, so to speak, his working-hours soul mate, denied this trivial sign of intimacy? I was privy to all the sordid drama of his personal life, yet I'd never been invited to call him by his first name! There was no sense to it. I wondered whether on the day we'd met he'd said, *Call me Thad*, as he apparently had to *everyone else*, and somehow I'd missed it? It was unlikely.

"He's earned the right," I said.

"Has he?" Calvin said, and I was grateful that the dusky parking-lot light obscured the expression of his face, so that I could tell myself it wasn't a look of pity he gave me. "I really don't see how."

❖ ❖ ❖

"Let me just see what's keeping him," I said to the couple sitting across from Dr. Thad's empty desk. They were tall and severe, and they kept their coats buttoned up to the neck despite the heat blowing gustily, and at great expense, from the vents in the ceiling. They looked, I couldn't help but think, very much like a younger version of the pair in *American Gothic*. There was no reason to panic. The clinic's funds were a little low, but we've always been dependent on a constant revenue stream. We were just one or two procedures away from being back in the black. All we needed was Dr. Thad and his above-average interpersonal skills, but he was nowhere to be found.

I sat down in Dr. Thad's wingback desk chair and dialed his number, using my office-issued cell phone, as there was less chance he'd pick up if he saw it was the clinic's main line. He answered on the first ring, but his voice was muffled, as if he were holding the phone away from his face. "Look, it's me! It's *me* calling *me*. Hello, Dr. Thad!" Dr. Thad said, more clearly, speaking into the phone now.

"We've got the Grantwoods here to see you," I said.

"What?" Dr. Thad said. "Who is this?" I studied the grim faces of Todd and Melissa Grantwood. They looked like they'd been raised in some kind of old-country religion, and were probably steeped in a no-nonsense farming culture that counseled patient endurance in the face of life's many, many disappointments. In short, they were the toughest of all possible sells, and yet it was essential that we collect.

"I understand," I said. "So your recommendations are—yes, as we discussed yesterday."

"Becky? Becky I've got my hands *full* right now," Dr. Thad said. I heard a squeal and what sounded like a slap on bare flesh. "You little—" then more squealing, and then the phone tumbling down onto what I had to assume was the hotel carpet, probably the Prescott Inn in Warlock. I'd heard enough. If I'd had any remaining illusions about the efficacy of Phocus for managing adult misbehavior, they would have been ripped away now. I put the phone on my desk and stared into the pale eyes of the Grantwoods.

"Dr. Thad has been unexpectedly detained in surgery. I'm so sorry. These things are just part of life for a physician." The Grantwoods nodded; they understood. They were familiar with this, the great lie upon which modern medical practice rests, that the doctor is always busy doing something more important than keeping scheduled appointments. They seemed to buy it.

I took a deep breath, prayed that the Grantwoods were not wearing wires, and prepared myself to practice medicine without a license. "*But* we discussed your case at some length yesterday, and Dr. Thad believes that with your ages and health history, IVF with donor eggs is the logical next step." I was fairly confident this would have been Dr. Thad's recommendation, had he been in the frame of mind to give one.

"We've got some really wonderful donors," I said, passing the book of dewy-skinned ovulators across the mahogany desk to them. Not a ripple of expression passed over the Grantwood faces. Perhaps the idea of going with genes obviously better than their own was too much to take in. They'd dreamed of raising dull, potato-faced children, and they weren't ready to give up hope of adding to the world's mediocrity via their own gametes. If only I'd gotten eggs from one of the Bandercook women. "I know it feels like a big step—and it is—but Dr. Thad and I believe that it offers an excellent chance of success."

"How much?" Melissa Grantwood said.

Honesty requires that I answer this question directly, but salesmanship demands that the number be couched just so, wrapped up in joyous dreams of bringing one's own child into the world. Dr. Thad is a master at this little balancing act; I am not.

I blurted out the number. The Grantwoods' heads swiveled on their coat-obscured necks, and they exchanged a look. "Will it work?" Todd said.

"We're very confident. The success rate in a case like yours is typically near 32 percent per cycle," I said.

"So . . ." Todd said, shifting in his chair, "it probably won't work."

"That's correct," I said, to be agreeable, though I thought it betrayed a very simplistic grasp of statistics on Grantwood's part. These people wanted a child badly, I knew that, and yet I could feel them slipping through my fingers anyway. "You have to understand, those are the industry numbers. But Dr. Thad is a remarkable physician. His personal success rate is slightly higher."

The Grantwoods said nothing, just sat there in the consult chairs like two bumps on a log. "IVF is a very difficult, a very personal decision. I won't tell you otherwise. But I will say, if you decide to make this choice, you are in very good hands with Dr. Thad. He is a brilliant, innovative, widely respected—"

A distant sound of muffled grunting interrupted me. It was coming from my phone, lying at my elbow on Dr. Thad's desk. The noises became louder and more rhythmic and were joined by high-velocity panting. I fumbled with the screen, cursing the day I'd password-protected this phone. The Grantwoods were no longer listening to me, they were staring at my innocent phone with as much disgust as their stoic faces could convey.

"Something must be wrong with this phone. I'm sorry—I don't know what that is."

"You don't know?" Melissa said, skeptically.

"Sure, I *know*, but I don't know where that's coming from or who could possibly be—"

"Looks like you forgot to hang up with Dr. Thad," Todd said.

"No, no, no. We hung up. This must be a new call—a prank call. Dr. Thad is in surgery." Mitchell had rearranged my apps again, and the function that gave this device its name, the actual *phone*, was eluding me. At that moment, a woman's voice screamed Dr. Thad's name, filling the office with her euphoria, just before my thumb could slide over "Disconnect."

The Grantwoods stood to go. "Well you're right about one thing," Melissa said, elbowing her husband in his large, sweatered stomach. "He sounds like quite the guy." I watched our money go walking out the door, hand in hand, smirking.

TWENTY-ONE

Mom, why aren't you married?" Mitchell said, spinning around in
a swivel chair, waiting for his breakfast. I was prepared for the
question from people in general. I fielded it all the time, and had done
so for years, until a birthday or two past my thirtieth. At that point,
people stopped bringing it up so much, out of compassion maybe.
Clearly, I'd missed my chance. Maybe I'd meet someone *years and years*
from now in a retirement home full of sexy seniors, but for the next several decades I was destined to be alone—that was sort of the consensus.
But Mitchell had never asked me this before.

"Because I don't want to be married," I said, with my mouth full
of toast. I slid a plate of toast to him and poured myself another cup of
coffee, running my eyes over the front page of the *Ward Caller*.

"Well, but why don't I have a dad?"

I put down the paper. This is what he'd been getting at all along, as
I should have seen. He'd been making an attempt at subtlety, because
this conversation, the Dad Conversation, rattled me, and he knew it,
though I did my best to seem calm and confident, at peace with all the
things we did and didn't have in our lives. The bite of toast stuck to the
roof of my mouth, and I washed it down with scalding coffee.

"Mitchell. We've been over this and over this," I said. This conversation was like rubbing salt on a fresh puncture wound, to me, and I could barely stand to imagine how it felt for him. He would go months without mentioning the idea, and then he'd hound me on the subject for days in a row, as if I'd stashed a co-parent in the attic like a chained-up Mrs. Rochester. Sometimes Mitchell seemed to believe that if he pleaded long enough, I would throw up my hands and say *Oh, all right!* and pull back a mysterious curtain to introduce him to a genial ball-playing father, some appealing composite of every TV dad who ever paced the screen, a hair-ruffling jokester, or a father from the days of black-and-white, someone who wore a tie, kept order, and doled out wisdom. Again and again, I'd assure him it was just the two of us.

At first, I'd be patient and sensitive: *It's OK to have those feelings, of course it is. Yes, everyone has a father in the scientific sense. But many people don't have a dad.* Then I'd do matter-of-fact: *Look it's just not going to happen.* Finally, exhausted with the topic, with a burning in my chest that might have been either heartburn or guilt, I'd point out that a lot of dads weren't so great anyway, and had he considered that maybe we were better off?

"But maybe we could just find him, if we really tried—"

"A biological father is not the same thing as a dad. And anyway, it's impossible, Mitchell. You know this."

"Mr. Holts says nothing is impossible."

"He couldn't be more wrong. There are lots of things that are impossible. Thousands of things. Millions. The number of impossible things may even be infinite. Nobody's really sure." Whenever we had the Dad Talk, I tried to be reasonable and businesslike, to assure him that this, the way things were, just the two of us, was all part of my plan. In fact, *the plan* was in tatters—not a single thing about our lives was the way I'd meant for it to be, and though I kept adjusting expectations downward, every new plan seemed to implode just the way its predecessors had done.

"I'm going to ask Mr. Holts about that." Mitchell was cutting up his toast into neat squares and eating them with a fork, as per usual.

"I don't think you should go running to Mr. Holts any time you have a question. There are a lot of things he doesn't know."

"Mom, he's a *billionaire*," Mitchell said. The five-thousand-dollar check Kevin wrote to Ranger Eric Underneedle as we boarded the van for home had nearly eclipsed everything else that transpired that weekend. Tales of Kevin's vast, sultan-like wealth were all the boys could talk about. On the whole, I was grateful.

"Ha," I said. "He's not. And anyway, money doesn't give you all the answers."

Mitchell took a swallow of orange juice. "Well, it seems like it does."

"It gives you some answers," I conceded. "But then it creates a host of other problems."

"Like what?"

"Oh, I don't know. It's complicated."

"Like where to store all your money could be a problem? Or protecting it from robbers?"

"No, I mean *real* problems, Mitchell. I just can't think of one right this minute," I said. I was not in a situation, bank account wise, in which the problems of those with a surplus of cash sprang readily to mind or seemed especially poignant.

"I want to be a billionaire, too," Mitchell said.

"Sweetie, he's *not* a billionaire. And the problem with money is that it can't really make you happy."

"I think Mr. Holts is really happy. He's always whistling," Mitchell said. "Sad people don't do that. You don't do that." Mitchell was swiveling his chair right and left, which he knows annoys me, especially first thing in the morning.

"I'm not sad. I just don't feel the need to go around whistling a moronic tune day in, day out," I said.

Mitchel sipped his orange juice. There is something incredibly galling about being regarded skeptically by a ten-year-old. I dipped into the vat of childhood memories for ammo. "You know, they say it's easier for a camel to pass through the eye of a needle than for a rich man to get into heaven."

"But why would a camel want to pass through a needle?"

"Well it wouldn't, most likely."

"So then it's not a problem," Mitchell said, spearing the last square of toast.

"Look, aren't you forgetting something?" I said. I was buttoning a pea coat over my scrubs, keys in hand. There was a brown paper sack full of food still sitting on the crewelwork doormat. We'd kicked off the food drive days ago, but Mitchell kept forgetting to bring in his bag.

"No," Mitchell said, turning to show me his backpack, into which he'd already slipped his completed homework.

"Look by the door. By the *front* door," I said, because Mitchell was drifting off toward the garage.

He craned his neck and squinted, an exaggerated pantomime of searching. "I don't see anything there," he said.

"Those are your cans for the food drive," I said. I had tied up the clinic's copy machine for an hour printing hundreds of food drive fliers. I had hung posters all over the Davis Elementary hallways. And Mitchell had remarked, with some justification, that I seemed to talk about canned food a lot these days. And yet, in spite of all these efforts, not a single can had yet been collected from Mitchell's class. I assumed that it was some sort of attempt to punish me for Pretty Johnny Flowers, the Duke, and I intended to press the issue and get it all out in the open.

"I think we should probably just keep those for ourselves," Mitchell said.

It was beginning to snow, so I pressed an orange ski cap down around his ears. It was a bad sign that he allowed this: he was choosing his battles.

"We don't need them. We have plenty of food, and there are people right here in Ward who don't have enough to eat," I said. "You can help them by taking these in to school."

Mitchell frowned into the grocery bag full of canned tomatoes and pumpkin puree and refried beans. "I know. But I still don't want to do it."

"You *don't want* to help hungry people? Or are you just"—I bit my lip to keep my composure—"trying to punish your mother?"

Mitchell looked confused. "Mom, I want to help you, I *do*. But if I bring in any cans, the kids in my class are going to kill me. They'll put me back in the cloakroom, Mom."

"Why would they do that? Do you know that the winning class gets a party?" I had just put up more posters announcing this incentive, deliriously hand drawing them after midnight, in an effort to spark some participation.

"Yes . . . but Mr. Holts says he'll take us to Pizza Planet if nobody brings in food. Then we'll get to eat pizza *and* play video games *and* bowl." The class party I'd been contemplating, boxed cookies and little cups of punch at their dreary desks, was a sad affair compared to the bacchanalia Kevin was dangling before their eyes.

"I'm sure he meant if *everybody* brings in food." There was no way that Kevin would oppose Calvin in such a head-on manner. Calvin wanted a *W*. Open defiance would jeopardize Kevin's data-mining project, and if there's one thing Kevin holds sacred, it's his own financial gain.

"He said *nobody*. He's against the food drive," Mitchell said. "He says they're unethical."

"Unethical? But we're going to be feeding hungry people with these cans."

"I know," Mitchell said. "That's why I can't do it. Also, I want to go bowling. I have to follow my conscience on this one." He slid his arms through the loops of his backpack and headed toward the car.

"Wait, Mitchell!" I said. I picked up the bag. "You care more about bowling than you do about people who don't have enough to eat? That is so . . . selfish."

"Mr. Holts says selfishness is a virtue."

"A *virtue*? There's nothing good about being selfish."

"I *told* him you'd say that. He said for you to schedule a conference if you have a problem with it."

"Well then that's what I'm going to do. Because I do have problem with it. I have a *big* problem with it."

"Mr. Holts said you probably wouldn't go through with the conference, for various reasons," Mitchell said. He looked up at me, trying to gauge my reaction. His soft brown eyes were bright next to his orange ski cap.

"What reasons?" I said, keeping my expression only mildly curious.

"That's what I wanted to know! But he just said that he makes you uncomfortable, and it's nothing for a kid to worry about. And I said, 'Is it grown-up business, Mr. Holts?' and he said it was, and then I said, '*You* said there's no such thing as grown-up business, you hypocrite!' And he laughed, and he told me I'm going to be a captain of industry one day, but he still didn't tell me the various reasons. Will you ask him and then tell me, Mom?"

"Sure. Zip your coat," I said.

❖ ❖ ❖

There was no question of having the Granada detailed at the car wash until Dr. Thad got back to work, so Mitchell and I were riding through the cold with heat pumping and the windows down. With the windows closed, the stink from the interior was just unendurable, but with the windows down, we were shivering. I put them halfway up and the smell was almost bearable, but fog began to spread over the glass. When we hit a red light on O and Fifty-Seventh, I took a moment to rub a fresh porthole in the windshield fog with my glove. On the street corner beside us, a woman with a mass of tangled gray hair pushed a shopping cart full of debris. A cardboard sign explained her predicament in rambling, hard-to-read detail. I stared at the traffic light ahead of me, but with the windows open, I was easy prey. She launched into a loud, whiskey-voiced ramble.

"Ma'am I'm homeless, I'm hungry, I'm cold, and if there's any way you could help me, just a dollar whatever you've got—" I lifted up in my seat, rolling my eyes, and fumbled in my pocket with my clumsy gloved fingers for some money. The woman began to shuffle toward the open passenger window.

"Get a job!" Mitchell screamed, from the backseat. The woman stopped in her tracks. The light turned green, and I sped through the intersection.

"Mitchell! How could you say something like that? I was going to *help* her. Why would you even think of yelling something so unkind?" I said. But I knew why.

"If she had a job, you wouldn't need to help her. She could help herself, and then you could save your money to fix our car," Mitchell said, spouting a ten-year-old's version of the Holtsian worldview, not substantially different from the forty-year-old's. "I'm *cold*," he added.

"Not everyone is as lucky as we are," I said. I could see my breath in the car. The heater was on max, but the warm air blew right out the windows as we drove. "It's not so easy to just *get a job*," I said thinking of what I'd do if things didn't turn around at the clinic. The holidays were nearly upon us, and nobody buys fertility services once pumpkin-flavored everything rears its clovey head. Thanksgiving to New Year's was a dead zone in which people spent their money on gift cards for their nearest and dearest and hoped to make miracles under the mistletoe instead of in the clinic. Usually, Dr. Thad and I hoard cash for the winter like squirrels do nuts.

We pulled into the drop-off line at Davis Elementary and it occurred to me, as Mitchell ran through the cold toward the front doors, that a Moment had just taken place. Yes, it had been one of those crucial times in which a mother, with a gentle voice full of love and wisdom, tinkers with her child's worldview, helping him to see things in a slightly different light, before his beliefs freeze into a twisted, hideous parody of an ideology, something so simplistic and grotesque that he is driven out of civilized society and forced to haunt the comments section till the end of his days. But I had blown it by any possible measure. Mitchell had insulted a homeless person, I'd promised her money, and then we'd just driven off. When I stopped for gas at the Fuel & Flee, my self-disgust was absolute.

I filled up the tank and then walked shivering through the doors, right into Hayes Bandercook, who was eating a gas station burrito for breakfast, a smear of queso sauce marring his handsome face, as well as the beginnings of a mustache. Maybe it was the burrito, maybe the facial hair, but whatever the reason, I felt nothing at all. *Wrong*. I felt strong. Resolute. I walked right past him toward the coffee machine, refusing to make eye contact. He followed.

"Rebecca," he said, standing behind me and breathing into my ear in a way that made my cold skin prickle, but I just stared at the coffee machine as it trickled syrupy black sludge from the night shift into my cup. "Hello?" he whispered, as I continued to ignore him. "Are you *mad*?"

I was more than mad, I realized. I was furious. Did a handful of (extended) liaisons at the Fox Motel give him the right to buy a giant box of store-brand condoms for possibly nonexclusive use with me? No it did not. Not by my estimation. Not when he also was shooing me out of windows and, let's not forget, never bothering to call?

"Use *vindicated* in a sentence," I challenged, wheeling around to face him with righteous indignation and a scalding cup of delicious burned coffee. I glared at him over my scarf. His surprised expression only highlighted the appealing symmetry of his facial features, but luckily his torso was entirely obscured behind an enormous work coat. If we kept this short, I could put this thing to bed—to *rest*, I corrected—once and for all.

"What? Why?" I was having a difficult time getting the plastic lid to settle over the bendy paper cup. Hayes took the cup from me and held it while I pressed the lid into place. I avoided looking at his hands. Too many memories.

"Exactly as I thought," I said.

"But why would I use *vindicated* in a sentence?" Hayes said.

I took the cup from him and turned my back, walking toward the door. I left him standing beside the hot dog rotisserie. "You wouldn't, because you *can't*." I said, loudly, not caring who heard me addressing him.

"Hold on, now. 'Why would I use *vindicated* in a sentence?' is a sentence. I'm right, aren't I? I'm right, and you know it. Rebecca!" He was laughing as if this were some kind of game, but I didn't slow my pace, and seeing how serious I was, he didn't follow.

On the way to work, I got stopped at the same light, with the cup of coffee rapidly cooling between my thighs. The same woman was standing guard over the same cartload of junk. I handed my coffee and some cash out the window to her.

"Turn your life around!" I said, looking at myself in the rearview mirror.

TWENTY-TWO

Like so many other desperate people before me, I found myself in the sunken waiting room of my sister's law firm. I sat on the smallest of the three orange vinyl sofas and opened a lifestyle magazine from the winter of 1979. I was alone and surprised to find how much this disappointed me. I suppose I had wanted to compare notes with someone else whose life was falling apart. *It's the end of the line for me. Don't know how I'll get out of this one,* a desperate person one couch over might have remarked.

I completely get it, I would have said, with absolute honesty.

The firm of Loos & Meer-Loos is like a mom-and-pop store that sells a bit of everything: "From Arson to Wire Fraud" is their slogan, and that's just their criminal practice. Between them, Ben Sr. and Madge handle every type of law but maritime. I found it very strange that not a single person in Ward had a court date to prep for or suit that needed filing on this fine wintry day. Maybe everyone was taking their business across the highway to Barton & Theotopolous.

I wandered over to the reception window. "If it's not a good time, I can come back," I said.

"Ms. Meer-Loos will see you now," Sara Beth said. She was very young, almost a girl, and yet too old for the long pigtails she was wearing.

"I didn't recognize you, Sara Beth. You're working here now?"

"That's right," Sara Beth said. "Aunt Madge is mentoring me so I won't make the mistakes my parents did." Sara Beth's father, Ross Loos, had trained as lawyer and worked briefly in the family business, but these days he was farming organic out near Daverly. He was a seeker, and what he was seeking was not the Almighty Dollar but a "different mode of living." He'd told me all this, unsolicited, when I bought a bag of runty eggplants from his stall in the chilly farmers' market behind the library, the last of the year. I followed Sara Beth down a hallway.

"I need your help, Madge," I said.

"I *knew* it. I have seen this coming for months. But I'm not going to say I told you so."

"I appreciate that," I admitted.

"First things first. These are my ground rules. I need absolute honesty from you," Madge said, looking up from an enormous varnished mahogany desk littered with papers and family pictures in thin silver frames.

"Of course," I said.

"Don't 'of course' me. I'm serious. If you've got a dead hooker in your trunk, I need to know that right away."

"That's not why I'm here," I said.

"It's a figure of speech, Becky. We've all got one, and if you've got any sense, you'll keep that trunk slammed tight and locked in front of company. But right now, I'm not just your sister. I'm your attorney. And when you're with your legal counsel, you bring out your dead. Got it?"

"Madge—"

"Because I can't help you with the dead hooker in your trunk if *I don't know* you've got a dead hooker in your trunk. Make sense?"

"Yes," I said.

"Now can I offer you a beverage? Coffee?"

"Please."

"Sara Beth!" Madge yelled. "Coffee! You know, I'm just putting this out there: I would love to handle the Sorensen divorce," Madge said. "I don't even have a preference which side . . . that's going to be a fun one. Whew! That's going to take some old-school, elbow-throwing, cussing-and-fighting country lawyering." Madge leaned back in her chair and contemplated the tiled asbestos ceiling. "Tell him not to call in some big city firm—that's a costly mistake. You want to keep a thing like that local."

"I don't think there's going to be a divorce."

"Ha!" Madge said. "Well, you may be right." She crossed her fingers. "But here's to hoping."

Sara Beth came in with a yellow Pyrex tray and two matching cloverleaf mugs.

"Thank you, honey," Madge said. When Sara Beth had closed the door behind her, Madge said, "So, I'm guessing the DA's office is about to drop charges, and you want to get out in front of that."

"Charges—why would they do that?"

Madge shrugged. "Because you shot an animal on a wildlife preserve."

"*I* didn't shoot it."

"That's good. That'll help our case."

"There's no case, Madge. It was just a regrettable accident."

"You know, you say that and I believe you, because you're my sister and I love you. *But* you've got one of those faces—always have. We'd have to work on it for a jury trial. I've got an excellent remorse coach based out of Des Moines. We could fly her in, but it costs. So, all the better if there are no charges pending."

I stared at my sister over the rim of my coffee cup and wondered, again, if coming here had been a terrible mistake. Madge's clients were, after all, mostly criminals—a population renowned for its poor impulse control and flawed decision-making processes. "Kevin paid the fine. The park service and I have settled our differences."

"OK, then what? Dead hookers, Rebecca. Bring 'em out. Put them all here on the table," Madge said, slapping her desk.

"It's about the food drive at Davis," I said. "Nobody is participating. I was hoping you might have some advice. How did you get buy-in when you ran it?"

"So the food drive—as your legal counsel, I'm forced to advise against that. Huge pain in the ass. Huge. See if you can pass the job off to someone else. That's what I'd do."

"It's too late to get out of it," I said. "I may have indicated to . . . uh . . . school administration that the drive was already in progress."

"Calvin Chester. I was hoping you'd bring him up. That's quite a story. Almost more than the deer, really."

"So you know about that, too," I said.

"Of course," Madge said. "I have discussed literally nothing else since the weekend. But I don't judge. It's the twenty-first century. I mean, *come on*. A Friday night in a pluralistic Western democracy with collapsing social mores and two-dollar pints? These things are bound to happen."

"I guess," I said shrugging.

"Frankly, I *admire* you. Your . . . fortitude. That guy? I just couldn't. The bow ties alone. I bet he's a spooner, too."

"Uh . . . ," I said, unsure whether I was expected to answer this question.

"I understand," Madge said. "Poor baby."

"This isn't really about Calvin. I want to do this for Mitchell. Kevin Holts has got him brainwashed. He thinks charity is a bad idea. He's yelling at the homeless, Madge."

"Jesus," Madge said. "Some of them are dangerous."

"We need to show him that compassion isn't just for losers."

"And to have compassion *for* losers. Hell yes," Madge said. "I'll do it. But you should talk to Holts. This is unacceptable."

"We're not on great terms," I said.

"Well, you never were. Although for a brief moment there, I thought you hated each other in a sexy way. Kind of a *Pride and Prejudice* type thing? But now it's just straight-up mutual contempt, right?"

I cleared my throat. "So Calvin wants to beat five thousand cans."

Madge whistled. "Shit. *Five* thousand."

"I have no idea where we should start."

"Let me make some calls," Madge said. "More coffee?"

"No, thank you."

"OK, I'll be in touch."

"That's it?"

"I've got closing arguments in Nee County tomorrow morning. But, don't worry. This is my priority number two."

TWENTY-THREE

I was at my desk, going over the final draft of Dr. Thad's speech for Fertile Con, which detailed our recent refinements in blastocyst banking—sure to be a crowd-pleaser—when I became aware of a person looming in my doorway.

"Where's Thad?" the person said, in a horrendous regional accent. I recognized immediately that it was Nina Flyte, who had somehow made it down the hallway to my office, where patients are not allowed. I smiled at Nina as if she were not both a nuisance and an intruder. Children were building the largest snowmen of the season in their monochrome yards, but thanks to the perfidy of Reyne "Hot Tub" Reynolds, she was no closer to becoming a mother than she'd been at the end of the summer. So if she looked a little frantic and distressed, I felt she had every right. A gentle answer was forming on my lips when it hit me. *Thad.*

"Where's *Thad?*" I repeated, with horror.

"I really need to talk to Thad, but he's not answering his phone," Nina said. In the scheme of things, it didn't really matter that she pronounced his name with a contracted vowel sound and an offensive nasal quality that had to be heard to be believed. We are all caught up in forces beyond our control, and Nina couldn't be blamed for the Northern Cities Vowel Shift. But it was difficult to imagine how anyone could bear to converse with her on a regular basis, especially about matters of the heart, and more specifically how *Dr. Thad* could bear it, because I realized then and there that Scenario Three—a volatile, dark-haired patient—had just walked in my office.

"Would you sit down a minute please, Nina. That's right. Close the door. Nina, I know you've been through a difficult time," I said, keeping my voice low. Nina is needy, brunette, and attractive, but I had never considered her as a serious candidate. She was, I'd assumed, too much a crystal-wearing, beet-juice-enema-using lunatic to captivate a man of Dr. Thad's intelligence. I'd underestimated him. But I had every confidence I could end this thing here and now, as long as we could both be discreet and keep our voices down. Then the Dr. Thad situation could be downgraded to something nearer what I'd planned for, and I could save Dr. Thad's reputation, his marriage, and his business—our business.

"I've been through *hell*," Nina said, too loudly. If Maryellen were anywhere in the vicinity, she would easily overhear, and then her curiosity would be piqued. She'd want an explanation. I indulged in the brief fantasy of chloroforming Nina and dragging her limp body out the back door before any of the gossiping staff could overhear her. Not that I would ever really *do* such a thing, of course. Besides the dubious legal and moral aspects of such a maneuver, the list of unpredictable outcomes created by such a risky plan would be as long as your arm.

"Yes, you have been through hell," I said, speaking very softly and hoping she'd take the hint and lower the volume. "And I understand that spending so much time with a man as charismatic and gifted as Dr. Thad can be . . . confusing."

"Oh, you do?" Nina said, raising an eyebrow.

"But there's something you ought to know. Dr. Thad is infertile," I said. Though I'd like to believe our Scenario Three patients are all driven by old-fashioned lust, frugality is also a factor. High-quality gametes are pricey, and this was not the first time a desperate woman had tried to save herself a few thousand dollars at the expense of Dr. Thad's feelings. Now was the moment for her to burst into tears and express remorse and self-hatred, but Nina just looked at me coolly.

"He's not infertile," Nina said. She was neither denying the affair nor apologizing for it—an absolute first in star-ampersand-star patient history.

"Nina, he is," I said.

"He had a vasectomy; it's not the same thing."

"He *told* you that?" This was unprecedented, and it threw me. It meant something that Dr. Thad had made this confession. Even I, who enjoy Dr. Thad's trust and confidence, had only learned this fact indirectly. I felt the stirrings of imminent panic. I inhaled deeply to calm myself.

"Not at first. But I got it out of him. It's the biggest regret of his life. But Angie doesn't want another child. She's a monster."

This was my own opinion as well, but I thought it would be disloyal to Dr. Thad to voice it, so I didn't. "The point is, Nina, that this relationship can't work. You want a baby. You *deserve* one. And you're going to be such a wonderful mother," I said, and I meant it, because ruthless scheming on behalf of the offspring is a quality at least as maternal as your garden-variety nurturing, and Nina was clearly a pro. "Think of the little pink toes and the gummy smiles. Don't throw away your chance at that."

"Oh, I haven't," Nina said. The confidence with which she said this caught me short. My eye drifted involuntarily to my desk calendar, where three large *X*s marred the month like the label on a vintage bottle of poison. (This is the notation I've reserved for Dr. Thad's days off.) He was heading to Omaha for his annual meetup with the local alumni of the Harvard Glee Club. I sometimes wondered whether this barbershop quartet was only a polite fiction. More likely, I supposed, Dr. Thad was conducting an illicit duet. But of course, I went to a state school, and I am not well versed in the many quaint and charming customs of the Ivy League. Now the gleam in Nina's eye painted the whole trip in an even more sinister light.

"He's actually quite phobic about medical procedures," I said. There are billboards outside the Omaha city limits promising a nearly painless vasectomy reversal, pioneered by Dr. Keith Richards, who, by fatal coincidence (so it now seemed), is a dear friend from Dr. Thad's Harvard days and lends his reedy tenor to the Glee. "There are certain risks involved," I said. I was practically begging her to call it off, as if that would do any good.

"He wants a child. I want a child," Nina said, with infuriating simplicity, as if life was about everyone getting what they want.

"Nina, Dr. Thad had that vasectomy for good reason. He's got a family history of violent psychosis."

"I think you're lying," Nina said. "He's one of the finest human beings I've ever met. He's got a beautiful aura."

"You should tell him so," I said. Surely that kind of nonsense would be a deal breaker for a man of Dr. Thad's intellect.

"I did. The very first night." She smiled in a way that made me queasy. It hurt me to imagine Dr. Thad having his aura read by an unnaturally flexible homeopathy nut.

"We're talking about a man who is only five foot seven!" I said.

"He's nearly five eight. And he's *brilliant*," Nina said, as if she were capable of truly comprehending the scope of Dr. Thad's gifts, which she is not.

"He's got that horsey laugh," I countered.

"You don't find it sonorous?"

"I do not," I lied. "I find it horsey. And Nina, you don't want that for your child. And Dr. Thad, whatever he may have said under the influence of Louis Roederer, doesn't really want to combine his genetic destiny with yours."

Nina flinched at that small detail, the Roederer. It was the sort of thing a person who'd been taken into Dr. Thad's confidence on this matter might know. "Did Thad ask you to tell me this?" Nina said.

I exhaled and passed my paperweight from hand to hand, as if weighing my words. "This is not the first time I've had this conversation, Nina. You could almost say it's part of my job."

This, I was glad to see, hurt her. They all think they're so special to him—it's just a way he has. He truly can't help it. I pushed a box of tissues toward her, but she had more mental toughness than her pre-Enlightenment worldview suggested, and her eyes remained dry.

"You're jealous," Nina said. This was uncalled for, but she was in a bad place, so I let it go.

"I just don't want to see you hurt again," I said. "*Or* Dr. Thad. And then of course there's Reyne to think of."

Nina actually rolled her eyes, which was out of keeping with the seriousness of our discussion. "Look, Becky," she said, getting up from her chair. "You're going to have to accept that there's another woman in Thad's life now, and it isn't *you*."

"There always is," I said to the back of her coat, but I spoke softly, and she may not have heard. When she was gone, I leaned back in my chair, chewing the eraser of my pencil, a bad habit that reemerges in times of stress.

There was no need to overthink this. If Dr. Thad had confided more, and promised more, to Nina Flyte than he had yet promised to any of the others, he would only regret it more deeply and quickly. The trick was to make sure no permanent decisions were made (or rather, *unmade*) while this temporary infatuation persisted. I did a quick search for "vasectomy reversal complications" and picked three of the most horrific, which I pasted into an e-mail titled "FYI" and sent to Dr. Thad. The whooshing sound from my outbox restored a measure of calm. If I knew Dr. Thad—and I know him *like my own soul*—Nina would have to find herself another supplier.

❖ ❖ ❖

"Becky, my personal life is . . ." Dr. Thad paused, searching for the right phrase. This was the day scheduled for his departure to Omaha, and in an abundance of caution, I'd gunned it out of the morning car line, peeling out with a hasty but affectionate wave to Mitchell, and proceeded by back roads to Dr. Thad's personal residence.

It felt furtive and shameful checking up on him this way, but I had to know whether his itinerary still included Nina Flyte and an ill-advised rewiring of the vas deferens. There was a pale light seeping from behind the curtains of his bedroom, the inner sanctum of Dr. Thad-ness. I parked my car across the street and killed the engine, staring up at the room where he and Mrs. Dr. Thad were only just waking, and for a moment, *I* felt like the one who was behaving unprofessionally. I said aloud, "A line has been crossed, Rebecca," and I could see my breath in the car. I very nearly drove away.

But it was a good thing I didn't, because a scant eight minutes later I surprised him loading a suitcase into the trunk of his car. Beside it, tossed in like an afterthought, lay a straw barbershop hat wrapped with a blue ribbon. He exhaled cold air through his finely shaped nostrils and began again. "My *personal* life is—"

"A total mess," I suggested. He frowned, as if this hadn't quite captured it. "Reminiscent of the worst of French cinema," I offered.

"Personal," Dr. Thad said. It was bitterly cold and dark. Although he was wearing his Nordic sweater and scarf set, I knew that he was suffering in the early morning chill even more than I, but he did not invite me to continue this discussion in his car, which is equipped with seat warmers. I eyed the leather passenger seat, where Nina's toned gluteals would soon take up residence, unless I could make him see reason.

"Dr. Thad, this is *America*," I said. He has a nearly European sense of refinement, and though one might wish that the people of the Midwest were worldly enough to consider his sophisticated ménages unworthy of comment or interest, this is very far from the case. It is only my talent for preserving secrecy that has spared him public disgrace thus far.

"I don't care, Becky. My personal life has no bearing on the quality of my work. It's asinine of you to imply that what's happening between me and *a very special lady*," he said, dropping his voice, "has anything to do with my professional reputation."

"Think of the metric system," I said, clasping his gloved hands in my bare ones. "It's a better system all the way around, isn't it? It's clean. It's logical. It's in use worldwide. But go over to the Old Cheyenne and order a beer in milliliters and you—even *you*, Dr. Thad—will get punched in the face. Because—don't you understand? This is *America* and nothing we say or do can change that."

"Goddamn it, Becky," Dr. Thad said, pulling his hands away. "Your fingers are like ice."

He reached for the door of his car. "You can't do it," I said, meaning the vasectomy reversal, which he had neither confirmed nor denied. "It's one thing to risk your career, but you can't risk your . . ."

"My what?" he said. He had the door open.

So help me, I balked. I just stood there in the driveway, staring at him.

"Becky, this conversation is over."

"Infection," I said. "Hematoma." He was sitting in the driver's seat now. "Fever," I added. He shook his head. "Scrotal discomfort!" I wanted to sink down to my knees to beg him not to do this, but I knew he wouldn't respect that. He slammed the door shut. "Impotence!" I yelled as he gunned it out of the driveway, raising a cloud of gravel and dirt in his wake.

TWENTY-FOUR

You really know your way around," I said to Madge as she steered her LeBaron over the crooked, potholed avenues of Nee. The streets of Ward are laid out on a grid, letters run east to west, numbers north to south. It's impossible to get lost, no matter how much you might wish to. But the town of Nee took a more freewheeling approach to city planning. Legend has it that the city fathers determined the paths of the streets over a jug of grain liquor, by firing randomly into the air and following the trajectory of the bullets.

"Well, I'm here a lot," Madge said. We were driving down Ed Barrelhouse Memorial Parkway past pawnshops and family restaurants. I wasn't entirely sure why Nee was "the key to everything," as Madge insisted. In fact I would have staked a lot on the wager that if Nee ever had the key, it had hocked it for beer money decades ago.

Ordinarily, I wouldn't bother going to Nee *for any reason*, least of all for answers. Problem solving is not one of Nee's natural resources, unless you have the type of "problem" that can be "solved" by hiring a bargain-rate hit man.

But Madge had caught me at a weak moment. I'd agreed to come without pointing out the insane futility of her plan, and now I was riding along without protest, with my head resting against the smooth red leather of the LeBaron, because I had just emptied my savings account to pay Front Desk and Maryellen, and what would happen next week was more than I cared to speculate about.

"How did things go with your trial?" I asked. This was slightly dishonest; I'd already heard Reyne Reynolds announce the guilty verdict on Channel 8, reporting live from outside Nee County Courthouse. The manic pixie defense had not held water with the jury, but Madge had rarely been saddled with a less whimsical client. The defendant simply wasn't believable as the kind of woman whose playful surprises might *accidentally* result in a man's death. Madge had done as much as anybody could have.

Madge frowned. "They handed us a conviction."

"I'm sorry," I said.

"Don't be. And don't shoot your manager in broad daylight in the middle of a crowded pizza place. That's the takeaway. It doesn't look accidental, not even in Nee."

"How do you accidentally pull off a shot like that while waiting tables?" Reyne and his co-anchor, Selma Cortez, had reenacted the scene in the pizzeria for the ten o'clock segment, using a water balloon to represent the trajectory of the bullet. It was a hell of a shot.

"I had a ballistic expert ready to testify that it was absolutely plausible, but on cross, my client admitted that she went out to her car to get the weapon *just before* accidentally shooting him with it. This fact she never mentioned to me. Jesus, I can't work with someone like that."

The houses of Nee rolled by with their cracked porches. Nee sits atop the Chisholm-Hawkes fault and its structures are prone to shifting and cracking. Wardians like to joke that one day the earth will open and swallow the place up. "Best thing for it," is the punch line.

"Why'd she do it?" I said, again somewhat dishonestly. I was no longer one of the average law-abiders who read a story like this over the morning cereal and wondered why someone might up and shoot her boss. As of late, I totally got it.

"Why?" Madge made a gesture that seemed to indicate that there is no greater mystery than the human mind—a mystery insoluble even to itself—and that to ask why anyone did anything presumed that we had access to a type of knowledge that is in fact denied us. I was going to venture to disagree with this worldview, but Madge said, "Brass tacks: he wanted her to work a double."

"Wow," I said.

"Well, she's got young kids. She couldn't just work a double with no notice like that. She had to think of their welfare, too."

"I guess," I said. "But now she's going to jail."

"For eighteen months. Could have been worse."

"Eighteen months for murder? Madge, you're amazing." I was very glad to have Madge in my corner. If she could work the school system the way she did our system of justice, five thousand cans for the food drive didn't seem like an impossibility.

"There were some serious mitigating factors. My client suffers from adult ADHD. It ruins lives, that disease."

We drove past a derelict park. A statue of Ed Barrelhouse, the town's founding father, with his hands in pockets, modest suit jacket billowing slightly in the back to suggest a westerly breeze, gazed out to the skeletal remains of some rusted playground equipment.

"Murdering people ruins lives," I said. "I can't believe a jury of our peers agreed that poor concentration is now a license to kill."

"My client was a valued member of the community until her disease got the better of her."

"So no priors?"

"I didn't say *that*. The point is we need to remove the stigma and help get more people in treatment. That's why I wear this gray ribbon from the Adult ADHD Fund—it's hope for a cure. You should consider giving it your support. Especially during these winter months. People shouldn't have to suffer the way they do this time of year."

"I'm not going to donate money to stop multitasking and the tilt of earth's rotational axis," I said. "There's just nothing we can do about it."

"That's what they said about smallpox, Rebecca. OK, here's our stop. Let's check that defeatist attitude at the door, shall we?"

❖ ❖ ❖

Our stop, apparently, was an abandoned Dross-Mart, specifically, the loading area in the back. Several objections formed on my lips, but I quashed them, not wanting to be called defeatist a second time.

"There's our guy. He's gotten me out of a few tough PTO situations before. Let me do the talking," Madge said. I pushed open the door of the LeBaron and stepped into an icy puddle, flooding my fur-lined plastic shoe with the murky contents of a Nee County pothole. Madge's heels were already clicking across the pavement toward a waiting blue-clad figure, so I followed behind her, sloshing. It seemed a bit late to voice misgivings.

Our guy was wearing business casual and a pointy blond beard. He exuded a casual criminality that did not reassure. An eighteen-wheeler with a painted-over logo was parked in the loading dock, the back door open to reveal stacks of wooden crates.

"I'm Rebecca," I said offering him my hand.

"No names," Madge said. "This is not a social call."

"Chase," our guy said, not shaking the hand I offered him, but actually clasping it with both of his. I was not sure what this gesture meant, but it seemed better to reciprocate, and so I did.

"I'm the manager here," Chase said, as if the Dross-Mart were not boarded up and dark. I couldn't help but think that a visit with Chase would make for a worthy class field trip, driving home a lesson about books and covers. Chase looked like the leader of a motorcycle gang, but apparently, his game was retail.

"So you got yourselves mixed up in a food drive?"

"That's right," I said.

"Shit," Chase said. "That's tough."

"Could be worse. Could be a bake sale," Madge said.

Chase spit onto the asphalt. "So here's the product. I've got one hundred sixty-eight cases, street value of three K, I'll sell to you for fifteen hundred."

"Let's take a look," Madge said. Chase pried open the top of the wooden crate. "As you see, this crate is fully packed. I guarantee you will not come up short. You're free to count it, of course."

"Of course we'll count it," Madge said.

"My reputation is sterling," Chase said.

"And we'll trust you until we don't," Madge said.

I picked up a can wrapped in an unfamiliar lavender label. Characters of a type I believed to be Chinese circled the can.

"What is this?" I said.

"It's lychee," Madge said. "It's a fruit."

"It's tasty," Chase said.

"Is it *all* lychee?" I said.

"There might be some straw mushrooms mixed in here and there," Chase said.

"It's going to look weird when so many of our 'donated' cans turn out to be lychee. I mean, what are the odds? Calvin is not going to buy it."

"He'll look the other way if he wants to win," Madge said.

"Maybe. What else do you have on hand?" I said to Chase. He was stroking his chin beard, and I noticed a gray awareness bracelet around his wrist.

"Windlow Elementary room mothers already cleared out the peas and corn stock. We're late to the game, Rebecca. It's lychee or lose," Madge said.

"Look at these numbers here on the bottom. I think these cans are past their expiration," I said.

"Keep in mind, that's by the Chinese calendar. That's a *lunar* calendar." Chase had an expert-on-everything attitude that would be hard to take in any sort of long-term business relationship. I was regretting our double-hand clasp already.

"It looks like this one expired two Februaries ago, by the Western calendar."

"Easy," Madge said. "Everybody be cool."

"Windlow bought two hundred from the same lot. They were good enough for *Windlow*," Chase said. Windlow Elementary has modern facilities. The children there paint pictures and play instruments thanks to their private lessons. They have access to flush toilets and science enrichment programs. Most of the time, I try to pretend there isn't a Windlow, but now Chase was throwing it in my face.

"Well, how interesting that *Windlow* of all places chooses to feed the hungry with black market, past-date cans. What a slap in the face. I wonder what Reyne Reynolds would make of a story like that." At least once a year, Reyne stepped away from features on adorable pets and did something more hard-hitting, "pulling back the curtain to reveal a side of Ward you may not want to see," as he put it. "All this stuff is stolen, isn't it?" I said.

"You said she was cool," Chase said. His criminality was looking less casual now, as if he'd switched an internal moral lever from the off position into active mode.

"She is," Madge said, laying a reassuring manicure on Chase's arm. She turned to me. "Rebecca, the provenance of these cans is not the issue. The issue is hunger. You can't sit up in your ivory tower, with a full stomach, and make these lofty moral pronouncements. If you want to make a difference, you have to get your hands dirty, like the UN," Madge said.

"Forget it. No deal," I said. I turned toward the LeBaron.

"You're walking away from me?" Chase yelled at my back.

"I'm walking away," I said, without turning around.

"*Nobody* walks away from me," Chase said, but I heard Madge clicking along behind me, so the claim didn't have the ring of truth.

❖ ❖ ❖

Madge and I sat in the LeBaron for a moment, in the grip of an awkward silence.

"Madge, there is no way I can buy all that expired lychee."

"Well I call that hypocrisy," she said. "You've put how many hundreds of humans on ice—do you worry about *their* expiration dates?"

"No," I said, rolling my eyes, because *assuming the power stays on* to run the nitrogen pumps, you can store embryos indefinitely. "That's apples and oranges."

"Then I'm not sure I can work with you," Madge said.

My stomach dropped. "It's the money," I said.

"You won't pay fifteen hundred dollars to spite Kevin Holts?"

"I don't *have* the money," I said.

Madge's dark eyebrows rose up to her hairline. People think of fertility as the ATM of modern medical practice, and *in general*, people are right. But we'd had to cancel four consultations with Dr. Thad this week alone. It's hard to make money without a doctor in the building.

"You're broke?"

"No, of course not. I'll pay you back soon."

"It's not a good time. To be frank, Barton & Theotopolous have got me over a barrel. Every screw-up and litigious asshole in town is filing into their office instead of mine. Goddamned upstarts."

"It's those commercials," I said. Barton & Theotopolous had been doing relentless late-night advertising, calling themselves "the Dual Fingers of God" while girls from the Prairie Fire Cloggers performed in the background. They were pretty compelling.

A can of lychee came crashing into Madge's rear window, thrown by Chase, who was running toward us with an armful of cans, throwing them one after the other and screaming something that was likely insulting, though the windows were rolled up and it was difficult to be sure. Madge peeled out of the parking lot and pointed the car toward Ward. I was going to have to win this food drive the old-fashioned way.

❖ ❖ ❖

Dr. Thad usually returns from Omaha with a spring in his step, but in this case, I was looking for a limp. I needed to know whether he winced as he sat down. He'd made it clear we weren't going to discuss the matter, so I had to keep my eyes peeled and look for context clues. Dr. Thad has an unusually high threshold for pain, and though the typical patient would be experiencing tenderness, swelling, and numbness, it was highly unlikely that he would telegraph his symptoms in any obvious way. I was on the alert for any signs of stoically borne discomfort when I walked into the break room and caught him filling a bag with ice.

"Stub your toe?" I asked.

"I'm not wearing sandals, Becky," Dr. Thad said. "I think you know how I feel about those."

Even on the sandy beaches of the Caribbean—a place he and I have never visited together, despite the biennial international fertility conference on Saint Kitts—you will not catch Dr. Thad schlepping around barefoot or in open-toed shoes. Angie's photos make this very clear.

"In fact, if you ever catch me in sandals you have my permission to"—he furrowed his brow, a gleam in his eye—"to ask me a personal question which is none of your business."

"No thank you," I said, rather coldly.

Dr. Thad looked at me sharply. "Oh, I see," he said. "Forgive me, I'd forgotten. Do you want to talk about it? I can lend a sympathetic ear, if need be."

"Talk about what?" I said.

"That's the tack you're taking? OK. You know me—I don't pry. Nor do I give credence to idle gossip. Nor accident reports. Nor matters of public record. Indifferent to all of the above. Now if you'll excuse me. I'm going to take this ice pack to my office . . . away from *prying eyes*."

Dr. Thad walked down the hall and just as he rounded the corner, I saw it—a very slight limp.

My grip loosened from the tiny handle of my demitasse, and it dropped to the carpet with a soft thud, sending a halo of espresso drops into the stiff fibers. If the spill were blotted immediately with a wet cloth, there was some chance of preventing a stain, but I could hardly see the point in bothering. Because, while I could hold out hope that the procedure had failed, as happens in up to 15 percent of cases, it was time to face the truth: within days or weeks, Dr. Thad would likely be producing sperm in a nonprofessional context.

TWENTY-FIVE

"I want you to know I didn't raise your mothers this way, boys," my mother said, sliding her meal along the metal bars of Wylie's Cafeteria tray slide, where we were preparing to eat Thanksgiving dinner. Our parents had flown in for the holiday and were appalled to learn they would not be served a home-cooked meal. "At the farmhouse, your grandfather would bring in a fresh-killed bird, and your mothers would help me pluck the feathers." This was absolutely true, and it had given both Madge and me a lifelong revulsion toward poultry. "And I laid a beautiful table," she said. "Back me up, Roger," she said, elbowing my dad in the ribs.

"Every year, she laid a beautiful table," my dad said. Madge and I glared at him, and he shrugged his shoulders. At one time, the two of them had argued from morning till night, but in his retirement, our dad had developed a habit of professing his instantaneous, absolute agreement with whatever she said. Now they were the picture of long-wedded bliss, or something.

The boys stared at their grandmother uncertainly. *She laid tables?* They went back to loading their plates, unsure what to make of it. Madge's youngest, Aidan, was too small to see the buffet, and so as he pointed at random, I filled his plate with whatever the contents happened to be, slopping beet salad alongside chocolate pudding, serving up turkey with Jell-O. The end result was something that might get us flagged at Child Protective Services, but Aidan seemed content. If we were raising them wrong, it was just too early to tell.

I was still deliberating over corn bread versus bread stuffing when I heard Mitchell yelp. He was at the end of the line, at the sliced pie, and Viola Holts had just run over his foot with her wheelchair. She scowled at him, by way of apology. Someone—presumably the caretakers, now off for the afternoon with their own families—had dressed her up for the occasion. Her silver hair was fluffed up and sprayed as stiff as a country singer's, and there was a turkey brooch made of yarn pinned to her ruffled blouse. Mitchell stepped away from her wheels and reached for a slice of pumpkin pie. Viola Holts raised her bony hand and slapped him viciously on the arm.

"Hey!" Mitchell yelled, wide-eyed and stunned. Viola put the slice on her own tray and began to wheel away.

"Are you OK?" I said. Mitchell's cheeks were flushed with surprise and hurt, his freckles obscured beneath the blush.

"Why did that old lady hit me?" he said, staring out across the dining room of Wylie's to where Viola Holts was headed with her stolen pie.

"She's doesn't know what she's doing," I said, although her movements had seemed deliberate and intentional. "She's probably got dementia. And I guess she really wanted that pie."

"There are six other slices of pumpkin pie here! That's so mean." It was true. A row of identical pie slices was there for the taking.

"She's a lunatic. She's out of her mind," I said, wrapping my arms around Mitchell to comfort him.

"Mr. Holts! Happy Thanksgiving!" Mitchell said, forgetting his pie grievance, because Kevin was coming toward us. He was pushing Viola in the wheelchair, though she was attempting, unsuccessfully, to stop him by deploying the emergency brake.

"Happy Thanksgiving, Mitchell. *Rebecca.* Mr. and Mrs. Meer. Mom has something she'd like to say. Go on, Mom," Kevin said. The old lady kept her lips pressed tight, eyes blazing.

"The truth is, Mom doesn't talk much these days, but I know that she wants me to tell you how sorry she is. She's uh . . . not herself. And she wants Mitchell to have the pie."

"It's OK, Mr. Holts," Mitchell said, "I've already got another—" But the old lady was holding out the pie plate to Mitchell, chastened.

"Just take it," I whispered.

Mitchell reached for the pie plate. When his hand touched the rim, Viola lurched forward in her wheelchair and spit directly onto the whipped topping.

"Jesus Christ, Mom. What is the matter with you?" Kevin said.

"That's OK. You can have it, Mrs. Holts," Mitchell said, backing a safe distance away.

"I'm so sorry, Mitchell. Mom is feeling ornery today."

"Kev! Why don't you join us? Our table is right over there," Ben Loos said.

"Yeah!" Mitchell said, happy at the prospect of sitting with an alleged billionaire and his favorite teacher, in spite of the wild-haired demon in the wheelchair.

"I appreciate that," Kevin said. "But we don't want to intrude."

"We'd be delighted to have you. I got us the table over there, right next to the Bandercooks," Ben Loos said. My brother-in-law was a genial, well-meaning menace. Kevin was looking at me, waiting for me to weigh in on the issue of his invitation, and Ben was sending unsubtle facial signals my direction.

"Of course," I said, with barely adequate warmth.

"Follow me," Ben said.

"If she touches my kid one more time—" I whispered to Kevin.

"I will euthanize her on the spot. I swear to you, Rebecca. It's only sentimentality that's held me back thus far."

"Fine," I said. Kevin positioned Viola out of striking distance, and took a seat next to Mitchell.

"Happy Thanksgiving, Kevin," Madge said. Her eyebrows were on the verge of summiting her hairline. Kevin returned the greeting, and then there was an uncomfortable silence. My mother was too busy eating to talk, and this gave my father nothing to agree with, so he stayed silent, too. Viola had apparently gone nonverbal in her decline, but she gurgled in an unsettling manner. Even the boys seemed uneasy, and were unusually quiet. Ben tried to fill the silence with cheery small talk, but none of his observations about the cold weather, the time of year, or the joy of being elbow deep in some good red clay were able to ignite the general interest.

The Bandercook table was so lively that I wondered if someone had smuggled in a flask—it was more likely than not. Chad Bandercook was winding up a tale that had everyone in stitches, and they seemed to be the picture of a happy family, though if history is any guide, there would be a brawl of some sort before the sun set on the holiday. I looked at Hayes, briefly, and he looked back, chewing thoughtfully on a drumstick.

Our mother started in on the Thanksgivings of old. "I rose before the rooster to get my pies in the oven. I bet your mother did the same, Kevin. Didn't you Viola?" Viola, of course, said nothing, but Kevin explained that in his view eating out was the only rational choice for the holiday, because the time and labor invested in producing such an elaborate, starch-heavy meal could not be justified by the level of enjoyment it produced.

"You think people appreciate your efforts, but they really don't," Kevin said, squirting squeeze-bottle ketchup onto his plate.

"That's absolutely true," my mother said.

"Everyone talks about outsourcing like it's a dirty word, but I don't want to spend *my* holiday basting a mutant monster bird," Kevin said.

"Hear, hear," Madge said, raising a glass of sweet tea.

The cousins began discussing the likely outcome of a battle between Tornado Man and Precipitation Girl. Madge and I commiserated quietly. We felt their recent obsession with the Weather Warriors was just another trial of motherhood, something that brought extra tedium to the family dinner table, but Kevin took an interest. He weighed in with a few observations that betrayed familiarity with the characters, their personal histories, known weaknesses, and preferred weaponry. The boys were floored. They tapped Kevin's arm, shouting out questions, and almost certainly smearing his cashmere sweater with gravy, but if he minded, he didn't show it.

"Remind me what your problem with this guy is," my sister said under her breath. I didn't reply; I just gave her a look that meant *watch this.*

"Kevin?" I said. He looked up in surprise. So far, the number of remarks I'd addressed to him remained a solid zero. "Since it's Thanksgiving, I was wondering if you might be having second thoughts about boycotting the school food drive. The need is so great this time of year and we"—I gestured to the splendor of the table before us, where every variety of mayonnaise-based salad was in evidence, and every Jell-O in the gelatin rainbow—"have so much."

"Second thoughts? Not a one," Kevin said. "I can't in good conscience encourage my kids to give of their own resources for the benefit of strangers. What kind of message does that send?"

"But aren't you giving of your own resources by teaching fifth grade?" Madge said. "Rumor has it you waived the salary."

"You know, Marjorie, teaching is not an expression of charity on my part. I'm not here to help anyone, per se. I'm just taking a stand against the whole progressive enterprise, this academia jet-set coalition that is hell-bent on diluting the American character."

"What?" Madge and I said, in unison.

"Look at the curriculum," Kevin said, getting heated. "Social studies—I call that passivity studies. Language arts—totally shot through with one very carefully calibrated message: dependence on government."

"But Kevin, the food drive. You've got your entire class brainwashed on this issue, and it's unfair. Even Mitchell won't help."

"I want to go to Pizza Planet!" Mitchell said.

"Brainwashed?" Kevin was losing the table, and he knew it. "That was never my intention. I just presented an argument, and the kids, to their credit, responded immediately. But I tell you what: I'll give you equal time. You come into room 304 and make your case. If you can sell it to my class, I'll change the terms of the Pizza Planet offer: we'll go only if we get full participation."

I looked at Madge. She was nodding vigorously: *do it.*

"OK," I said.

Soon the Meers and Looses, habitual speed-eaters, were fork deep in pie slices, but Kevin and Mitchell were still slowly eating turkey, slicing it into bite-size pieces and dipping it into ketchup. My pecan pie stuck in my throat: they were doing it in nearly perfect sync. Aidan looked up from his pie plate. He'd been eating it hands-free, and he now wore a little goatee of whipped cream on his chin. My worst fear was realized: Kevin and Mitchell laughed in unison. Conversation dried up. My parents exchanged a look. Viola Holts's eyes blazed. She made a guttural sound deep in her throat.

"What is it, Mom?" Kevin said.

"Stupid!" she said, apparently to Kevin. Her voice was raspy and hoarse. "Stupid!" she repeated.

"Be nice," Kevin said, as if Viola Holts had ever been nice a day in her life.

Viola raised a thickly veined finger and moved it slowly around the table, pointing at Kevin, then me, then resting at last on Mitchell. *"He,"* she croaked. She was trembling all over with some strong emotion. "He is *your*—"

"Mom, what?" Kevin said, half rising from his chair. "What's wrong?"

I grabbed a fork and stuffed a large bite of pumpkin pie between Viola's open lips. "Student. That's right," I said, smiling and adopting the singsong tone generally used with the demented. "Kevin is Mitchell's *teacher*."

Viola spit the pie onto her chin, and it dribbled over the napkin Kevin had tied around her neck. She sank back in her chair, as if exhausted from her effort at speech.

"*Go!*" Bill Bandercook yelled, slapping the table with his palms so hard that the dishes shook. The entire Bandercook table, save Rusty, dashed through the back door and into the parking lot, whooping and yelling.

"Oh no you don't!" Wylie screamed, puffing after them in her kitchen apron and chef's hat. "Not this year!"

A moment later, she came back through the doors and handed Rusty the check. "And there you are, sir."

"Thank you for being respectful of our traditions," Rusty said, opening his wallet.

"Thanksgiving dine and dash? What kind of tradition is that? Your family is messed up."

"Now, Wylie, why do you think I don't have kids of my own?" Rusty said, winking at me as he paid the tab.

Kevin insisted on paying for our entire table, but Mitchell and I didn't wait for the check. Madge and my parents and even Ben Loos, who famously couldn't buy a clue on clearance, were staring at me as if they expected I might rip off the mask they'd taken for my face and reveal my true, alien nature. I said something about having "lots to do," and hustled Mitchell into the car.

TWENTY-SIX

I'd imagined that the food bank would be a grim place where nobody looked anybody else in the eye, but just barreled past with their caps down low, huddled over a bag of cast-off groceries. It was exactly like that, but even more depressing. Folk music of the sixties was playing on an ancient radio and a couple of gray-haired hippies, thin and bent, doled out provisions and smiles. My first thought had been to ask one of the volunteers to speak, but one look at them, with their long gray braids and roomy jeans, and I knew Kevin would chew them up and spit them out in under two minutes.

The truth was, I had no business as the public face of doing the right thing. I had more or less become the face of doing the opposite. After Thanksgiving dinner, I'd planned to avoid calls from my family indefinitely, but they hadn't even tried to get in touch or demand any answers. Nobody was saying a word to me on the subject of Kevin or on any other subject. I had an uncomfortable, pariah-y feeling and so I needed to find someone else, someone who could speak with moral authority on the subject of hunger. And I needed them today, before Mitchell's last shreds of compassion were plowed under the wheels of Kevin Holts's cartoon version of America, in which a positive attitude and a decent work ethic were all it took to put food, maybe even vast wealth, on the table.

A young mother pushing a stroller turned to speak to me. "You're a doctor? I've never seen a doctor getting food here before." Her two children were dressed in sweatshirts with dinosaurs on the front. Both of their noses were running, but their tiny faces were powerful compassion magnets. I wanted that.

"Well, I'm not a medical doctor. And I'm not getting food—this is for school. I'm looking for someone to speak to the fifth grade about the food bank."

She bit her lip, taking this in. "So you're *not* here for groceries?"

"No, as I said, it's sort of a class project—"

"A *class project*." Something sarcastic had crept in to her tone. "So, we're like animals at the zoo? You want to show us to your class so they can learn something about poor people?"

"No, you don't understand. If you could just share your experience—"

"*You* don't understand. You want to parade me and my kids in front of a bunch of little kids like sideshow freaks? Because my family's problems are educational? How dare you."

She looked like she meant business, so I took a couple of steps back.

"I'll do it," the person behind me said. He was young, tall, and nearly skeletally thin, and also wearing a coat with a winged skull on its back. His blond hair was filthy, but he was a good negotiator. "Five hundred bucks," he said.

"I've got fifty."

"Fifty and a gas station burrito," he countered.

We shook on it.

❖ ❖ ❖

"I was like you once," Cody said, backwards-sitting on a chair at the front of the classroom. He pushed the hood of his skull coat back to look the children in the eyes. "Did my homework, got good grades, all that shit." Cody spat on the floor, and one of the Eubanks triplets gasped.

"What the fuck?" Kevin mouthed at me from the back of the room where he stood, arms crossed, shaking his head.

I shrugged. *"Equal time,"* I mouthed back. To the front of the room, I said, "What would really help, Cody, is if you could explain how you get by. Tell the kids about the vital role the food bank plays in your life, and how their donations can help."

"Y'all want to help me?"

The children nodded vigorously. They were mesmerized by Cody—his garish tattoos (the one around his neck read "Warrior"), his foul language, the smell of cigarettes and must that seeped out of the lining of his hoodie, gradually filling the classroom.

"OK then, real talk. I don't want your stank-ass cans of beef stew."

The bolder of the children giggled at this colorful phrase, the rest of them just stared, frozen in their desks.

"How am I supposed to heat that shit up? I don't have a mother-fucking house."

"Let me just interrupt, Cody, if I may, and point out that not all people in need of food assistance are homeless. Just today at the food pantry I met a mother who lives not far from here. She works full time—"

But the children's heads swiveled away from me, back to Cody.

"I operate in a cash economy, understand? If you want to help me, give me money. Or give me something I can get money with. I'm talk-ing scrap metal, copper wire, shit like that. But you want my advice?" Cody said.

"Yes!" Mitchell said. Several of his nearest classmates giggled. I gave him a look, and he shrugged, *What'd I do?* The picture of innocence.

"Don't waste your time on charity. It's a cold fucking world. Look out for yourselves, little bitches." With that, Cody pushed out of the chair and sauntered from the room.

"Let's show Ms. Meer some appreciation for bringing in such a fascinating guest speaker," Kevin said.

The class broke into loud applause.

"And now I think it's time we get out our math books."

"Wait. What about the vote?" I said.

"You're serious?" Kevin said, dropping his voice. "You want to do the vote? That freak who just stank up my classroom was the crudest stereotype of a poor person I have ever encountered. If you had created him in a work of fiction, you would be justifiably pilloried. Nobody's mind was changed here."

"Do the vote, Kevin," I said.

"Listen up, class. I know we've decided not to participate in the food drive, but Ms. Meer thinks that after meeting Cody, maybe you've changed your minds. And that's OK. So if that's the case, if you *want* to help people like Cody get their fix—"

"Food," I said.

"*Food,*" Kevin said, "then I'll change the incentive. If you want, and *only* if you want, I'll take everyone to Pizza Planet for *participating* in the drive instead of boycotting it. So who wants to help Cody? Show of hands."

Nearly every hand in the classroom shot up.

"Huh," Kevin said, looking with surprise at all the small waving arms. "Congratulations, Ms. Meer. Fifth grade is now on board."

TWENTY-SEVEN

It's a funny thing, what stress can do to a person. I ought to have been in panic mode, but instead a profound sense of peace washed over me. I sat at my desk, making a small sculpture out of paper clips and whistling to myself. I was like a mountain climber slowly freezing to death near the summit, admiring the way the light glints off those lonely peaks in the clouds. Nina had just left my office, and her pregnancy test was positive. Someone was going to have to break it to Dr. Thad.

"We need to talk," I said, opening the door of Dr. Thad's office without knocking. He was sitting at his desk, watching grains collect in wavy patterns at the bottom of his sandscape.

"Becky, I'm just drained. Emotionally, physically drained. Angie and I worked out years of conflict last night. I cried, she cried. We recommitted."

"That's great, Thad," I said, in what I hoped was a natural manner. His eyebrows shot up. "I think you mean *Dr. Thad*, Becky?"

"No, I mean *Thad*," I said.

"Well, I didn't spend nine years at Harvard to be just *Thad.*" He spun the frame of his sandscape, creating a small tornado of colored sand that leveled all the previous structures.

"Why not? Why am I the *only* one who can't call you Thad?"

"I think it's prudent to keep a certain professional distance, don't you?"

"In front of the patients, sure, I'll call you Dr. Thad. But right now, when it's just you and me, why am I not allowed?"

"I think you know very well why not," Dr. Thad said, leaning forward with the solemn expression he uses to deliver bad news.

"No, I don't know. It seems to me that I'm the only person in Ward who isn't on a first-name basis with you, and to be perfectly honest, it hurts my feelings."

"Ah, your feelings," Dr. Thad said. "You know, I didn't ask for this charisma. It's something of a curse, really. And your *feelings* are precisely our problem. The likelihood of us acting on our longstanding mutual attraction, deeply suppressed in your case, grows exponentially the minute I let you call me Thad. I've probability-modeled it and—it's just a no. It's for your own good."

"You think I'm attracted to you?" I said. "You're impulsive and irresponsible and childish and a solid 40 percent of my working hours are spent cleaning up whatever mess you've made that threatens to drive this clinic into the ground."

"It's true," Dr. Thad said. "It's all true. It's why I've got to shut you out. Because you deserve better than me. And because without you and your moral authority, only slightly compromised by your subconscious longings, I wouldn't even *be* Dr. Thad. I'd probably be sleeping under a bridge—and alone, at that. Don't you see, Becky? I was never meant to do this, not in real life. In many ways, I would have been more at home on the set of an emergency room television drama, where horrific trauma injuries can't put out the flame of sexual tension."

"You're wrong," I said. In spite of it all, the thought of Dr. Thad hanging up his real lab coat in exchange for a lab coat costume was enough to bring me to my knees. "But you are such an egomaniac, Dr. Thad. It's a little bit revolting."

"Is it?" he said. "I think we both know what lies just on the other side of revulsion."

"Well I'm glad you've worked things out with your wife. Maybe she'll be in a forgiving mood when you let her know about your baby."

"What baby?" Dr. Thad said.

"The one you're having with Nina Flyte," I said.

Dr. Thad chuckled. "Frankly, Becky, I don't even want to have *dinner* with Nina Flyte, much less a child. All that new-age business . . . it simply became too much. I could never really love anyone so pre-Enlightenment. You've always understood that about me."

"Nonetheless," I said. "In about eight months, there's going to be a brand new Sorensen. A little unvaccinated, natural-remedies bundle of joy with a new-age wacko for a mother."

"Impossible," Dr. Thad said. "I'm infertile."

I sat down in his consult chair uninvited. "So the procedure failed," I said.

"I never had it! Your dire e-mailed warnings and my innate physical cowardice quickly overcame my passion for Nina. Which turned out to be fleeting, oddly enough."

"I'm keenly aware that Nina is not a logical woman, but if you never had the procedure—does she believe she reversed your vasectomy . . . *homeopathically?*" It was a serious question, but Dr. Thad howled with laughter. The sound was like a stable full of vocalizing horses, all snorting and whinnying at once.

When he had composed himself, he said, "I hesitate to explain this to you. I'm afraid you'll think less of me."

"That's simply not possible, Dr. Thad," I said.

"There are three pillars of the Glee . . . harmony, secrecy, and *brotherhood*."

"You and Dr. Richards *faked* your vasectomy reversal?"

"How thoroughly you understand me. We hardly need words, you and I, do we?"

I shrugged. It was true, but I was in no mood.

"The whole thing—let's just say it was a shameful chapter. I'm not proud of it. But Keith got his licks in, believe me. He made me sit in an ice bath for half an hour. So I feel I've more or less atoned for that already. I'm ready to move on."

"There's still the problem of Nina, who believes she is gestating your fetus."

"Nina is all wrong for me. I think it's best we cut off contact."

"I assume you want me to tell her."

"Would you?" Dr. Thad's best smile was all over his face, but I was unmoved.

"Absolutely not," I said.

He crossed his arms over his chest, like a pouting child. "My relationship with Nina began following your blunder at the insemination. If not for your tactless comment about Reyne Reynolds's sperm, I would not have been required to comfort her in a way that inevitably became physical. You practically drove me into her arms, Becky."

"If you had taken the advice I gave you in your driveway that morning—"

"Your advice? Let's talk about your advice. After becoming involved with Nina, I then reconciled with Angie, as you are always urging me to do, placing myself in the middle of a very uncomfortable love triangle. I think if you're honest with yourself, you'll see that you bear some responsibility in this situation."

"I don't see that *at all*," I said.

"Nonetheless, can we—can you—trust me to do it? Isn't it more likely than not that when faced with Nina's tears and howls of despair, I will do the noble thing and resume the affair, like a gentleman, despite my own preferences? And *then* where will we be? Think it over, Becky. Now if you'll excuse me, I'm going to put the finishing touches on this little speech you've written up. It's dry as toast. Not many applause lines, are there?"

I rose from my chair without replying. At least he was working again. It wouldn't be long before the clinic resumed posting a profit. Meanwhile, I'd made a list of pawnable in-office properties to tide us over.

❖ ❖ ❖

I drove to the Prescott Inn in Warlock with the office espresso maker, three desk chairs, Maryellen's laptop, and the break room microwave rattling in the back of the Granada. Dr. Thad was really going to hit the roof about the espresso maker, and so I had thrown it in mostly out of spite. I was going over to Barrelhouse Pawn in Nee to get a loan to keep the clinic doors open, but first, I wanted some reassurance that this was all worth it. I'd seen Dr. Thad in so many compromising situations; now I wanted to see him do something right for a change. He was a terrible husband, a wretched business partner, but, when he put his mind to it, a brilliant doctor. We'd made real breakthroughs together, and now Dr. Thad was going to share them with the world, or at least, with interested health-care professionals in the tri-city area attending the Midwest Fertile Con.

The Prescott Inn had spared no expense. There was a welcome banner plus the usual conference trappings—expo booths, piles of free lanyards and promotional pens, and a person of indeterminate gender wearing a foam uterus costume who stood at the door, waving and getting the crowd fired up for the panels and speeches that awaited within.

In the Prescott's main ballroom, Dr. Thad took the podium and let the chatter die down, smiling. Whoops and applause came from several enthusiastic pockets of the room. Dr. Thad acknowledged them with a nod. He is a charismatic presenter, a liberal user of visual aids, and a canny deployer of PowerPoint effects and animation—people knew they were in for a treat. I took a seat near the back of the room and smiled. *It's about the science,* I said to myself. At the end of the day, that was what mattered. "Innovations in Blastocyst Banking" shimmered on the screen behind Dr. Thad's head.

"I know you came here today to be informed about my innovations in blastocyst banking—but that's nothing we can't cover at the mixer later. Now, if you'll indulge me, I'd like to speak to you on another subject, one which concerns all of us very nearly, and is quite dear to my heart. My subject is nothing less than the future of the Middle West, my adopted home." Dr. Thad clicked to a map image of America's central region. He let the image linger, while the crowd opened notebooks and settled into chairs. Then with a whirl of stars that prompted oohs and aahs, he transitioned to the next slide—a cartoon depiction of fetuses growing in podlike incubators. It was a provocative choice, but if anyone could make it work, it was Dr. Thad.

"Eugenics is a dirty word. But, may I ask, why? The science of human improvement has a troubling history, but I tell you, friends, it also has a bright future. At my clinic, we have set ourselves the goal of improving the intelligence, the ability, of the average person in the Midwest region through an aggressive program of high-quality gamete collection. We need not exterminate or sterilize the dull-witted among us." Dr. Andrea De Mott, a devout Catholic, clapped robustly at this sentiment.

"Through advances in science the unfit may be *made to bear* the fit." Dr. Thad was making emphatic gestures. His hair was becoming mussed. I could not have sworn that his lips weren't flecked with spittle. He used a dramatic fade-out effect to get to the next slide, which was a line of alarmingly Nordic individuals in snowflake sweaters. By the way they stood, hands on hips, all clear blue eyes and strong jaws, it was safe to assume they were hell-bent on global conquest. (It occurred to me later that Dr. Thad had simply copied and pasted his own image into the frame again and again.)

The image was blown away, as if by the wind, and a close-up of pistons in a factory of some sort took its place, clearly meant to rep progress. "Society as a whole rises to a higher level. The rare genius— not so rare anymore. America, with her bloated midsection and low-performing underbelly, can at last tone up. This great nation will shrug off the shackles of mediocrity and fulfill its imperial destiny. A new breed of Americans will press her borders north and south, until the dream of a united continent is achieved at long last."

A new slide unfurled from the top of the screen, like a flag. It was all of North, Central, and South America decked out in stars and stripes. The health-care professionals began to shift in their seats. They had complimentary bottles of water and each table was laid with several bowls of munchies, but even so, this was straining the boundaries of Midwestern Nice.

"This guy," someone whispered at the table next to mine, and she received some concurring uh-huhs from her colleagues. Nobody wanted to *bad-mouth* him, a nice guy up there, doing his best, but his talk was, in the Midwestern sense of the word, "interesting."

Dr. Thad continued on in this vein, speaking too loudly and too quickly, laughing too heartily at his own jokes, and generally behaving like a man who has just done a line of coke. Dr. Thad had not used the words *national socialism* or *Untermensch*, but even so, his speech featured enough eugenics red meat to garner at least polite applause in Germany circa 1939.

I dropped my head and covered my ears, wanting to scream. Dr. Thad was out of his damn mind—that much was certain. But for how long had he been a raving eugenics nut? And how had I missed it? I had devoted twelve years of my life to him, and I had literally nothing to show for it, beyond a beat-up stink car filled with pawnable items. I felt like Hitler's gardener, who'd explained in the course of an extremely awkward public television documentary I'd seen, that, sure, he'd noticed Herr Adolf had a certain tendency to harp on "racial purity" when he'd had enough schnapps, but somehow he'd just never really put the pieces together and realized for whom he was planting all that edelweiss. People shook their heads and marveled at the old man's willful blindness to the megalomaniac who signed his paychecks. I'd thought the same thing that night on my couch, eating popcorn and muttering something about the banality of evil.

I lifted my head from the table. There were raised voices coming from the back of the room, and my first thought was that the conference attendees had finally run out of corn chips and patience and were planning to tar and feather Dr. Thad, or run him out on a rail, or however they handled this kind of thing in Warlock. But the scuffle was too contained to be the beginnings of mob violence. At the back of the room, two middle-aged nurses were trying to hold back a small, mousy-haired woman I didn't recognize. She was very worked up. She kicked the nurses viciously and broke free, bursting into the main aisle.

"You're a liar," she screamed, heroically taking issue with all or at least some portion of the talk, while the rest of us just sat there eating corn chips and feeling uncomfortable. "The lies stop now!"

"Can?" I said.

"My name is Jan!" Front Desk screamed, before Prescott Inn's security team tackled her into the ballroom carpet.

TWENTY-EIGHT

The CLEAVER was only days away. Already the bundled tests and scorecards had made their way via ground freight up from the publisher in Texas, driven by a single long-haul trucker who rolled the windows down to stay awake and peed in paper cups to make good time. Calvin and Rusty were unloading the test bundles in a secure location on the Davis campus. Just knowing that those booklets full of multicultural children running neighborhood recycling drives *(If Vladimir recycles four bottles and Xanti recycles twice as many as Lok . . .)* were lying in wait had plunged the entire school into a deep funk. Teachers looked out over rows of unpromising children and knew that their livelihoods depended on the right bubbles being filled by those small, unwashed hands. It was paramount, everyone agreed, that the children not be made nervous.

Teachers administered practice tests, reading from the included scripts—SAY: *Today we are going to answer some questions to see how much you have learned. Some of the questions will be difficult for you.* Construction-paper cleavers appeared on the bulletin boards, representing students hacking through the state grade-level-proficiency standards. Calvin strode through the halls with an encouraging smile as tight as spandex.

Once, as I counted cans for our tally, I thought I heard the sounds of muffled sobs coming from the principal's office. I stood for a moment, my hands wrapped around some pickled beets, and wondered if I ought to check on him, but I thought better of it. We had nothing left to say to each other. Before long, the reams of bubbled paper would be on their way to the scoring center in Texas, out of our hands. Calvin would be packing up his things in a small cardboard box soon enough.

❖ ❖ ❖

Maryellen and I were loading up the Granada with everything I hadn't packed up on the day of the Fertile Con. Dr. Thad had, true to character or lack thereof, been carrying on an affair with poor Front Desk. He was taking an "indefinite leave of absence" to work through his issues. The story was captivating the entire town. Nobody seemed to talk of anything else.

"You know where they'd meet? The *Fox Motel*," Maryellen said. I stared straight out my enormous windshield, my hands at ten and two, while Maryellen leaned in the driver's window, trying to make eye contact. "Did you hear what I just said, Rebecca? You know that nasty little place off I-80 by the slaughterhouse? The Fox. He took her *there*. I mean, really."

"That's alarming," I said, truthfully. Local sentiment was running mostly in Dr. Thad's favor. Front Desk was a calculating temptress who'd taken advantage of a vulnerable older man. That's the way people saw it. The fracas had erased his deranged presentation from the public mind entirely, and now people saw him only as a brilliant, handsome doctor ensnared and humiliated by someone with below-average looks and a GED. I felt somewhat responsible for not warning her about Dr. Thad's character, but Jan had kept her dysfunction and volatility so artfully hidden beneath a bland, forgettable exterior that I had never considered her to be at risk.

"He told her she was *special*. Do you know how that sounds to a twenty-four-year-old?" I said.

"Like the truth," Maryellen said. "Poor baby. She believed she was special, and yet, you and me, we couldn't even remember her name." Maryellen blew her nose loudly. She'd been taking this hard. Maryellen and I had treated that girl like a phone-answering automaton. Was it any wonder she had fallen into bed with the first person who recognized her humanity?

"Don't beat yourself up, Maryellen." I backed out of the clinic lot, probably for the last time. The building and its equipment, even the contents of my beloved lab, were all up for sale.

❖ ❖ ❖

"Who died in there?" Ed Barrelhouse Jr. said, staring down into the Granada's roomy trunk, which was packed with the wreckage of my professional life. Ed was a scion of Nee society, son of the founding family. He had a gray flattop haircut and a needle-thin tie, baby blue in color, and he was wearing only a short-sleeved dress shirt with red stripes outside in this cold without seeming to feel it. The man was a marvel.

"Nobody, so far as I'm aware," I said. I was shivering with my coat zipped up, but Ed didn't appear at all uncomfortable. His face was alight with the thrill of the deal.

"That's a *roomy* trunk," Ed said, hooking his thumbs in his pants pockets. "A trunk like that could serve a man well in many situations."

"Plenty of storage space," I agreed.

"How much you want for it?"

"Not for sale," I said. We agreed on three hundred dollars for the contents of the car. When we'd unloaded the remains of my life with

Dr. Thad, I turned the key in the ignition. The heater blasted to life, pouring the car's gut-turning scent into our nostrils with such force that even Ed, who looked as if he'd smelled the inside of a correctional facility or two, took a quick step back.

"Good God. What *is* that?" he said. "You got a dead cat under the vinyl?" Ed poked his head in the window and surveyed the interior.

I shrugged my shoulders. "Could be," I said.

Ed twirled the air fresheners with his finger. There were three stylized pine trees and one red apple with a worm hanging from the rearview mirror. "These here are not cutting it. Hold up. I've got something can help you."

A moment later, Ed emerged with a black aerosol spray can. "Close your eyes and cover your mouth," he said, and I did so. He sprayed and sprayed until the can sputtered, and when he was finished, the car smelled somewhat less offensive than before.

"It's no garden of roses, but at least you don't smell like the inside of a morgue in there," Ed said.

"It smells kind of tropical," I said. "Thanks."

❖ ❖ ❖

I drove three blocks, enjoying the absence of the car's customary stink, before the new scent became overwhelming. "Oh my God," I said, rolling down the windows as quickly as I could. "It's Player Pour Homme." My heater was now billowing out a spicy, masculine fragrance. It smelled like the men who traveled in packs in their tight T-shirts, heading out into the night with grim determination to return to their sad apartments neither alone nor with each other. It smelled like coconuts. It smelled like hugs held a beat too long, uncomfortable eye contact, and dancing with an unnecessary amount of pelvis. It was the very fragrance of sexual desperation, and it was billowing out my windows into the streets of Nee like a summons. It wasn't long before it got an answer. I was stopped at the light on Barrelhouse Parkway and Grifter Ave, and Hayes Bandercook came running down the street toward me, screaming my name. My name and also *Help me!*, which, given that he was a Bandercook, could mean so many different things.

"Do you need a reference for community college? Or is it legal trouble of some kind?" I ventured to ask.

"I only wish it were," Hayes dropped his hands to his knees, panting hard. "It's Big Country. Rebecca, if our time together meant anything to you—and I realize it may not have"—but even in his distress, Hayes smirked in a way that indicated he'd doubt that claim—"get me out of Nee. My life may depend on it."

"OK, hop on in," I said.

Hayes shook his head. "*Nuh-uh.* You're too visible. This car is a goddamned eyesore, no offense. Let me ride back to Ward in your trunk."

"Whatever," I said, popping the trunk. I had been too tactful to suggest the trunk myself, but my strong preference was not to be seen cruising with Hayes Bandercook in my large green car through the pickup line of Davis Elementary. This was better all the way around. Hayes jumped in the trunk, and I ran out into the street and slammed it shut over him. The light turned green, and a heating and AC repair van behind us began to honk its horn. I flipped them off, since it was Nee, and we sped toward the highway.

❖ ❖ ❖

I sat in the car line waiting for Mitchell, wondering what best to do with the Bandercook in my trunk, but there was some sort of holdup at the front of the line. Minivans and SUVs with stick-figure family decals were snarled as far as the eye could see. I was making no progress. I backed the Granada up over the curb and pointed it in the direction of the school's side lot, exiting the line. I would go in and pick Mitchell up myself, and while I was at it, check on the haul for the food drive. We'd seen a modest uptick in donations since the fifth grade had adopted Fifty-Eighth Street Cody as a sort of room mascot. The total collected so far was solid, but we needed more than solid to win the food drive. We needed unprecedented altruism at the elementary school level, and I think everyone realized we weren't going to get it.

I walked across the parking lot, allowing myself a sigh. Everything seemed to be falling apart, and nothing new was emerging in its place. I had no idea what I would do when the clinic was put to rest. Dr. Thad was at a medical spa receiving treatment for "exhaustion," leaving all the painful decisions of the clinic's closure to me, which is probably just what he'd have done if he were here, too. But he was not my problem. It was Mitchell I was worried about. He wasn't sleeping well lately. He was silent and tense. His usual energy had flagged. He spent long quiet moments scribbling in a notebook, with a worried look on his small face. The transformation was sudden and painful. No longer did he leap from the furniture or bound down the halls. His constant chatter had dried up completely. We ate our dinner in silence, and when I couldn't stand hearing only the noise of our chewing a minute longer, I'd drop my fork and make him some bold, vague promise.

"Mitchell, it's going to be OK. We're going to be fine," I'd say. He would nod, but he was too old to believe it. I needed to tell him not only that it would be OK, but *how*, and the truth was, I had no idea.

A small crowd of children was loitering near the back of the building, just outside the doors. I saw no teachers anywhere in sight, and I wondered for a moment if they'd been accidentally locked out in the cold. Then I noticed a boy in a familiar orange ski cap, who had climbed up a ladder that was leaning against the garbage bin. He was throwing things into it.

"Mitchell, what are you doing?" The scene was dreamlike and impressionistic: orange ski cap, brown trash bin, the roiling winter clouds in the long prairie sky. Mitchell looked self-consciously resolute and solemn, like a TV president.

"What we *have to* do, Mom. I know you don't understand." There was a can of extra-fancy petite peas in his hand, and he dropped it into the stinking abyss of garbage. Three more thuds of canned food followed. The children were working in an efficient assembly-line manner, handing up creamed corn and golden mushroom soup to Mitchell, who disposed of them as quickly as he could.

"Stop it!" I said grabbing at Mitchell's coat. "Mitchell, get down from that ladder right now!" Some of the children began to scatter at the sound of a raised adult voice.

"Loretta. Ethan. Emma T. We're not finished," Mitchell said, in the calm voice of authority, and to my amazement, the children resumed working.

There is so much randomness in the world, whether sperm will meet egg, which genes will dominate, and which will recede to subtle lines of face or hidden tendency toward disease. But at this moment, I felt the whole thing was rigged. Someone had flipped a weighted coin, and Mitchell, my beloved child, was no more like me than a stranger on a bus.

"Oh yes you *are* finished here," I said, positioning myself between the ladder and the children, but I did not have my son's charisma, which was not garden-variety magnetism, but something so potent it might serve him well as CEO of a cult or a tech start-up, and nobody listened. I had a vision of my child, full grown, jogging onto the stage with a chin mic while *Thus Spake Zarathustra* swelled through the speakers and a crowd of investors clapped, or worse yet, wearing aviator glasses in a steaming third-world hell hole, passing poisoned cups of juice to his flock on the eve of some arbitrary apocalypse. Maybe he was as bad as everyone—as Calvin—said, and I had never seen it till this moment.

"You can't waste all this food!"

"Giving it to the food bank is a waste," a tiny girl with two dark braids said. Emma T., if memory served.

"The class voted. I thought you decided you wanted to help people?" I said.

"We do, but . . ."

"It can't *help* anybody if it's at the bottom of a garbage bin."

"But helping people just hurts them," the little girl said.

"Like what happened with the toads," one of the Eubanks triplets said.

"The toads." For the first time, it occurred to me that the toad episode might have been Kevin's doing. Possibly he had engineered the toadsplosion as an object lesson in the harmful effects of charity and compassion.

"People have to become self-sufficient," a boy said, "before they drag this whole country down."

"But there are little kids in Ward who don't have enough to eat. You don't expect little kids to be self-sufficient, do you? What about old people? Shouldn't we take care of them?"

"We just don't want to hurt anybody," Emma T. said.

"So we have to do what's ethical," Mitchell said. "Even if it means losing our trip to Pizza Planet."

"So all of you here buy your own food? Maybe your parents should stop feeding *you*."

"Mom, that's a different situation. And paternalistic government is nobody's friend," Mitchell said, throwing a can of chunky beef stew into the trash. "Open your eyes!"

"Mitchell," Calvin said, in his nightmare voice. At the sight of their principal, all the children scattered, Mitchell included, and raced back to the building from which their indifferent monitors had allowed them to wander. I was left standing next to the ladder, a few stray cans of chicken broth at my ankles. I reminded myself that human beings are not capable of exploding, because Calvin looked as if he were ready to join the Davis toads in death by spontaneous combustion. He seemed

to be having trouble drawing the necessary breath to speak, but after a moment he said, "Don't *ever* bring him back here, Rebecca."

"Wait!" I said, kicking cans out of my path as I followed behind him.

"Oh, no," Calvin yelled over his shoulder, bringing his hands down with a decisive slice. "This is over."

❖   ❖   ❖

Mitchell followed me out to the car, his backpack slung over one shoulder, the other strap dragging behind him in the dirty snow. His face was flushed with shame, and all up and down the car line, heads craned to stare at us as word spread. The word. *Expelled.* Mitchell slid into the backseat and covered his face with his lunchbox. I started the car, but I felt unable to drive it. I sat there in the parking lot, beginning to cry, as "The Greatest Love of All" came on the radio, crushing my last bit of optimism under its melodic heel. It was a fatal mistake.

Kevin Holts rapped at the window. I lowered it. "I want you to explain something to me," Kevin said, ducking his head in the window, invading my personal space. If he noticed I was crying, he didn't react to it. His tone was polite, but there was something in it that put me on notice.

"Explain what?" I said. I looked right into his eyes without blinking, though mine were streaming tears, and my nose was turning red and swelling up.

"Would you step out of the car, please, Rebecca?" Kevin said, noticing the weeping ten-year-old in the backseat. "We need to discuss"—I exited the Granada—"this," Kevin said, thrusting something under my chin. It was just a piece of notepaper with some sort of incomprehensible flow chart drawn in pencil. At that moment, it was the last thing I cared about.

"I'm not even sure what this is," I said, taking it from his hand and giving it a once-over.

"Exactly. That's *exactly* what I'm talking about." Although I have seen Kevin in a variety of situations, until this moment, I had never seen him truly angry, and the transformation was shocking. He was a tall auburn column of fury. "You know, you're holding it upside down."

I flipped the paper around and squinted at it. It didn't seem to help. "So what is it?" I said.

"That is a little something called a business plan. And this particular one is for selling the canned food directly to the homeless *instead of donating it.*"

"Oh my God," I said, connecting the dots. "Mitchell did that?"

"He did," Kevin said. "They made thirty bucks before Calvin shut them down. The homeless were buying at a discount, then returning the cans to the store at full price and using the refund money to buy booze. It's all here in Mitch's plan. You really don't see it?"

I shook my head. I saw nothing but a random series of boxes and arrows, and those were now wavering through even more of my tears, because I knew what Mitchell had been trying to do. That thirty bucks was for us, for the day not long from now when we had nothing left. That's why he was hurling cans into the garbage—he was angry and afraid. I was making a gesture toward ending hunger, but what could I really do about it? I couldn't end hunger. I couldn't, he believed, even take care of him.

"There are people pushing shopping carts full of rags and talking to flagpoles who understand this," Kevin said.

"Well, it doesn't really matter now," I said, sniffling.

Kevin dragged a hand through his hair and glared at me. "Explain to me how it's possible that someone like you—someone who has, what? a 20 percent share in a business where she does 98 percent of the work—"

"Ten percent share," I said. "But we're out of business now anyway."

"Jesus Christ," Kevin said, snatching the paper from my hands. "That guy is such a dipshit."

That, I thought, was an understatement.

"Explain to me how someone like *you* is capable of producing a child like Mitch."

I didn't have an answer for this. I just stared, speechless, into the freckled fury of his face.

"He's *mine*, isn't he?" Kevin said. He looked as if he already knew.

I'd invested so much in denying this. It was for the best, I'd believed, that Kevin have no part in Mitchell's life. But Kevin had inserted himself in our lives anyway, even without that knowledge.

"Yes," I said.

In spite of his tirade, my answer seemed to shock Kevin. Even his lips paled. His world was ripping apart and re-forming itself, the way mine had, nearly eleven years before.

"You had no right to keep him from me," Kevin said.

"Why would I think you *wanted* him? Your life"—I pointed at the sky—"was on an upward trajectory. Whereas mine . . ."—I pointed down to the dirty parking lot snow. Kevin stood, blinking, considering this. I wondered whether he remembered that final conversation as well as I did. It was not lost on me that all his predictions about me had more or less panned out.

"Whatever I said or didn't say, he's *my son*. And I really had no idea," Kevin said, looking sadly at the dirty snow that lined the curb.

"Mitchell has to be told," Kevin said. I thought of the alternatives. Leaving town in the middle of the night, putting my car in reverse and running Kevin down where he stood. Neither of them were good. "And I want to tell him myself. I assume that's not too much to ask."

"Fine," I said. "I guess you heard that Calvin just expelled Mitchell from school."

"Don't get hysterical," Kevin said, rolling his eyes. "Mitchell's a passer."

"What does that mean?"

"I would think that a woman who is literally in bed with administration would be better informed—forget it. That's neither here nor there. A passer means he's one of the students we can count on to pass that fucking test. You don't expel a passer."

"Kevin, are you not hearing me? He already did it. He caught Mitchell throwing away donated food—and it's over," I said, inadvertently quoting Calvin.

"He *expelled* Mitchell because of his principled stance against the food drive? That's bullshit. That will not stand. Let me handle Cal. As you may have noticed, he's got very mixed feelings about you."

The Granada began to shake. Hayes was still in the trunk, kicking and pounding as if his life depended on it.

"Oh Jesus," I said. "Excuse me." I walked to the back of the car and unlocked my trunk. Hayes Bandercook emerged gasping for breath, his eyes wide with terror.

"You left me to die in there!" he screamed.

"Hayes, I'm sorry. I just forgot."

"You forgot? You *just* forgot," Hayes said. His arms cartwheeled around him as he tried to regain his balance and his composure. "You and me—never again! Spend your time at the Fox Motel with someone else. It's over!" Hayes screamed. He ran toward the chain-link fence that encircled the school, scaling it with the agility of a man who often scaled fences, and in a hurry, possibly with law enforcement hot on his heels.

Mitchell's nose was pressed against the window. His eyes were soaking up the scene, but I hoped the radio was loud enough to drown out Hayes's parting words. Kevin looked as if he'd been hit upside the head with a piece of rebar. He leaned against the car and stared at me.

"At some point Rebecca—and now is not that time—we're going to have to talk about your choices."

"OK," I said.

"Because something is very wrong with you. Do you have an explanation for yourself, I wonder? Your entire goddamn car smells like Player Pour Homme. You have a Bandercook, an actual *fucking Bandercook*"—I winced—"riding around in your trunk, and it wouldn't have been too much longer before you had a dead Bandercook in there, the way that exhaust pipe is angled. So what we're going to discuss at some future point, when I'm confident I can keep my temper, is why you're like this. Because a person doesn't just end up like you—there has to be some triggering event. Because *you are*—"

I didn't care to hear whatever was coming next. "The *mother of your child*," I said. It stopped him cold, because, unfortunately, the truth of this statement was now indisputable.

"OK. Fair enough," he said, and he turned and walked across the parking lot toward the school buildings, carefully folding the business plan and putting it in his pocket.

TWENTY-NINE

I transferred custody of the sperm and ova and all our chilly little embryos to Dr. Beatrice Roane, the clinic's new owner, who would care for them with at least as much moral seriousness as we had done. I bit my lip to keep from begging her for a job. I knew what the answer would be by the frosty triumph in her eyes.

I was as depressed as I had ever been, and I chose to spend most of my newfound free time on the couch, wallowing. It's easy to see life's early disappointments as bumps on the road to inevitable success, but I was already old enough to acknowledge that my future might be quite a bit less bright than my past. Madge, surprisingly, took a different view.

"Nobody could have done as well with that psycho Thad as you did. You made that place work for years. Against impossible odds, Becky. And now you're free."

"But free to do what, exactly?" I said, peering out from the afghan I had wrapped myself in.

"Something without a lot of people contact. You never belonged in a clinical setting, in my opinion. Can't you just work in a lab somewhere?"

I dropped the bag of marshmallows I'd been binge eating and stared at her, in the simultaneous grip of a sugar rush and an epiphany. It really wasn't a bad idea.

"Madge," I said, washing down the last of a jumbo-size marshmallow with a sip of warm orange juice, "there's something I have to tell you about Mitchell."

"Oh, is there?" Madge leaned toward me, cocking one eyebrow.

"He's not a designer baby," I continued, grabbing another marshmallow for courage. "I didn't even use a donor."

"Oh. My. God." My sister was more shocked than I have ever seen her.

"I thought you knew? After Thanksgiving . . ."

"Everyone's been calling Mitchell 'mini Holts' since Wylie's Cafeteria. But I just assumed—we all assumed—that there was a medical middleman involved."

"Nope," I said. "Just the low-tech method." I found her bewildered expression a little irritating.

"You and Kevin Holts. *You* and *Kevin*." Madge was having trouble wrapping her head around the idea. I was on record as a Kevin Holts hater, but what of it? As Dr. Thad had said, passion and revulsion were two sides of a coin. I was a complicated woman who was not always going to conform to expectations. She should try to get used to the idea and keep her judgment to herself.

"Madge, have you ever taken a rash step you couldn't later explain?" I said.

"No," Madge said, helping herself to a marshmallow. "But I guess Kevin Holts has. Jesus."

❖ ❖ ❖

The last disagreeable errand that I had to dispatch for the clinic was spreading her weird pink toes across a purple foam mat. Nina Flyte was leading a group of retirees through a sun salutation. I waited in the hall until class broke up, and Nina walked over to me with her bare feet.

"I know why you're here," Nina said. She had the wild-eyed look of a frequent radio caller.

"I very much doubt it, Nina," I said.

"You want me to break things off with Thad. Well, the answer is no. No today, no tomorrow. Forever no. Got it?"

"Just one minute," I said before she could dash off impetuously. I realized that I needed to speak to her in her own language, so I took a deep breath and prepared to emote all over her. "Do you know what comforts me on dark days, when the wind howls outside like it's going to tear the roof off my house and send it smack into the Glass's place across the way?"

"Alcohol?" Nina said. I wondered if I was just going to have to embrace my new identity as the town drunk, because rumor had it, correctly, that Bold County Lager had played a starring role in my "romance" with Calvin.

"*No.* Reyne. I know that no matter how bad it gets, unless the power goes out, I can turn on Channel 8 and Reyne is going to be out there with the hood of his yellow raincoat corded to max tightness, yelling into the camera about wind velocity. I may not understand what he's saying, over the din of the storm, but I understand what he stands for. Integrity. Courage. It takes a special kind of man to do what Reyne does. He puts it all on the line every tornado season."

"I suppose. But he's in my past. I left him. I've moved into my mom's place—just until Thad and I work out the details of our new life," Nina said, looking suddenly dreamy, and entertaining a vision of peaceful domestic bliss, which Dr. Thad is utterly unqualified to deliver.

"About that. Dr. Thad has had a change of heart."

"What's done is done," Nina said, pointing at her belly, which was still Pilates flat at this point. "He can't walk away from this."

"I'm happy to refer you to a reputable ob-gyn," I said. "I think Dr. Kreutz out in Warlock would be an excellent choice to finish out your obstetric care. She'll let you play trance music and sit on a rubber ball and all that sort of thing. You'll love her."

"I mean he can't walk away as this child's father. He's in my life for good, for better or worse."

"Nina, that child isn't his. It can't be."

Nina pursed her lips. "Um, I think I know who the father of my child is, Rebecca."

"And I think you don't. You see, Dr. Thad never had the vasectomy reversal." Nina widened her eyes, pushing her sweaty headband back from her forehead.

"He most certainly did," she said. I wonder what he'd put her through in terms of his "post-op" and tried not to imagine.

"Nope," I said. "It was an elaborate ruse, because he didn't want to lose you *or* his sterility. You know, he's got charisma, sure. But he's something of a dipshit," I said. "Seriously."

"But he *couldn't* have faked it. What about the ice baths? And the limping?"

"We are dealing with a thorough and dedicated practitioner of medicine *and* deception," I said. "You should expect nothing less from a person like Dr. Thad." It was really tragic, how completely overmatched she was by the man she claimed to love. She might have just as reasonably claimed to love particle physics—she had the same chance of understanding either of them.

"So this is Reyne's baby?" Nina said. "How can that be?"

I shrugged. "Human reproduction is a complex and mysterious process—"

Nina threw up her hands. "But then nothing you did helped."

I've heard enough refund requests in my life to see where this was headed. "We'll never know that for sure," I said, though it did seem to be the case. Despite his love affair with hot water, Reyne had finally triumphed, on his own terms. "But the more important question is—where do you stand with Reyne?"

Nina sighed and made a gesture that seemed to indicate the situation was too delicate and complex to put into words, which was just incorrect. "I don't see how the two of us can reconcile." Nina, I realized, was like a very toned and flexible Madame Bovary, and her perfectly balanced chakras couldn't sate her need for drama and chaos.

"Your other option would be to raise this child alone."

"A *single mother*?" Nina said, in the same tone of voice people reserve for the phrases "crack whore," or "Jehovah's Witness."

"We're no longer required to wear distinctive clothing and live on the outskirts of town," I pointed out. "It's really not so bad."

"Not so bad? It's not so bad to be a bitter, lonely alcoholic with a weird kid? Having pity sex with the principal? Well, I don't want that to be my future."

"Then, Nina, *go to him*," I said.

"I think I will," Nina said, tightening the cap on her coconut water.

❖ ❖ ❖

"Can we talk about his name?" Kevin said, yelling to be heard over the racket of crashing pins. "Because I think you've done him a real disservice."

"He's in the fifth grade, Kevin. It's a little late to change it."

"But *Mitchell* . . . it's just Michelle with a *T*."

"That's his name," I said. "Accept it." I had accepted a lot of things in the past few days, so I spoke with a certain moral authority. In appearance and attitude both, my son was a miniature Kevin Holts, and my consuming love for my child made it difficult to hate his father the way I once had. I understood Kevin's odd way of looking at things now, because Mitchell's mind worked in such a similar way. My life was more or less in shambles, and it was obvious to me as it had never been before that so many of Mitchell's good qualities—his talent for order and structure, his even temperament—he had *not* gotten these things from me. The secret wouldn't keep any longer. In a year or two, when Mitchell was a teenager, the resemblance would be so strong that casual strangers would pick them out as father and son.

I was at peace—more or less—well anyway, I was *resigned* to Kevin unveiling himself as Dad, but the question of Mitchell's reaction tormented me. I'd had trouble sleeping lately, imaging how hurt and angry he would be. I feared he would never forgive me. Kevin certainly hadn't and wouldn't, though he was coolly civil to me, in his low-drama way.

"Fine. I accept it. He can have his name changed when he's older. Pizza's here!" Kevin called. The three of us had gone to Pizza Planet, along with most of the fifth grade, to celebrate Davis Elementary's domination of the district food drive. Our win really had improved morale. Kids were hurling bowling balls down the lanes with a pure, joyful violence. Maybe they were high on the notion that they could make a difference in the lives of their fellow citizens. Maybe they were just happy to beat, for once, those stuck-up snots who attended Windlow Elementary—their more fortunate peers who accepted all the world's honors and awards as their birthright. Either way, they shrieked with delight whenever one of them sent pins crashing down into the pit at the end of each lane.

"Well here we are," Kevin said, smiling broadly as he served pizza slices to his former students. He himself was eating only a tiny bowl of bare salad greens. He'd tried to convince the kids to follow his example, but, I was glad to see, even his persuasive powers had their limits. All the kids had opted for steaming slices of grease-soaked carbohydrates. When they were busy eating, he looked at me. "I think it's time."

"Go for it," I said, pushing my slice away. I was too nervous to eat it. Kevin called Mitchell over to our table. "Have a seat," he said. Kevin cleared his throat. "Mitch, I know your mom told you that your dad was an anonymous stranger who couldn't succeed in the sexual marketplace. And I know how that must have made you feel. Like a freak, right? Like a total loser?"

Mitchell nodded.

"You see, the trouble with your mom's job—former job—is that it allows losers to procreate," Kevin said.

"Losers have always procreated," I said.

"Not now, Rebecca," Kevin said. "That's a debate for another time. Anyway, Mitch, buddy. I have good news. Your mom may not get an A-plus for honesty or for the responsible use of contraceptives, but I want you to forgive her for that. Because she's your mom, and she loves you. So can you do that for me?"

I was tearing up. Under the circumstances, it was an incredibly generous thing to say.

"OK," Mitchell said, with his mouth full of crust.

"I know you're mad as hell. I'm mad as hell, too. But we have to forgive her, because for all her faults, she did one thing right. Do you know what that is? Can you guess?"

"No," Mitchell said.

"Mitch, I am your father."

"Really?" Mitchell said.

"Really," Kevin said.

I could hardly look at him, but I forced myself to, dabbing tears with my thin Pizza Planet napkin. Mitchell was utterly delighted.

"So . . . do I get to call you Dad?"

"Absolutely," Kevin said. "And I want you to know that I can't imagine a kid I'd be prouder of than you."

"Thanks . . . Dad," Mitchell said. He was beaming. "So, are you going to live with us in our house?"

"Well, no. You see Mitchell, I don't believe in monogamy. It's just total bullshit. Don't get me started. But just because I have no intention of conducting an exclusive sexual relationship with your mom, that's no reason I can't be a good dad to you, is it?"

"I guess not," Mitchell said. Kevin tousled his hair, which in a certain light, has a definite auburn cast.

"Here, open your present," Kevin said. He retrieved a large box from under the table. Mitchell ripped off the paper and screamed. It was the Phantom.

"How did you know?" I said to Kevin.

"I just did. I got one for myself, too, Mitch. We can try them out tomorrow."

"I'm going to head over to the bar," I said. "I'll catch up with you guys later."

I ordered a pitcher because Kevin was driving us all home in his Porsche and I was hoping to be sick in it, and I took it out to the patio and sat down under one of the heaters. The day was unseasonably warm and springlike, and the icicles that lined the deck were dripping onto the parking lot below.

"That's not all for you, is it?" Calvin said. He was wearing a bowling league shirt that said "Cal" on the pocket, with his unzipped coat thrown over it. Kevin had quietly resigned and Calvin had replaced him with an idealistic young grad named Kylie Hywhistle, whom he predicted wouldn't last the quarter.

"Have some," I said, filling his pint glass with pale bowling-alley beer. He sat down in the chair next to me, looking rather surprised at the invitation.

"Only because I'm in a celebrating mood. I just signed a contract for a pretty sweet data-entry-manager position in Ames. I start end of school year."

"That's great, Calvin," I said, and we clinked glasses. I meant it. Davis hadn't met its benchmarks, but neither had any other elementary school. After some reconfiguring and back room dealings, the state board of education had decided to "phase in" the new scoring standard, meaning that for this year, Davis had passed. But Calvin was too clever to take this temporary reprieve for more than it was; he was off to greener pastures.

"I credit our food drive win. Without that one shining victory, my résumé had nothing but the reek of desperation and failure." I drank a large swallow of Bold County in lieu of responding.

Kevin had personally donated ten thousand cans to the food bank on behalf of Davis Elementary, a gesture which he feared would be perceived as compassionate, though in fact it was nothing more than a deal he'd cut with Calvin. Mitchell was finishing out his elementary career at Davis. Still, even the appearance of such generosity cut Kevin to the core, and he'd been too ashamed to show his face at the last meetup of the Ward Objectivists.

I was impressed in spite of myself. Kevin had ordered the canned goods from some obscure Objectivist canning facility to ease his pangs of conscience at such an altruistic act, even one done as a quid pro quo. All ten thousand cans were John Galt Brand Fancy Sliced Carrots, which was either an oversight on Kevin's part or an attempt to brand the needy by giving them orange complexions. This large-scale gesture of compassion had also made a serious impression on Mitchell, which Kevin felt was the worst thing about it.

"Best of luck, Calvin," I said. The drip of icicles onto pavement was audible. I unwrapped the scarf from my neck. The portable heater was so warm I felt my skin tanning. A bird flew over our table, a cardinal carrying a French fry in its beak. We drank our Bold County Lagers in silence. Across the parking lot, a bearded man in a ragged coat was kicking a can in irritation and muttering to himself, "Who the fuck is John Galt?" Calvin and I shared a wry smile.

THIRTY

Viola Holts choked to death on a piece of beef at the Musk Rose Inn on her eighty-fifth birthday, turning purple and clattering down over the china- and lace-laid table, overturning a boat of gravy, which dripped steadily into the plush pink carpet as all efforts to revive her failed, in full view of a full dining room. The manager was going to have to run coupon specials for months to get even a half house. Kevin was outside taking a call when it happened. His tall red-headed sisters, Rose and Lynn, back in town for the old lady's milestone, ran out to the snowy gazebo where he was conducting business and screamed at him. They kept screaming as he hurried into the Musk Rose and recognized the woman who had birthed him, face down in a plate of mashed potatoes and rare beef. His eyes filled with tears; he'd planned to tell her the news about Mitchell while she enjoyed her slice of birthday cheesecake, but now he'd never have the chance. As he stood over the slumped body of his mother, he plucked a roll from the bread basket and began to eat it, absently, but nobody blamed him. He was in a state of shock.

"Imagine tackling a rib eye with an eighty-five-year-old jaw. What *joie de vivre*," Dr. Thad said, when I ran into him at the Handy Farmer. He had spent six weeks in striped pajamas, drinking fresh juices and playing lawn tennis under the palms of an exclusive California sanitarium, and now he was loosed again upon the world. I excused myself after a minimum of pleasantries.

❖   ❖   ❖

I parked the Granada in the lot of the Fox Motel and waited, as instructed, until Big Country saw fit to join me. Two young guys in hoodies paced the parking lot—his personal security, I assumed. When they finished their patrol, they both spoke into their cell phones at once. A few minutes later, Big Country emerged, casting his rotund shadow over the parking lot, blinking in the noon light like a mole. I got out of the car.

"These are yours," I said, dropping the keys to the Granada into his soft fleshy hands.

"That's my ride," Big Country said, smiling with real pleasure. He'd been forced to sell his beloved Green Dragon when faced with a shortage of liquid cash. "You've taken good care of her. She smells excellent," BC said, leaning in through the enormous window and filling his lungs with the scent of Player that clung to the vinyl like rust to the door, or even more closely, because the rust at least flaked off bits of metal from time to time.

"So we're cool?" I said.

"We're cool," Big Country said, and we shook on it. Hayes Bandercook had run up a serious debt with Big Country, which was why either his life or his kneecaps were in danger, depending on who you spoke to. Accounts differed as to whether the sum involved was for Xanadu or losses at the unlicensed casino Big Country ran out of his mom's basement, and I preferred not to know. I was offering the car to settle Hayes's outstanding bills. "I'll put the word out that Hayes can come out of hiding," Big Country said. "I know where his skinny ass is anyway. He's living in Rusty's garage. Dumb fuck."

"Excellent. But if you don't mind—please leave my name out of it. Let him think you bought the car from me. We're not on the best of terms—which is for the best."

Big Country smiled. He was even more terrifying with his teeth out. "Shit. You're a *mama*. No reason for you to spend your time with the likes of him."

"Well said, Big Country." We parted friends.

❖ ❖ ❖

"Mom, if I tell you something, will you promise not to tell Dad?" Mitchell was sitting at the kitchen table with a spiral-bound notebook, doing his homework, or pretending to.

"Of course I promise," I said. My track record of not telling "Dad" things was stellar, and I was vaguely insulted Mitchell would even need to seek reassurance on this point.

"The thing is . . ." Mitchell looked down at his hands, as if he didn't know how to put it. "I don't want to let Dad down, but I just don't want to live low carb," he blurted in a confessional rush. Then he blushed.

"Who *would* want to live low carb?" I said, grabbing his hand. "It's just a stupid fad, sweetheart. Before low carb, it was low fat. Before low fat, it was an earlier version of low carb. Low carb is already post-peak. Next year, mark my words, your dad will be eating platefuls of pasta and screaming in terror if somebody butters his toast. Which he will also then be eating. *And that's OK,*" I added.

Kevin and I had been going to see a counselor named Vee, who wore a gray bob and cat-eye glasses and sat cross-legged in a slipcovered chair. She gave us exercises to do so that we could "more effectively co-parent." Many of them involved imagining ourselves stretched out on the warm sand of a deserted beach, a thought exercise which usually led me to an unplanned nap. Whenever we ran aground on one of our many, many differences of opinion, we were to turn to each other, acknowledge how appalled we were by the other's views, and then say after a deep, cleansing breath, "but that's OK." It shocked me how well this worked. Short of our furtive encounters so many years ago, Kevin and I had never had more positive interaction.

I'd found work in a lab, just miles from the site of Kevin's latest venture, an obnoxious steel and glass building he referred to as "corporate." Mitchell liked to go and spin around in Kevin's futuristic desk chair, above which hung, to my surprise and horror, the taxidermied head of Pretty Johnny Flowers, the Duke.

My project at the lab involved a promising compound, which seemed to increase concentration, decrease erratic behavior and impulsive sexuality, and generally grease the mental wheels of the lab animals who consumed it, all without sending their salivary glands into overdrive. We were years away from human trials, but I was cautiously optimistic that one day, a drugged-up humanity would behave only with logic and decorum, and then so many of society's problems would be solved. Although sometimes I reflected that *my son* was the result of a series of impulsive, poor decisions, and that when they didn't destroy lives, careers, and civilizations, sometimes bad decisions were the best of all.

"So you're saying we *can* order a pizza?" Mitchell said, raising his eyebrows hopefully as I continued to dissect all that was wrong with his father's dietary superstitions.

"Call it in," I said, feeling I'd just been played. At moments like these, I knew that he was not *all* Kevin's child.

Mitchell wrapped his arms around my neck and kissed my check. Then he picked up the phone and ordered a large everything pizza with double crust.

ACKNOWLEDGMENTS

Thanks to my agent, Noah Ballard, for being a true creative partner in this project. Without you this book would be just another slightly unhinged Word document. I'm so grateful for all you did to make this happen.

Thanks to my editor, Carmen Johnson, for believing in the book. Your incisive edits have made all the difference. I'm lucky to have worked with you and everyone at Little A.

Thanks to my friend and writing mentor, David Liss. I owe so much to your encouragement and advice. To say that I'm lucky to know you is an appalling understatement.

Thanks to my talented friends: Amy Mikler, photographer to the fast-blinking and unwilling; Veronica Goldbach, for crucial writing advice; Keegan Chopin, who makes me laugh every day through the miracle of the internet; Cristen Peterson, arbiter of cool; and Melissa Nobles, who kept my children alive, fed, entertained, and out of the room.

Thanks to my family: To my parents, Joe and Kathy De Mott, whom I can never repay, and I'm talking primarily about the childhood library fines. And to my brother, John De Mott. You're my Ethan. Unless you want to be Joel?

To my daughters, who valiantly watched untold hours of TV during the writing of this book. Without your boundless appetite for glowing screens, none of this would have been possible. Now go outside.

Finally, to Lance Curtright, for more than I can ever say . . . unless I learn power chords and write a hair-band ballad.

ABOUT THE AUTHOR

© 2015 Amy Mikler

Eileen Curtright was born in Lincoln, Nebraska, and currently lives in San Antonio with her husband and three daughters. *The Burned Bridges of Ward, Nebraska* is her first novel.